Praise for *In the Lion's Mouth*

"*In the Lion's Mouth* shows Flynn on top of his form."
—*Fantasy Book Critic*

"For those who like fantasy elements in space wars, intrigue, resource spies, and thrillers."
—*SFRevu*

"Flynn's incorporation of Norse and Celtic mythologies into SF adventure and romance makes this a popular choice for fans of David Weber's Honor Harrington series."
—*Library Journal*

"Flynn is amazing. I haven't gotten this drunk on sheer words since I read *Bone Dance*. . . . This is space opera at its best."
—*Connotations*

"Fascinating and intelligent."
—*Kirkus Reviews*

IN THE
LION'S
MOUTH

MICHAEL FLYNN

A TOM DOHERTY ASSOCIATES BOOK
NEW YORK

This is a work of fiction. All of the characters, organizations, and events portrayed in this novel are either products of the author's imagination or are used fictitiously.

IN THE LION'S MOUTH

Copyright © 2011 by Michael Flynn

All rights reserved.

A Tor Book
Published by Tom Doherty Associates, LLC
175 Fifth Avenue
New York, NY 10010

www.tor-forge.com

Tor® is a registered trademark of Tom Doherty Associates, LLC.

ISBN 978-0-7653-6283-4

First Edition: January 2012
First Mass Market Edition: December 2012

Printed in the United States of America

0 9 8 7 6 5 4 3 2 1

Margie, again

CONTENTS

MAIN CHARACTERS

Francine Thompson	d.b.a. Bridget ban, a Hound of the Ardry
Graceful Bintsaif	a junior Hound
Lucia D. Thompson	d.b.a. Méarana, a harper, daughter of Bridget ban
Ravn Olafsdottr	a Shadow of the CCW
Donovan (the scarred man)	d.b.a. the Fudir, sometime agent of the CCW
Rigardo-ji Edelwasser	a bonded smuggler
Swoswai Mashdasan	garrison commander on Henrietta
Dawshoo Yishohrann	leader of the conspiracy
Gidula	an old Confederal Shadow (black, a white comet)
Oschous Dee Karnatika	field marshal of the rebel Shadows (scarlet, a black horse)
Geshler Padaborn	a revolutionary
Poder Stoop	the Riff of Ashbanal (blood red, a Maltese cross)
Tina Zhi	a functionary in the Gayshot Bo

Rebel Shadows

Little Jacques	another rebel Shadow (swallowtail, red with border)

Manlius Metataxis	"brother" to Dawshoo (sky blue, a white dove)
Domino Tight	a young Shadow (tawny, a lyre proper)
Big Jacques Delamond	a large Shadow (white, a blue trident)

Loyal Shadows

Shadow Prime	Father of the Abattoir (black)
Ekadrina Sèanmazy	field marshal of the loyal Shadows (black, a taiji)
Epri Gunjinshow	a protégé of Prime (forest-green, a yellow lily)
Pendragon Jones	a loyal Shadow (silver, a golden mum)
Jimjim Shot	the Beautiful Name, the Mayshot Bo

Retainers, smugglers, boots, sheep, magpies, couriers, Shadows, Names

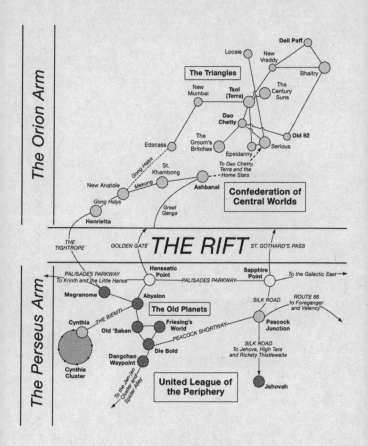

MAP OF THE
CONFEDERAL BORDERLANDS

Planar projection of the Confederal Borderlands and the Triangles. View is from Galactic North. Not all worlds or roads are shown. Worlds are not all on the same plane.

MAP OF THE
CONSECRATED BORDERLANDS

Having dressed and painted their passionate dream of a beautiful life with all their powers of imagination and artfulness and wealth and molded it into a plastic form, they then pondered and realized that life was really not so beautiful—and then laughed.

Johan Huizinga, *The Autumn of the Middle Ages*

IN THE
LION's
MOUTH

PROCESSIONAL

Sing, O harper, the anger of Donovan buigh,
That graced us all with boundless grief,
And left brave men a prey to dogs and kites
As we foresaw upon that fateful day
When Donovan buigh and Those of Name
First fell out.

When his wrath at first arose 'twas I he fixed
    it on.
Oh, yes. 'Twas I who hauled him from his
    happiness
Off those same Jehovan streets where once he
    walked,
And had he not his eye upon more distant joys
    affixed,
We'd twain lie dead in those same gutters,
    gutted
By each other's skills. But he foreknew, and so
    forbore to fight
And did submit him to my plea. But know this
    now, O harper.

It was to thee that he was bound when I untimely
  snatched him up.
Attend my tale and learn
Why once great cities burn.

PROLEGOMENON

The winds whistling o'er the breasts of the Dōngodair Hills carry much of the loneliness that can be found in those remote peaks and scatter it like pollen across the eastern plains, so that the Beastie boys, and the Nolan Beasts they tend, suck it in with every breath, and even the bluestem and inching grass, and the rip-gut in the wet bottomlands whose leaves are serrated knives soak up despair like sunshine and release it to the breeze. Thus it is that the rustle of the tallgrass can wring a sigh from a strong man and drive a lonely woman to weeping.

When night falls over the gloaming prairies of the Out-in-back, it falls complete. The city lights, such as they are, glow like hearth fires on the far side of the Dōngodairs; but their gleam does little more than limn the crests with a narrow pale-white band. Otherwise, green is simply another kind of black, and for half the year even the sky holds little more than a second pale band: the distant shore of the Orion Arm across the Rift of stars. It too is the glow of distant hearths: the ancient home-stars of mankind.

Amidst such engulfing shadows, what is one more shade drifting o'er the heath?

Clanthompson Hall sits an oasis of light on a swell of the prairie atop a deep, clean well; but the light is tightly held within fortress walls, and leaks out only through slits and windows. Her towers bespeak an earlier epoch in the history of Dangchao Waypoint, when her stone facing was more than mere decoration, and warring clans fought over water rights and control of the open range. The range wars are long over; and over the generations the squat functionality of her battlements has softened to more graceful and moderate lines. She stands now a stately matron, surrounded by her family of outbuildings, barracks and mess hall for the ranch hands, repair shops, a helipad, orchards, and a few tastefully hidden gun emplacements.

Oh, she is still a fortress in her heart! For Clanthompson Hall is the keep of Bridget ban, a Hound of the Ardry, and therefore for some a target. The rise the Hall sits upon is not much to speak of, let alone to speak of it as a hill. It does not so much as bear a name. But from it, and for miles around, nothing can approach unseen.

Or almost nothing.

It is called a "sitting room," but two of the three women in it are standing. The first is Francine Thompson, d.b.a. Bridget ban, mistress of Clanthompson Hall. She stands by the large bay window that overlooks the endless prairie, though she herself overlooks nothing. The curtains are drawn open and the night without is held at bay only by lamps burning bravely on tables. Even so, night has won his victories here and there, in darkened corners, in shadowed alcoves. Bridget ban wears high riding boots and a casual, loose-fitting blouse in the reds and yellows that the Thompsons favor. Her hair is a bright red and her skin a deep gold. She stares into the night, her back to the room, while she listens to the report.

Graceful Bintsaif, who is delivering the report, is a junior Hound and wears the powder-blue undress uniform of that grade. It bears at present only a single blazon, but it is a worthy one and, quite properly, she will not speak of how she won it. She is lean as a whippet and seems always to be straining forward, as if against some unseen leash. She interrupts her report to say, "Shall I kill it?"

"Not yet," says Bridget ban, who does not turn from the window.

Lucia Thompson, the third woman present, is seated on a stool. She is an ollamh of the *clairseach*, a master harper, and plays under the name Méarana, which means both "fingers" and, by a shift in accent, "swift." She is her mother, stamped at an earlier age, though with sharper corners, and with flint in her eyes. She has, it is said, a cutting glance, and she turns that gaze toward the window. "Where is it now?"

"By the maintenance yard. Behind the baler. Continue, Bintsaif."

The junior Hound stands with arms clasped behind her back and feet slightly spread. She has already loosened the flap on her holster. "The Bartender on Jehovah," she says, "is convinced that Donovan has left the planet. Furthermore, he believes that Donovan left voluntarily. He had spoken earlier of . . . coming here."

Bridget ban turns her head to look at the junior, and then snaps her attention back to the yard outside. But she is too late. The shadow is no longer by the baler. Her eyes search and do not find it. So she sighs and takes a teaser from the drawer in a lamp-table and checks the charge.

"Does this ever grow easier?" asks Graceful Bintsaif, drawing her own weapon.

Bridget ban tosses her head. "No. What else did you learn?"

"The Terran Brotherhood did not expect Donovan's departure. They had begun negotiations with him over a venture, possibly an illegal one."

Méarana stifles a laugh. "An illegal venture? In the Terran Corner of Jehovah? I may die of shock."

Bintsaif glances at her curiously. "Is it wise for you to linger here?"

The harper smiles. "And where might one be safer than between two Hounds?" She herself is no Hound, though her mother has taught her a thing or two.

The junior Hound shrugs and continues her report. "Port Jehovah records show that a petty thief tried to use the ticket Donovan bought, but his identification papers proved to be forgeries. He had killed a man in a burglary gone bad and was anxious to leave the planet. He claims to have found the chit fortuitously, lying by the walkway outside the terminal, and so seized the opportunity for escape." Bintsaif cocks her head, listens, then moves to stand beside the door from the Hall. "The Jehovan proctors believe he killed Donovan precisely to steal the chit, and Donovan's body lies now somewhere in the waste tunnels below the city."

Both Bridget ban and Méarana snort derision, a gesture so alike in mother and daughter as to bring a smile to the otherwise sober lips of Graceful Bintsaif. "Yes," she says. "The Terran Brotherhood is likewise skeptical. Not that Donovan cannot be killed, but that he cannot be killed by such a quotidian man as the proctors arrested." Bintsaif shrugs and holds her teaser straight up from the elbow. "I cannot say he impressed me, the one time I met him." She nods to the harper. "But then I can't say that you impressed me, either. Not then. In any case, Donovan has thoroughly disappeared from League space."

Bridget ban turns sideways to the door so as to present the smallest target. "We'll see what it wants first." And she aims her teaser directly at the door.

Their hearts beat, their breathing slows.

The door eases open, and the shadow that had crept over the heath slides into the room.

Méarana lifts her arm *just so* and a throwing knife snaps into her grasp from the harness in her sleeve. It is a different sort of plectrum with which she might pluck the heartstrings. Death is in the room, and ready, but not yet do they slip his leash.

Nearly as thin as Graceful Bintsaif, clad in a black, form-fitting body stocking, and coal-black also in her skin, the intruder is a portion of the night that has come alive, a bit of the darkness that has slipped into the light. Her eyes are twin moons. She holds both hands up, palms out, and says in the hooting accents of Alabaster, "I haff noo waypoons," this being as big a lie as anyone has ever spoken in Clanthompson Hall.

The white flash of the intruder's teeth is her most vivid feature. "Boot, you moost admeet, that in the mooment I entered, I coold have keeled . . . oh, two of you, I think. Yes, Gracefool Bintsaif, even you behind me."

No one lowers her weapon, and the intruder cocks her head. She shifts to the birdsong twitter of Confederal Manjrin, and there is no hoot in her voice when she does. "You situate very nice. No one in fire line of other. But, if I step, just so . . ." And she slides with a cat's grace. "Hounds cannot fire without perhaps hitting each other."

"My knife's flight remains unhindered," Méarana points out.

"Ah. So. But, you throw knife . . ." A flip of the wrist. "I catch knife. Now, if Bintsaif is finish her most excellent and respectable report, I fill in rest, and tell you fate of man Donovan." She tugs her hood free, revealing close-cropped, bright yellow hair.

"You're Ravn Olafsdottr," says Méarana, pointing. "You were the Shadow agent sent to kill Donovan a case of years ago." In the dodeka time used in the Old Planets, a case is twenty-four.

"Ooh, noo, noo, noo," again in Alabastrine. "Nayver to keel him—oonless he fell his dooty. May I seat? If you be nervoos, you strip me naked, tie me oop. Once I helpless be and you oonafraid, you can listen to my tell. Plans have change. All plans have change. There is stroogle in the Lion's Mouth."

That a Confederal Shadow, even bound and naked, would be the second-most dangerous person in the room, no one doubts for a moment. But no one doubts either that if assassination had been her object, Ravn Olafsdottr would have acted in the moment when she had stepped between the two lines of fire and both Hounds had for an instant hesitated. That she is not to be trusted goes without saying. But there are degrees of distrust; there are scales to suspicion. It is not yet clear in what way they should mistrust her.

They search the Confederal with consummate care, and she submits to this with cheerful indifference. She had expected as much, and would not have come but that she had resigned herself beforehand to its indignities. They discover scars on her body that evidence harsher searches, more insistent interrogations; and some of those scars are fresh.

Finally, the Hounds are convinced, not so much that Olafsdottr is weaponless, but that short of amputation she cannot be further disarmed. They sit her on a broad sofa of soft brown-and-white Nolan hide, but do not bother to strip and bind her. That offer, they ascribe to a certain whimsy on the Ravn's part. But the sofa is a subtle thing: one sinks into it, and cannot rise without a struggle, a safeguard against sudden attack by anyone sitting on it. Hounds and harper take seats on three widely spaced chairs surrounding her. Olafsdottr shows her teeth again. "Be not afraid," she says. "I am a courier, true, but Death is not today my message." But she knows they are only exercising normal prudence. In its way, it is a compliment to her skills that, outnumbering her three to one, they remain wary of what she yet may do.

Graceful Bintsaif laughs from a seat behind the courier. "I'm not afraid."

Olafsdottr turns her head. "Then you are a very foolish girl."

The junior Hound flushes but Bridget ban intervenes. "You've been tortured," she says.

The courier waves a hand. "Soom people, I pay them soo leetle mind, they moost ask more insistently to gain my attentions." She flashes teeth, relaxes on the sofa, and spreads her arms across the back of it. She looks in turn at each of the three women. It is nicely arranged. To keep any two of them in view, she must turn away from the third. This thought broadens her perpetual smile.

Bridget ban, coming to a decision, lifts her voice slightly. "Mr. Wladislaw? Could you bring some assorted nectars and four glasses to the sitting room, please?" Then she turns her attention to her importunate guest. "Explain, then. How do ye know what happened to the Donovan?"

"I know his fate because I took him to it."

It is a rhetorical trick, this abrupt dropping of the hooting accent, but no less effective for that. It freights her pronouncement with greater significance. Méarana starts to say something, but her mother halts her with a show of her hand. "You mean he has resumed the service of the Confederacy?" There is a hardness in her question that she has not shown even to Olafsdottr. One no more despises an enemy than the knife despises the whetstone. But a turncoat—that is another matter.

Olafsdottr smiles. "He foond the leeps of my dazer most eloquently speaking. He soobmitted, and a small droog assured that his secoond thoughts would come too, too late to matter. But interesting . . ." This, in Manjrin. "That betrayal rather than death first cross your mind."

"So, he *was* coming here," murmurs the harper, and she gives her mother a glance that the Hound chooses to ignore.

"Very well. Ye kidnapped him," the Hound acknowledges. "But that seems a long risk to run to pluck such meager fruits."

"Ooh, I think there is a flesh beneath the skin of that oold fruit, however dried and wrinkled he seems; and perhaps a hard noot at the saint-er."

"Yet, here you are; and he is not."

"He woonted to coome, boot he was tied oop." The teeth flash once more.

The door opens and Wladislaw enters with a silver tray balanced on his right hand and a projectile pistol gripped in his left. He pauses in the doorway and assesses the threat level in the room before he steps forward and places the tray on the low table before the sofa. He steps back and speaks to Bridget ban without taking his eyes from the Confederal. "Will there be anything else, Cu?"

"Yes, pour the nectar for us, Mr. Wladislaw. All from the same pitcher."

The butler fills the goblets one by one with a frosty

pear nectar. Olafsdottr ducks her head sidewise to look at him as he bends over.

"Are you truly left-handed?"

Wladislaw glances at his pistol. "Ambidextrous, ma'am." He sets the pitcher back on the tray and steps away.

"Ooh, I would give my right arm to be ambidextrous!"

A faint smile twitches the butler's lips. "Will that be all, Cu?"

"Yes, Mr. Wladislaw."

"Mr. Tenbottles asks that I tender his apologies for allowing this intrusion. No one saw . . ."

"They were not intended to see. Was anyone hurt?"

"Only their pride, Cu."

"Then the scab may serve them well."

After the butler leaves, Ravn Olafsdottr rubs her hands together as she contemplates the four glasses. "All from same pitcher," she says in Manjrin. "Such gracious assurance drink not tinctured." She reaches out and takes not the drink directly before her, but the one closest to Méarana. Then she settles back on the sofa. She does not sip the nectar yet.

The Hound smiles briefly and takes the glass in front of Olafsdottr and waits until the others are similarly settled. She too allows the nectar to sit untasted.

"Noo, harper," says the Confederal. "This will be a tell to tangle your strings, oon my word; but I will give it to you in my oon way and reveal things in their oon time. Life is art, and must be artfully told, in noble deeds and fleshed in colors bold."

I. RIFTWARD: THE FIRST COUNTERARGUMENT

> Swift we sped, your Donovan and I,
> Toward the Rift that rends the stars
> Apart, we plied the boulevards that bind them.
> Sooner far than I had sought for
> Woke he from those slumbers so awarded
> That he should wake when waking no more
>   mattered.
> Wroth he was at being thus abducted
> And for some time the issue lay in doubt
> Between us. E'en I must sleep,
> And in that sleep lie open to his guile.
>   But hold!
> I shall place distance 'tween my tale
> And me, and speak of Ravn as I do of others;
> And thus relate as would a goddess grand
> Who sits benign atop the world and, glancing
>   down,
> Sees all things in her ken with even eye.
> And so . . . It begins.

The scarred man awoke muzzy-headed in a dark, close
room, confused at where he was, and tangled in wires

and tubes. The last clear thing in the jumbled closets of his mind was his buying of a ticket to Dangchao Waypoint, and for a fuddled moment he wondered if he might be within that very ship, already on his way.

But if so, he was grossly cheated, for he had purchased third-class fare on a Hadley liner and, of the many things his present accommodations were not, a third-class cabin on a Hadley liner was one. The room was barely large enough to contain the thin, hard bunk on which he lay and, when that bunk had been stowed into the wall, the room grew paradoxically smaller: a pace and a half one way; two and a half the other. It was the half pace that galled.

It was a room for keeping prisoners.

"Fool," said the Fudir, once he had removed the catheters and intravenous feeding tubes that spider-like had webbed him in his cot. "We've been shang-haied."

"How long were we asleep?" Donovan asked.

There is this one thing that you must know about the scarred man; or rather, nine things. It is not his hooked chin, nor his sour humors, nor even the scars that interlace his scalp and leave his preternaturally whitened hair in tufts. It is that he is "a man of parts," and those parts are the pieces of his mind, shattered like a mirror and rearranged to others' whims. It is in the nature of the intellect to reflect upon things; and so a mirror is the proper metaphor, but the scarred man's reflections are more kaleidoscopic than most.

The singular benefit of paraperception is that the

paraperceptic can see different objects with each eye, hear independently with each ear, and quite often the right hand knows not what the left is doing. This has advantages; and would have had more had the scarred man's masters not been ambitious or cruel.

Early in Donovan's service to the Confederation, the Secret Name had gifted him with a second personality, the Fudir, which enabled him to live masqueraded as a petty thief in the Terran Corner of Jehovah while Donovan ran Particular Errands for Those of Name. But if two heads are better than one, ten heads must be better than two, and the Names had later, after Donovan had displeased Them in some small matter of galactic domination, split his mind still further. They had slivered his intellect and made of him something new: a para*con*ceptic, able not merely to perceive matters in parallel, but to conceive ideas in parallel. This was the ambition.

It was also the cruelty. They had imprinted each fragment with a complete, if rudimentary, personality, expert in some particular facet of the Espionage Art. The intent had been to create a team of specialists; though the consequence had been instead a quarrelsome committee. For the hand that split his intellect had misstruck; and the blow had split his will as well.

Though perhaps the blow had been true, deliberate, a part of his punishment. Perhaps at the last Those of Name had flinched from the prospect of too great a success. Those had made an art of punishment, and the connoisseurs among Them would often contemplate the intricacies of a punitive masterwork with something close to aesthetic joy. "Kaowèn," they called it. The scarred man had been conceived initially as a human weapon. But who would build such a weapon without a catch?

"Fool," said the Fudir. "We've been shanghaied."

"How long were we asleep?" Donovan asked.

I'm not sure, replied the Silky Voice. *I seemed to fight the drugs forever.*

The Pedant rumbled and blinked gray, watery eyes. 𝔦𝔣 𝔞𝔰𝔩𝔢𝔢𝔭, 𝔫𝔬 𝔪𝔬𝔯𝔢 𝔱𝔥𝔞𝔫 𝔱𝔥𝔯𝔢𝔢 𝔡𝔞𝔶𝔰. 𝔦𝔣 𝔰𝔲𝔰𝔭𝔢𝔫𝔡𝔢𝔡, 𝔞𝔰 𝔩𝔬𝔫𝔤 𝔞𝔰 𝔱𝔥𝔯𝔢𝔢 𝔴𝔢𝔢𝔨𝔰.

The Sleuth eyed the life-support equipment from which they had so recently disengaged. *We were in suspension* he deduced, *not asleep.*

That could be. Suspension would affect even me, back here in the hypothalamus.

<Ravn Olafsdottr!> remembered Inner Child. <She slipped up behind us. And slipped something into us.>

Yeah? said the Brute. **And where was you? You're supposed to be the lookout.**

Now is not the time for recriminations, a young man wearing a chlamys told them. We must start from where we are, not from where we might have been.

The Brute grunted, unmollified. He tried the door, found the jamb-plate inactive, and struck it in several likely places. Donovan did not expect it to open, and so was not disappointed when it failed to do so. A young girl in a chiton squatted nearby on her haunches, her arms wrapped around her legs and her chin resting on her knees. We can get out of here, she said.

Donovan turned control over to the Sleuth, who went to their knees for a closer study of the jamb.

The Pedant recognized the locking mechanism from his databank. *A Yarbor and Chang lock. This ship is Peripheral-built.*

"Probably hijacked by our gracious hostess," muttered the Fudir.

Which means this room was not *designed* as a prison cell, said the girl in the chiton, whom Donovan liked to call "Pollyanna."

So. Retrofitted ad hoc, said the Sleuth, and likely in haste. Yarbor and Chang . . . so what?

Its central processor has a design flaw. A notice went out from their corporate headquarters on Gladiola two metric years ago. I remember reading it.

You remember everything, the Sleuth complained. He took the scarred man's right arm and pointed. *Pedant's design flaw indicates that an electrical current passed across these two points—here, and here—will set up a magnetic field within the processor that resets the lock to zero.*

"That's nice," said the Fudir. "So if we had a generator in our pocket, or a battery, and some wires, and could maybe do a bit of soldering, if we had a soldering gun—and some solder—there's a chance we could get out of this room."

"At which point," said Donovan, "we would find ourselves in a ship. A bigger cell, is all."

Hey. At least we'd have room to stretch.

"And where would we find wiring?"

<There's an Eye in the wall just above the door.> *And it's not pitch dark in here.*

He means there is a power source.

"I know what he means. Sleuth always has to be clever and elliptical."

When he ain't bein' obtuse! The Brute laughed.

That the Brute was making obscure geometric puns irritated Donovan. Sometimes he didn't know his own mind. Ever since his sundry selves had reintegrated, they had been learning from one another. The Brute was no longer quite so simple as he once had been; though it was not as though he had blossomed into the New Socrates.

The Fudir climbed atop the bunk, studied the Eye, unscrewed a housing with *a convenient tool* he kept cached in his sandal, detached the live leads—*See? We didn't need a power source*—and pulled the cable, while simultaneously Donovan and the others considered what they might do once they had broken free of their prison.

"Take over the ship, I suppose," Donovan said. "Slide to Dangchao Waypoint. See Méarana . . . and Bridget ban."

<How many does Olafsdottr have in her crew?>

Don't matter.

"Well, it might, a little."

I wonder why she shanghaied us, said the Sleuth.

The lamp that was lit has been lit again.

What's *that* mean, Silky?

Something she said. Something I remember from a dream. Pedant? You remember everything.

The corpulent, watery-eyed version of Donovan shook his massive head. 𝔉𝔞𝔠𝔱𝔰 𝔞𝔯𝔢 𝔪𝔶 𝔪é𝔱𝔦𝔢𝔯, 𝔫𝔬𝔱 𝔡𝔯𝔢𝔞𝔪𝔰.

The Fudir applied the leads from the Eye to the

doorjamb, one above, the other below the point that the Pedant had identified. *This ought to work,* the Sleuth commented.

Of course it will, said the girl in the chiton.

Current flowed. Magnetic fields formed. Somewhere inside the door, registers zeroed out and reset.

Or were supposed to. The door remained shut.

The Brute stood and, perforce, they all stood with him. He pressed the jamb-plate—and the door slid aside into the wall. The scarred man felt a huge satisfaction.

<Careful> warned Inner Child, who took control and peered cautiously into the corridor. To the left it ran four paces, ending in a T-intersection.

To the right . . .

To the right stood Ravn Olafsdottr with a teaser in her hand and a splash of white teeth across her coalblack face. The teaser was pointed at Donovan's head. "Ooh, you nooty buoy," she said in the hooting accents of Alabaster. "Soo impatient! I wood have let you oot in the ripeness of time. Now you have brooken my door!"

"You should stop somewhere for repairs, then," suggested the Fudir. "I was on my way to Dangchao, so you can drop me off on Die Bold if you're going that way."

Olafsdottr patted him gently on the cheek with her free hand. "You are a foony man, Doonoovan."

Olafsdottr fashioned him a dinner of sorts. Food preparation was not her forte, and the results could best be described as workmanlike. However, three weeks in suspension had honed an edge to the scarred man's appetite, and he ate with surprising relish.

The refectory was small: essentially a short hallway with a door at each end, a table running down the center, and a bench on either side built into walls of a dull, ungracious gray. "This is not the most comfortable ship," the Fudir complained.

Olafsdottr stood in the aft doorway, a double-arm's reach distant, and her weapon still ready in her hand. She said, "One seizes the moment."

"And the ship."

The vessel is a monoship, the Pedant decided. Small enough for a single pilot.

She's alone, then.

That's good news, said the Brute.

Why?

Means we got her outnumbered.

There were few personal memorabilia aboard that he could see, but they were not Ravn's memorabilia. Confederal agents traveled light and took what they needed when they needed it.

The Fudir waved a spoonful of a chickenlike puree at the bench across from him. "Have a seat," he told his captor. "You look uncomfortable."

"Do I also look foolish?" she replied.

"Afraid I'd try to jump you?"

"No."

"Then . . . ?"

"I meant I was not afraid, not that you would not try."

Donovan grunted and returned his attention to his

meal. So far, he had not asked the Confederal her reasons for kidnapping him. He was a past master at the game of waiting. Either Olafsdottr wanted him to know or not. If she did, she would eventually tell him. If not, asking would not win the answer.

"I will be missed, you know," he told her.

The Ravn's answer was a flash of teeth. "I think noot. The Bartender, he is already sailing your drinks to oother lips. 'Tis noo skin oof his noose who buys them."

"I was on my way to Dangchao. The Hound, Bridget ban, is expecting me. When I don't arrive . . ." He allowed the consequences of his nonarrival to remain unspecified. A Hound of the League could be many things and anything, as adroit and dangerous as a Confederal Shadow, and Bridget ban not least among them.

But Olafsdottr only smiled and answered in Manjrin. "Red Hound missing many years. Some associates claim credit, though I believe their bragging empty."

"You were right to doubt them. She has returned and awaits me even now at Clanthompson Hall."

"Ah. If so, associates much red-faced." Olafsdottr laughed and switched to the Gaelactic that was the lingua franca of the League. "But she hardly awaits you, darling. Detestable in the ears of Bridget ban falls the name of Donovan buigh. Old grudge?"

The Fudir grimaced. "Old love."

"Same thing, no?"

Donovan shrugged and smiled, as if to say that even

old grudges had expiration dates. Olafsdottr might not believe that Bridget ban would come looking for him. Neither did Donovan; but why not sow doubts?

The Long Game between the Confederation of Central Worlds and the United League of the Periphery might be played on a chessboard of suns, and in it this agent or that might be as a grain of sand on a broad beach; but where the agents stood "in the blood and sand," matters were more particular, and interstellar politics only the medium in which they swam. Personal loyalties mattered. Personal grudges mattered. In the sudden flash of the barracuda's teeth, what significance has the vast and swirling ocean?

After Donovan had eaten, Olafsdottr locked him in the ward room. It was decorated to resemble the cabin of an Agadar sloop, a sailing vessel much favored on that watery world. It was longer than it was wide, and paneled in light woods. A holostage with a play deck and swivel chair adorned one end. To its right hung a set of wall-mounted nautical instruments that, the nearest ocean being rather distant, were certainly more decorative than functional. Cabinetry and cushioned benches ran along the walls, including a bunk recessed into the wall. Two comfortable chairs occupied the middle of the room. The overall effect was "taut."

"Stay poot," Olafsdottr said, wagging a finger before she closed and locked the door on him. "Plainty in there to amuse you," she added from the other side.

And so there was. The Fudir's primary amusement

on Jehovah had involved the opening of locked doors. He set to work. "Not very difficult," he judged.

It's a monoship, the Sleuth reminded him. *Why would a one-man ship have high-end locks?*

Why would it have locks at all? wondered Donovan.

𝔚𝔥𝔞𝔱 𝔦𝔰 𝔱𝔥𝔢 𝔰𝔢𝔠𝔬𝔫𝔡-𝔪𝔬𝔰𝔱 𝔣𝔯𝔢𝔮𝔲𝔢𝔫𝔱 𝔲𝔰𝔞𝔤𝔢 𝔬𝔣 𝔪𝔬𝔫𝔬𝔰𝔥𝔦𝔭𝔰? asked the Pedant.

What is the most frequently annoying personality we have to share a head with? the Sleuth answered.

Funny that *you* should ask, the Brute said.

Private yacht?

𝔖𝔢𝔠𝔬𝔫𝔡-𝔪𝔬𝔰𝔱 𝔣𝔯𝔢𝔮𝔲𝔢𝔫𝔱, 𝔖𝔦𝔩𝔨𝔶.

Donovan sighed. Sometimes his head seemed a very crowded place. On occasion, he remembered that he had been the original and the others remained in some sense tenants, and he remembered that he had once been alone.

Perhaps, said the young man in the chlamys. But the "I" that cooks up schemes, and the "I" that remembers everything, and the "I" that is master of every martial art, and . . . all the rest of us . . . We are all the same "I," aren't we? We're closer to you than your skin.

Donovan said nothing. He was not especially fond of his skin, which stretched sallow and drumhead tight across his bones. He still owned that gaunt and hollowed-out look that long years in the Bar of Jehovah had given him. He wondered if he might have always looked that way, even in the flush and vigor of his youth. Assuming he had had a youth, or that it had been flushed with vigor.

We'll remember someday, Pollyanna assured him.

Donovan was less sure. Sometimes matters were lost past all retrieval; and maybe happily so. Some memories might best remain covered than recovered. "I liked it better when you had all fallen silent," he said, and wondered if the drug that Olafsdottr had given him had also upset the delicate truce he had reached with himself the previous year.

"Smuggling," snapped the Fudir, distracted from his inspection of the lock. "Smuggling and bonded courier work. All right? Now quiet down and let me work."

Bonded couriers. Precisely. There is a popular show on Dubonnet's World called Samples and Secrets, in which the unnamed pilot of a monoship brings each episode some package—a secret, a visitor, a treasure—that changes the recipient's life for good or ill.

It's why they're sometimes called "schlepships," the Sleuth said.

The Fudir pulled his special tool from the hidden cache in his sandal and set to work on the lock mechanism. The Pedant had been right. These were not high-security locks. The door opened onto the main hallway.

Ravn Olafsdottr was waiting outside. "Really, Donovan, where do you expect to go?"

The Fudir grinned. "Admit it, Ravn. You would have been disappointed if I hadn't come out. If you wanted me to stay put, you would have had better locks installed."

"I was in a hurry. But I may do so, if you do not behave yourself. You were not supposed to awake so soon. Annoy me too greatly and I will soospend you once more."

"And forego the pleasure of our company?" He looked up and down the corridor. "You have Eyes all through the ship, don't you?"

The Confederal shrugged a little, as if not to belabor the obvious. "And motion sensors for your restlessness. You move about, I hear the ping of your processions."

"Then what does it matter if I stay in one room or not?"

Olafsdottr scratched the bright yellow stubble of her hair. "Who can say? Perhaps you sneak up behind, garrote me, have your wicked way, and take ship back to Jehovah." A foolish notion, her smile said. "We will be good friends sometime, you and I; but that time is not yet."

"Don't be so sure I would want my way with you," the scarred man grumbled. "I've been with more toothsome wenches than you in my time."

"Ooh! Boot do they bite so wail with those tooths?" She gnashed the dentition in question and switched to Manjrin. "You stay ward room now. We past Dangchao. Be on Tightrope soon. Not jog pilot's elbow on such road."

Inner Child chirped with alarm, but Donovan maintained the scarred man's composure. "The Tightrope," he said casually. "No wonder you snatched a monoship. Anything bigger couldn't take that road."

"A narrow way, but correspondingly swift," his kidnapper said in Gaelactic, "as Shree Bernoulli commanded. And speed is of the essence. Urgent matters await us on Henrietta, and the game is worth the candle."

Donovan cocked his head attentively, but Olafsdottr did not elaborate on the nature of the candle. The Pedant volunteered that Henrietta was the sector capital of Qien-tuq, in the Confederal borderlands. Once in the Confederation, escape would become problematical.

"I've heard it said," Donovan suggested, "that the speed of space on the Tightrope is so great that one can cross the Rift standing still."

"Ooh, that is exaggeration, I am thinking! But the walls are close and the subluminal mud encroaches on the channel. It is a bad way and a treacherous one. But one unpatrolled by League corvettes."

"Sounds like a good reason to seize control of the ship before you get us on it."

"Ooh," said Olafsdottr, "you are a foony man, for sure. Should I kill you now and save myself soospense?"

Donovan grinned. "You won't do that. You went to all that trouble to sneak into the League, nab me, and commandeer a handy ship when you could have injected me with something fatal and been done with it. That means you plan to keep me alive, and that means you're taking me somewhere. I'm a valuable cargo."

"Valuable," Olafsdottr admitted, "but not priceless. Don't make your inventory cost greater than you be worth."

That evening, before he turned the lights out, the scarred man removed a particular hologram from his scrip and studied on it.

Four figures sat at an outdoor café table on the sun-lit cobbles of the Place of the Chooser, the great public square in Èlfiuji, in the Kingdom on Die Bold. Bridget ban sat in the middle turned at three-quarters but with her head fully facing the imager. Her smile, broad; her eyes seducing the viewer; her red hair captured in midflight, as if she had just then tossed her head to look at the artist. Her left arm draped Little Hugh's shoulders; her right hand covered the Fudir's on the table. Greystroke's hand rested on her shoulder.

A fellowship, and a good one. He missed them all terribly. The four of them back then had been in search of the Twisting Stone, and the singular tragedy was that they had found it.

"She's not expecting us on Dangchao, you know," Donovan told himselves after restoring the image to his scrip and speaking the lights out. "It was a spur-of-the-moment decision to visit her. She won't know it when we don't show up."

Oh, the harper will know, said the girl in the chiton. She knew we were coming before we did.

"It was going to be a surprise," the Fudir whispered.

No surprise now. No expectation of the harper's broad and welcoming smile. No possibility that the daughter's smile would infect the mother. The fellowship in his hologram had been broken, and broken by his own actions. He had abandoned them, had abandoned Bridget ban, with no word and no explanation. One such desertion might be reparable; two would never be, and even the harper could lose her smile.

Unless he could take the ship from Ravn Olafsdottr.

Snug in his bunk, neatly boxed into the wall, Donovan discovered that the bed was not especially user-friendly. Between the thin pad and the short length, he turned and twisted in pursuit of an elusive relaxation. Perhaps a thicker pad would have settled him; perhaps not. But one of the twists—or one of the turns—brought him against the panel that formed the inner side of the bunk; and the pressure must have been just right, for something went *snick* or *click* and the panel slid aside, and Donovan fell off the bunk on a side that he hadn't known it had.

He found himself in a narrow passageway between the wall of the ward room and the wall of the utility room next to it. There were pipes, ducts, and cable runs, as one normally finds in walls; but there was also crawl space and, here and there, shelves and bins. Inner Child glanced quickly fore and aft, saw nothing in the darkness, but kept watch—for seeing nothing in the dark was hardly a comfort to him.

Oho, said the Sleuth. *The Rightful Owner was a* smuggler. *There are probably caches, passages, and hidey-holes like this all through the ship.* Tyrants and democrats had escaped the people's wrath cocooned in such ships. Secret treaties and covert agreements had traveled secure in their bosoms. Prototypes and patents had been hustled to subsidiaries—or competitors—on sundry worlds.

After this fortuitous discovery, the scarred man took to wandering the monoship at odd hours, investigating its nooks and crannies. He wondered how long the ship had been in Olafsdottr's possession. She might know of the nooks, but perhaps not of the crannies.

Using the secret passages, he could make an end-run around Olafsdottr's security and come upon her from an unexpected direction. Her reflexes could not be markedly inferior to his own, nor her mastery of the arts mortal. His main advantage was that she did not wish to damage him, and this might cause her to hold back if it came to that.

But not every imagined possibility is a real one. The two places where Olafsdottr spent most of her time were the two places where the passages did not run. First was the pilot room, which was in any case too small and cramped for a struggle that included a survivor. The second was her sleeping quarters, where she was most vulnerable, but which was inaccessible from the hidey-holes that otherwise swiss-cheesed the ship. Not all the caches connected. To approach her sleeping quarters meant crossing the spinal corridor, and that was alarmed by her ad hoc security system. It was not an impossible task to circumvent the system, but it would require deactivating several sensors; and that deactivation would in itself consti-tute an alarm.

It irritated Donovan considerably that such a won-derful discovery could not be put to immediate use.

Olafsdottr continued to be wary in his presence, and when they ate together, it was at arm's length. In ex-asperation at the blandness of her cooking, Donovan one day programmed a dinner of Chicken Joe Freezing that had a bit of a bite to it, but Olafsdottr would not taste of it.

"Who knows what wicked spices you have rubbed into that poor hen?" she asked. And never mind that the meat from the protein vats had never gone through the formality of actually having once been a hen.

But even when he had divided his own serving in two and offered her the choice of halves, she demurred, and he wondered if it was not the spiciness itself rather than the possibility of being drugged that put her off.

"I am wounded," he said, "that you do not trust me." Later, he vomited the poison in the ward room's lavatory. Taking the antidote beforehand was risky in any case, and he resolved to find another tactic.

Olafsdottr allowed him some limited exercise time. "Idle hands, devil's tools," she explained, and led him to a fitness room equipped with a variety of machines. Donovan expressed his amazement and gratitude and did not hint that he had already seen the room. The mirror on the back wall was one-way and provided anyone in the passage behind it with an excellent view.

Olafsdottr stood as usual in the doorway, and made helpful suggestions for his exercise regimen. The Brute especially enjoyed the activity; and the Silky Voice used it to work on her enzyme control. But at the conclusion, as he was toweling off, he noticed a handled insert used as a shim for changing clearances on the machine beside him. Save that it was not sharpened, it would make a fine knife. He pulled it out as if to change the forces on the pulley, and found that it had good hand-balance.

Without turning, he threw it at Olafsdottr. The Confederal twisted sideways and snatched it out of the air. She examined the slug of steel in her hands, then looked at Donovan and grinned. "You like play catch?" She slung it back at him on a flat trajectory aimed at his face. "More fun with knives," she added.

The Brute dropped into a crouch and, thrusting his hand up, grabbed the handle as it passed overhead. Careful, he said. Ya don't want ya should break the mirror. That's bad luck.

As he rose, he sent the shim spinning back to Ravn. The courier spun to her left and somehow directed the pinwheeling slug back toward Donovan with barely a twitch to its motion.

Inner Child heard a sound behind them and stepped aside, so that the Brute very nearly missed catching the projectile. He tossed the shim up, caught it by the flat of the blade as it fell, and threw it on a long, lazy turn-and-a-half toward his captor.

"Oh, excellent move," the Confederal applauded. She had to sidestep and reach behind, since the shim was coming at her blade-first. She returned the shim the same way. "But 'crouching-ape' catch better."

On the next round, though, as the shim hurtled toward her, an alarm tripped and a series of sharp chimes sounded through the ship. The Ravn jerked her head around, remembered in time the deadly projectile, and dropped "boneless" to the floor, striking with the flats of her hands to reduce the impact. The shim shot through the space her skull had occupied and rang against the wall across the hall from the doorway.

She had rolled on falling, of course—the body has reasons the mind stops not to ponder—and she came out of the roll into a crouch onto the balls of her feet just as Donovan reached her. Her teaser halted the scarred man an arm's reach away.

"Ooh, that was very clayver, sweet. You play me friendly game of threw-the-knife and betray me at crucial mooment. You play me, and not shim."

Donovan held his hands where she could see them. "What betrayal? I ran over to see if you were all right."

"Not even scratch, my sweet. How you kick oof mootion sensor from here?"

Donovan shook his head. "Must have been a malfunction. Your whole system is jury-rigged. I'm surprised you haven't had false positives before now."

By the guarded look on Olafsdottr's face, he judged that there had been previous false positives, perhaps while he had been in suspension. He said nothing, preferring that any doubts about system reliability be spread by her own mind.

The Confederal waved her weapon. "You go before me. Left at refectory."

The scarred man did as was told. *Idea*, the Sleuth said.

I hope it's better than playing catch with a blunt instrument.

Quiet, Silky. The Ravn's got a "no-not-me." It damps the motion sensors in her vicinity. If we can steal it, or the Fudir can duplicate it, we can sneak up on her when she's asleep; not set off the alarms.

Oh sure, thought the Fudir, Olafsdottr will give me the run of the machine shop.

They had reached the T-intersection. The long stem of the T ran past the ward room and the closet in which he had first awakened all the way to the exterior air locks. The cross-bar led to the refectory and, beyond that, the pilot's saddle. Olafsdottr looked down each corridor, pursing her lips.

The alarm came from here, the Sleuth concluded. *There must be a location code in the alarm pattern. The long and short beeps.*

Dissatisfied, Olafsdottr marched Donovan back to the ward room. "You be a good buoy," she said, "and stay in room." And she closed and uselessly locked the door.

Travel time between stars was long—weeks, sometimes even months, depending on the local speed of space—and there was little to engage the attention save when entering and leaving the Roads. Consequently, the ward room was well stocked with what the great 'Saken philosopher Akobundu had called "the grand continuum of culture"—literature, music, art, travel, the enjoyment of nature, sports, fashion, social vanities, and the intoxication of the senses— though the Rightful Owner's tastes seemed to have run more to the lower strata of that continuum. There were seven cardinal sins, Bridget ban had once told him—and the entertainment center catered to no less than five of them.

More entertaining by far, the Fudir was able to use the play deck to hack into the ship's navigational system, from which he learned that they would be a fortnight on the Newtonian crawl through the high coopers of Abyalon. Olafsdottr would not resume the pilot's saddle for a while. What better time for taking the ship?

Of course, if he realized that, so did his adversary. She would be more alert than ever during the next week and a half.

And so, Donovan set himself to learn about the Rightful Owner. He had no guarantee that such an education would gain him an advantage; but there was a chance that the monoship *Sèan Beta* had additional capabilities of which Olafsdottr was as yet unaware. A weapons cache, perhaps. As far as he knew, Olafsdottr's teaser was the only formal weapon on board.

Of informal weapons, there were of course a plenty.

Time was growing short. After Abyalon, came the Megranome crawl. And after Megranome, the Tightrope branched off and it would be too late to turn back. There was no exit off the Tightrope until it debouched onto Confederal space at Henrietta.

The evening after the Fudir had ferreted out the name of the Rightful Owner—*Rigardo-ji Edelwasser of*

Dumthwaite, Friesing's World—and the refreshingly honest name of his company—*Bonded Smugglers, LLC*—Donovan won the game of waiting.

"It does not grow, does it?" Olafsdottr said from her usual cautious post at the door between the refectory and the pilot's saddle. She had of course eaten earlier, and stood by now while Donovan did the same.

The scarred man had programmed a meal of tikka and naan, and ate noisily and sloppily, using the naan as mittens to pick up the chicken pieces. He looked up at her. "What doesn't?"

"Your hair. It never grows."

Donovan scowled and ran his hand along the tufts that spotted his scalp. "Oh, yes, missy," he said in the Terran patois. "Names very budmash fella, but save him this-fella planti on haircuts."

Olafsdottr nodded gravely. "I have heard this tell. You have soofered great harm." She reached forward, almost as if to tousle the scars in Donovan's hair; but he pulled back, and she was not so foolish as to lean closer.

"Great harm," she continued in doleful tones, "and I speak as one expert in great harm. You are not the only Shadow to feel the nettles of their whims. It is a poor master who beats his dogs. Beat them too much and they will turn on him, as some of us now have. There is a struggle in the Lion's Mouth."

Donovan grunted and applied himself to his naan.

"Do you understand what I have said?" Olafsdottr said.

He looked up, his mouth dripping. "And what is Hecuba to me, or I to Hecuba?"

His captor seemed uncertain of the Terran reference. "Do you know the Lion's Mouth? I have been told that your memory is . . . uncertain."

"You mean 'wiped.' It's your version of the Kennel where the Hounds train; except you breed rabid dogs."

Olafsdottr crossed her hands over her breast. "You wound me, Donovan-san. Am I a mad dog? Well, perhaps so." She spoke more intently. "Some of us are mad enough to challenge the Names. There is civil war among us."

Donovan returned his attention to his meal. "Good luck then to the both of you. Let me know how it turns out."

"We are bringing home all agents from the Periphery."

"You've made a mistake then. We're not an agent. We've been retired."

"Ooh. Our retirement plan is very singular. There is oonly one way to retire."

Donovan did not ask her what that one way was. "You forget Those of Name discarded us."

"Then when you join with us you may take your revenge for that, and sweet will be the taking, I think."

"Very sweet, but I had it in mind to watch from the sidelines. Revenge is a dish best served cold—and by someone else."

Olafsdottr shook her head. "No sidelines this fight."

Donovan wiped up the last of his sauce and stuffed

the naan in his mouth. He had gotten hints of this last year from Billy Chins. "How many of you are in it?" he asked around the bread.

"Almost half have lit the lamp."

"Almost half . . ." He swallowed. "Oh, *that's* encouraging. Half the Lion's Mouth against a regime in power for centuries, with total control of the police, the Protectors, and the . . . What of the 'boots,' the military? Where do they stand?"

Ravn cocked her head. "We conduct this war as we always have—with stealth, with intrigue, with assassination. Some boots," she allowed, "may know a civil war is broken out. But there are no bloody battles; no planets bombarded. No great stupid mobs rushing about shooting at one another . . . and missing."

"Not yet, anyway." Donovan tossed his napkin into the fresher and took his dishes to the sink, where he scraped the remnants into the recycler. He turned abruptly and faced her. "Why me?" he said. "What good would I do the rebellion? I'm one, broken old man."

"Not so old as that; and broken pieces have the sharpest edges."

A facile response, Donovan thought. That her people meant to use him in some manner, he had no doubt; but in what manner was as yet unclear. *Perhaps as no more than a knife thrown by one side at the other.*

"You think on what I have told you, Donovan," Olafsdottr said as she marched him back to his nominal prison cell. "You will see it is the right thing to do, and you and I will be famous comrades."

That argument, more than any of the others, planted caution in the heart of Donovan buigh. For he had never heard an agent of Those of Name cite "the right thing to do" as an argument in favor of anything.

CENGJAM GAAFE: THE FIRST INTERROGATORY

Méarana strikes the arm of her chair with the flat of her hand. "I knew it! He was coming here, after all. To see you, Mother. You know what that means?"

Bridget ban tosses her head. "That he's a masochist?"

The harper makes a moue. "He wanted a second chance."

"He's had that already."

"A third, then. What difference does the count make?"

Bridget ban sets her face and turns to her. "This is something we can discuss later." And a motion of her eyes indicates both Olafsdottr and Graceful Bintsaif.

The harper shrugs. "As you will. But I think there are no surprises for the tale-spinner."

The Hound gives her attention back to the—Prisoner? Guest? Visitor? "Tell me," she says, "how you can know the thoughts of Donovan buigh, when I doubt even he knows them so well?"

The Confederal smiles. "You must grant me two

things. The first is many weeks of conversation between us, in which he may have revealed his mind to me."

"That would be quite a revelation as I understand things. And second?"

"And second, you must grant me some poetic license." Olafsdottr nods at the glasses of nectar that stand before each of them. "You have not drunk from your glass. Do I take that as evidence that the glass set initially before me was tinctured with sooth juice? Oho! I have not heard Graceful Bintsaif behind me lift her glass, either."

"Oh, for pity's sake," says the harper. "Here!" And she drinks from her own glass and then reaches across the table to hand it to the Confederal. Bridget ban hisses, but the agent makes no move to snatch her daughter. It might come to a struggle later—at some point they must all give thought to whether and how Olafsdottr would leave the Hall—but for now she has come merely to talk.

The Shadow swallows the rest of the nectar. "Ooh. Very tasty. Stoorytelling is dry work."

"How much of the story so far has been true?" asks Graceful Bintsaif.

Olafsdottr turns to look at her. "Soo untroosting, you are. All of it true. Perhaps not all factual."

The junior Hound snorts. "A contradiction."

"On the contrary! What is factual is what is done, accomplished. A verdict. But what is true is what is faithful, and loyal. Perhaps all facts are true, but not all truths are fact." She turns to face Bridget ban and the harper. "A story may be true to life."

"Verdict," says the harper, "means 'to speak truth' in some ancient tongue."

The Confederal tilts her head sideways. "Does it? Oh, there are languages older than the oldest tongues! Why do you not fetch your harp? He toold me how well you play, how well you improovise on a theme."

The harper looks to her mother. "I think she tells the truth. The Donovan she describes is a man I recognize. If she has embellished his thoughts, she has not done so falsely."

Bridget ban considers this for a time. She folds her hands flat together and tucks them under her lips, and her eyes grow hard and distant. Her lips move, just a little. Finally, she makes a sign with her right hand and lays both hands flat on the arms of her chair. "I will be no barbarian. You came to us unafraid. You may remain in the same manner. Mr. Wladislaw, bring Miss Lucia's harp to the sitting room, please. And . . ." She nods to Olafsdottr. "May I serve you some coffee?"

The Confederal's eyes widen; then she laughs. "Of course. I come expecting to drink more than that."

"And bring coffee, also," the mistress of the Hall tells the Ears through which her butler listens.

"I don't understand," Méarana says to the smiles she sees on the other three women. "What is so funny about coffee?"

Olafsdottr answers. "It is what we say in the Confederacy, lady harp, when we bring someone in for questioning. Cengjam gaafe. 'Invite in for coffee.' There are other phrases—samman, kaowèn, or worst of all duxing kaoda. La, we have more ways of asking questions than we have questions to ask. Ooh, here come faithful retainer with harp and coffee!"

Mr. Wladislaw accomplishes this Herculean task by carrying the harp in his own hands. It is a *clairseach*, a lap harp of the old style, with metal strings played with the nails. It is draped in a velvet cloth of royal purple and Méarana believes she can hear the strings singing to her. Likely, it is the breath of the air passing through the chords as the butler carries it; but Méarana prefers the poetic to the mundane. The passage of air explains *how* it sings; it does not explain *that* it sings.

The coffee is brought in a more pedestrian manner by the butler's assistant, who wears white gloves of all things and pushes before him a gravity cart with a silver coffee service upon it. If the Confederal wonders that the coffee has already been waiting to be fetched, and that Bridget ban has orchestrated the meeting to achieve this gesture, she does not show it on her face, which is as cheerfully concealing as ever.

"You smile too much," Bridget ban tells her.

Olafsdottr's grin broadens. "I will try to be more dooleful as my tale unwinds. Most people, I think, would wish more opportunity to smile than what their lives give them."

"A man may conceal with a smile more effectively than with a great stone face. The stone face may not reveal much; but it will always reveal that it is not revealing. The smiling face appears open, which makes it the greater lie."

The Confederal nods. "I see you do not lie."

Bridget ban stiffens for a moment. "Being kidnapped could have been no reason to smile for Donovan buigh. Have you no regrets at what you deprived him of?"

"Ooh, I have many regrets; as many as I have winters behind me. The Fates deprive a man of nothing but that they do not grant him something else. What have I deprived him of? You? By your own account, he did not have that when he left Jehovah."

"When you *took* him from there," Méarana corrects her. She has been tuning her harp to the second mode, for Olafsdottr had told a sad onset to the tale. Father ripped untimely from his own intentions, on the very verge of coming home. What, she wonders, could be more tragic than that?

"But how closely do you attend me?" the Confederal asks the room. "He had great fun, the scarred man did. Opening my locks. Poisoning my food. Throwing metal slugs at my head. Planning my ambush and death. What more fun may a man have and live afterward? As you have orchestrated this tête-à-tête, so did I orchestrate our little voyage. He woke too early, I grant you. But . . . have you ever danced with a cobra? Sometimes, in a life grown hardened to danger, one must seek the greater risk to enjoy the greater thrill."

Méarana hums a tenor F, pauses to adjust one of the half intervals on the strings (for her chords are no more well tempered than she), and then pauses expectantly and looks around the room at the others.

Graceful Bintsaif has been watching her with some incredulity. Perhaps she wonders at playing music with a cobra in the room. But music, by long tradition, eases the serpent's bile.

Bridget ban, for her part, has waited patiently. She is long inured to her daughter's eccentricities. And well so, for had not one of those eccentricities impelled her to seek out her father and to rescue her mother from utter oblivion? And all that with no small risk to herself. Bridget ban does not fear death, for she holds to a belief that death is not the end. But unending suspension in a lost and derelict ark was no more death than it was life. Rather, it was some awful schrödingerian halfway point, partaking of the worst features of both.

When all seems settled, the Hound, who has never once taken her eyes from her guest, pours out a cup of coffee and hands it to Ravn Olafsdottr. "A small question," she says.

Olafsdottr drinks the hot brew without hesitation, even though its bitter taste could hide a thousand potions that in pear nectar would curdle its sweetness. "Ask," she says.

"For all his games at escape, for all his secret passageways, and picked locks, and poisoned Joe Freezy, I see that Donovan buigh . . ." She spreads her arms to take in the room. ". . . is not here. And this tells me that all such attempts failed. Else, he would be telling me this tale—and with far more relish, as I recall the man—and you would be sitting less comfortably."

Olafsdottr's laugh is like the trilling of a bird on the wing. "Noo. The Fates rule all, and some things are not to be. Our two destinies were intertwined. I meant what I said, that he and I would become great companions; although the Fates are cruel and have a sense of humor, so that while the foreseeing was true, the companionship was not what anyone expected. The joke, as always, is on us; though seldom to our amusement. Play, harper, and your strings our tale promote and with your chords catch out the discord note."

II. RIFTWARD: THE FROG PRINCE

The next day, the Fudir broke Rigardo-ji's security code and entered the smuggler's files. These proved as dull as any collection of legitimate invoices, as the sundry planetary and state governments around the Periphery were notional in what goods they chose to blockade. During the Great Cleansing, the peoples of Terra had been scattered widely on the hither side of the Rift and unequally gifted as regards terraformation. Some worlds had in plenty what others lacked entire. Thus, it was worth a rich man's purse to smuggle boxes of oatmeal cookies from Hawthorne Rose to Ramage; or tobacco sticks onto Gladiola.

The smuggler's most recent invoice was for the delivery to Foreganger Prime of a secret protocol entered into by Abyalon with the People of Foreganger. He had been returning to Abyalon with the chopped protocol—and a gift called "the Frog Prince" from the People to the Molnar of the Cinel Cynthia deep in the Hadramoo.

The People's Navy swore revenge on the pirates of the Hadramoo, the Pedant remembered, after the hijacking and massacre of the tour liner *Merry b Starinu*, four standard years ago.

Perhaps the gift is a peace offering.

The Fudir was doubtful. "The People of Foreganger make peace on their own terms, usually after some notable vengeance."

"One way or the other," Donovan said, "Foreganger won't be happy that their present was hijacked along with the courier's ship. Pedant, where was the *Starinu* hijacked?"

Off Abyalon.

<And Abyalon and Foreganger have entered into a secret protocol.>

How much you want to bet, said the Sleuth, *that this "Frog Prince" is some sort of vengeance weapon that Abyalon hired from the People to use against the Cynthians?*

"No bet," said Donovan.

A bomb, do you think?

"Wonderful," said the Fudir. "A bomb on board. We didn't have near enough problems."

If we can find where it's stashed, the Brute suggested, we maybe can use it to knock off Olafsdottr and take the ship from her.

"If it's a big enough bomb to take out the Molnar," Donovan pointed out, "it's too big to set off aboard a monoship. A takeover weapon must be one that can kill or incapacitate the Ravn without killing or incapacitating us."

<Someone in the room!> cried Inner Child.

The scarred man swung abruptly away from the holostage, saw nothing, turned the other way.

More nothing. The ward room was empty.

Where did you see it, Child?

<From the corner of our eye. To the right of the stage.>

"Sleuth, you and Fudir check it out."

The Fudir took control of the scarred man and went to the back wall, where the nautical instruments were mounted.

The wood paneling was genuine, and done up in a basket-weave pattern of vertical and horizontal slats, so that the wall seemed some vast sort of wicker-work. The Fudir glanced toward the console's swivel chair. If Inner Child had glimpsed something in this direction . . . The Sleuth did the geometry . . . it would have stood approximately—here. He ran his hands along the interstices.

You're thinking a secret door, ain't ya, Sleuthy?

It was a logical deduction, and logic was the Sleuth's forte. The smuggler's ship was riddled with such things. The Fudir's explorations had already found secret cabinets with jewels and stolen artwork intended for clandestine delivery in the Old Planets. Nothing to use as a weapon, except perhaps for the Peacock vase.

I just thought of something, said the Sleuth.

And you're gonna tell us.

The road to the Hadramoo splits off here at Abyalon. What happens if we don't deliver this "Frog Prince" thing to the Molnar?

Who cares?

No, I don't mean what will the Molnar do. Or even what will the Abyalonic Council or the People of Foreganger do. I mean, what will the Frog Prince do?

The scarred man paused in his examination of the wall. If the Abyaloni and the People were deploying a vengeance weapon against the Cynthians, there might be a delicate matter of timing involved.

As in time bomb?

<That could kill the messenger.>

"Abyalon wouldn't agree to that," the Fudir muttered.

"Foreganger might," Donovan replied, "without telling Abyalon."

Wonderful. If the Frog Prince were a bomb set to detonate when it reached the Hadramoo and Olafsdottr took the ship to Megranome Road instead, the thing would detonate instead when they were on the Tightrope.

Who says it's on a timer? asked Pollyanna. Or even that it's a bomb?

<Right. It could be poison gas. Something, you give it to the Molnar and he opens it, and—poof— he's dead.>

If Silky had not heightened the scarred man's senses with a cocktail of enzymes, he might not have felt the light puff of air that wafted from between two vertical slats. If Inner Child had not mentioned poison gas, he might not have flinched from it. The Sleuth explored the slats with his fingertips and identified the edge of a door; and once he had the edge of it, the rest of the outline followed easily.

No obvious handle. The Fudir began to push and twist the various instruments fastened to the wall.

It's probably not booby-trapped, Pollyanna said.

The scarred man hesitated.

"Pollyanna!" said Donovan.

She's right. What sort of fool booby-traps his own ship?

<A smuggler who has left for a night carousing in the Bar of Jehovah?> Inner Child suggested.

Nah. He'd set locks, not bombs. The Brute twisted the chronometer, jiggled the barometer, pushed the binnacle. It was only when he turned the knob on the compass that they heard a *click* and the panel swung gently inward.

"You can come out now, Ravn, dear," he cooed.

But no one stepped forth and when Donovan entered he saw it was not a cache but a passage. The back wall was a blind. To the right a short connection joined a second passage that seemed to run lengthwise up the ship—probably the one behind the cabinets. To the left, was a narrow corridor and it was from that direction that he heard the soft sound of a closing latch.

Inner Child edged around the blind, saw that the passage was empty and crept gingerly through it. The Fudir made no sound with his footfalls; and even his breath was still as death.

Was this an elaborate ambush? But Olafsdottr had no need of ambushes. She could have executed him at any time. She was keeping him alive because her side wanted to use him in their civil war. So what was this about? Just playing stealth games? There were more exercises than the merely physical, and boredom was a wondrous motivator.

The passageway made a dogleg and, passing through a second door, Donovan emerged into the cold well of the pantry, surrounded by cuts of harvested meats, vegetables, and juices in rows of low-entropy receptacles. The door he had come through had masqueraded as a rack of shelves.

Leaving the cold well, Donovan passed into the pantry. A wintermelon, an arm's length long, sat on the carving board. Succumbing to impulse, he pulled a carving knife from its scabbard and, holding the blade by the point, threw it from the far side of the pantry. The blade performed a satisfying somersault before sinking to its hilt into the melon.

By now, the motion sensors would have alerted Olafsdottr to activity in the pantry. But he had stayed out of the ambit of the room's Eye. He reentered the cold well and thence returned to the ward room.

"Well, that was entertaining," the Fudir said when they had seated himself again at the play deck. "It seems our Ravn is a bit of a tease."

<Will she wonder if a knife is missing?>

"She'd be a fool if she hasn't kept inventory; and the motion alarm will pique her curiosity. It may puzzle her to find the knives all accounted for and the wintermelon assassinated. I can only hope it drives her mad wondering what else might be missing."

He awoke the holostage and noticed immediately that the files he had been reading were gone. A few minutes of searching failed to relocate them. Not just closed, but gone.

The Fudir stared purse-lipped at the hidden door, now also closed. "A roundabout means to get me away from the console," he muttered. "She could have waltzed in, held her teaser to my head, and taken the files any time she pleased."

Something does not add up.

At dinner that evening, while Donovan ate a concoction of soybeans and bilberries, Olafsdottr announced that they would enter the Abyalon–Megranome Road in four days. Abyalon's network of Space Traffic Control lasers was already pushing the ship toward the Visser hoop that was its entrance ramp. In the final sprint, the ship's onboard Alfven engines would engage, grab hold of the "strings of space," and vault the ship over the bar into the superluminal tube. That would be a bad time to bother the pilot. Were the ship to miss the hole, it would pass Newton's-c in flat space and go out in a Čerenkov blink.

The ancient god Shree Einstein had decreed that nothing could move faster than the speed of light. But he had also decreed that space had no objective existence. And so, since it was no thing, space as such could move faster than light. At this concession, his rival, Shree Maxwell, had loosed his demons, and created convection currents within the æther of Ricci tensors, shaping the network of Krasnikov tubes known as "Electric Avenue." So while a ship hurtling down such a tube was still constrained by the speed of light, within the tube local-c might be arbitrarily high.

Nor could Shree Einstein see how his commandments had been flouted. The tube walls formed a Visser Skin, laminas of progressively slower space called the subluminal mud, which decoupled the interior causally from normal space. In a sense, a ship in the tube network was no longer "in" the universe, but "underneath."

All this had been understood in ages past, in the old Commonwealth of Suns; and being understood, had been well engineered; and being well engineered, understanding no longer mattered. The formulas worked, and machines could be taught to work them. That was all a man need know.

On his return to the ward room, Donovan noticed that a steel bar had been welded to the outer door and, when turned on a pivot, would prevent the door from opening. Donovan raised an eyebrow to his captor.

"Simple means often best," she announced. "Have not had good night's sleep since you awoke."

"If you don't like my company, you can drop me off at the transit station in Abyalon's coopers and I'll catch the next liner back to Die Bold."

Olafsdottr smiled. "You be a foony man, Doonoovan. I have said soo many times." Then she ushered him in and closed the door behind him. Donovan heard the steel bar slide into place. A metric minute later, the door opened again and Olafsdottr stuck her head in. "Peekaboo," she said. "Joost checking you stay poot." She grinned, closed the door, and shortly the steel bar slid into place a second time.

The Fudir arranged pillows on the bunk and pulled the sheets up over them. Then he took up a station in the corner beside the hidden door and waited.

One reason why the scarred man excelled at the

game of waiting was that most of him could sleep while the rest took turns on guard. Inner Child and the Brute stood sentry while the Silky Voice marshaled and concentrated the requisite enzymes. Genistein and isoflavonoids from the soybeans, anthocyanocides from the bilberries, she sent them off to fortify the night vision of the retinal rods. It would not be fair to say the scarred man could see in the dark, but "you are what you eat," and it would not be right to call him blind, either.

After some time had gone by and the night was well advanced, the door slid open and Inner Child nudged the Fudir awake. A figure slipped into the room, paused to assess motion, and flowed swiftly toward the bed on which the scarred man ought to have been lying.

Partway there, it paused in watchful silence, and the Fudir noted a club of some sort in its hand. Then, apparently satisfied, it backed away and strode to the holostage, where it seated itself at the play deck. The scarred man slipped up behind it in the dark and placed one hand over its mouth and with the other plucked the club from its hand.

"Rigardo-ji Edelwasser, I presume," he whispered into its ear.

Donovan felt the man stiffen, try to turn. "*Nu, nu, nu,*" he said with the Silky Voice. "*Gentle, my good sir. Be not afraid. You are Rigardo-ji, the Rightful Owner of this vessel? Nod your head.*" The head bobbed once in his grip. "*I will release you, but you must make no move nor cry. I have destroyed all the Eyes in this room, citing my modesty, and she has assented by not replacing them. But we will speak in whispers, in case she has salted this room with Ears. She is accustomed to my self-conversations, but speak too loudly and she might wonder if I speak with too many voices. Do you understand?"*

Again, a single, spastic nod of the head.

"Good, good. We are in the same boat, you and we. There is no need to struggle."

When Donovan unloosed his hold, Rigardo-ji turned to face him. "Are you a madman? I've been watching, and I think you are mad. That's why she locks you in here."

"Wouldn't that make *you* mad? Why have you been lurking in the wainscoting all this time?"

"Am I a fool? A poor, honest smuggler, me, just trying to make a living. I'd been drinking and, when I heard her bang through the lock, I hid in one of my . . ."

"One of your hidey-holes. Go on."

He shrugged. "And I passed out. Came to after we were under way. Guess she never realized I was still aboard. I figured out what she was, toot sweet, and I ain't no match for a Confederal Shadow. I didn't dare try to take her on myself. 'Sides . . ." The smuggler flipped his hands. "She was going the right direction, so there wasn't no rush. I come out now and then just to check the headings. I figured if I just waited, something would come up."

"And something did."

"Yeah. You."

"But you're not sure about me, or you would have approached me sooner."

"It was pretty clear you were her prisoner. That

made you her enemy, but it didn't make you my friend. For all I knew, you were Confederal bound too, and you'd gang up on me if I showed myself. I overheard some of what you two was saying, but I don't speak birdsong, and I wasn't always where I could eavesdrop."

Donovan considered the man before him. He could see, even in the dim-lit darkness, the tightness of his mouth and eyes. "Why come out tonight?"

"I thought . . . it was time we made contact."

Liar, the Sleuth said. *He checked the bunk to make sure we were sleeping—and had a club in case we weren't.* But Donovan only said, "You didn't wake me. You went to the console."

"I've been dead reckoning. I needed to check our position, and it's safer to do that here than in the control room. I been out a coupla times, but sometimes I have to cross a hallway and that sets off her damn motion sensors. How does she bear? The ship, I mean."

"Four days out from the Megranome Road."

"Oh." The smuggler's concern was palpable. "That ain't good. We need to take the Biemtí to the Cynthia Cluster."

"To deliver a geegaw to the Molnar."

Donovan felt hesitation in the smuggler's posture.

"You read through my work orders," Rigardo-ji said. "I thought I snatched them in time. Look, that's top secret—need-to-know—and the penalty clauses Foreganger lays down . . ."

The Brute tightened his grip on the smuggler. "**Keep the voice down, I toldja.**" Then Donovan said, "I promise not to tell the People. I scanned your current invoices, to see if you had anything aboard I could use as a weapon. Short of breaking a vase over her head, I didn't find anything."

"There may be something we can use," the smuggler allowed. "I can read between the lines when I gotta. With two of us, we got a chance. I'll go get it out. Then you distract the 'Fed, and I pot her. No offense, good buddy, but you've had three chances already to kill her and passed up each one."

Donovan thought about it and reluctantly agreed that the roles had to split that way. If Rigardo-ji suddenly appeared from nowhere, Olafsdottr would recognize it precisely as a distraction and the element of surprise would be irretrievably lost.

"You'll only get one shot," Donovan said.

"I'll only need one. But it's got to take her by surprise. I woulda tried something already, but I got no illusions. A microsecond's warning, and I wouldn't even get the one shot."

Donovan did not know how good a shot the smuggler might be. Many an eye and hand, steady on the range, grew uncertain when a living person was in the target hairs. Rigardo-ji sat rigid, Donovan's arms upon him, eyes wide, stinking of sweat. Slowly, as if disengaging, the scarred man released him, stepped back.

"It will have to be soon," he said. "Before we enter the Roads." *And before you lose your nerve.* He did not voice that thought.

"Tomorrow," the man said. "After dinner. There's a T-intersection where . . ."

"I know it." It was where the false alarm had been tripped the other day.

"There's a storage space behind the cross hall. Sometimes, they bring containers up the long hallway, and I open the panel and they dolly them straight in. It's empty right now. I can make my way into it. You come past, turn up the long hall like you do. Your backs are to the panel. You get her to stand still. I slide the panel open and . . ." He made a gun of his fingers. "Pop. Pop. I got her."

Donovan said nothing, and after a moment the smuggler looked at his fingers and self-consciously wiggled them, as if throwing the imaginary gun away. "That's the important thing," he said. "You gotta distract her while I open the panel or else she'll hear it. I mean these are cargo doors; they ain't exactly stealthed."

"In the back," Donovan said.

"Safer that way, don't you think? I don't wanna give her the chance. Confederal Shadows, they're ruthless. I've read the stories."

"Do you have something nonlethal, something to disable her instead? I know some people on Dangchao who wouldn't mind getting her as a sort of house present when I visit."

"Who do you know that would keep a Confederation agent as a house pet?"

"People who ask Questions."

Rigardo-ji shrank from him and made Ganesha's sign to ward off bad luck. "I shoulda known you was no ordinary prisoner. Yeah. Yeah, sure. There's something in my stock. It'll knock her out, but not kill her, if that's what you want."

Inner Child heard the scraping of a steel bar. "<Quick,>" he whispered through the scarred man's lips. "<She's coming!>" Donovan added, "Tomorrow, after dinner."

The smuggler vanished like smoke. The panel beside the holostage clicked shut. Donovan threw himself into one of the chairs and sat twisted on the cushions.

Olafsdottr opened the ward room's door and entered just behind her teaser. Her left hand slapped the lights on and Donovan pretended to be flustered by the sudden light. He raised his head, as if he had been dozing in the chair, and shielded his eyes with his arm.

The Shadow looked about the room, grinned, and said, "Good night, Doonoovan-buoy. You have a very crowded head, boot noo moor whisper. Sleep tight."

The next day ran slow. Donovan read a book from the ship's virtual library, but afterward he could not have explained what it was about. He participated in a simulation of the battle of Mushinro, taking the part of the doomed Valencian general Kick. It was widely assumed that Kick had the battle won and it was only his hesitation at a crucial juncture that had permitted the victory by the Ramage-led coalition. But Donovan's attention was not on the simulation and his own hesitation at a different juncture lost the battle yet again. Only when the dinner hour at last approached, did the scarred man realize the root of his unease.

He did not trust the smuggler, Rigardo-ji.

It was a small thing, but the devil, it was said, lurked ever in the details. There had been a hint of thuggishness beneath the fear, and there had been that moment when, simulating a gun with his fingers, Edelwasser had said, "Pop. Pop."

Two shots.

A second shot just to make sure? Or a second shot to tie up the other loose end?

Last meals, it is said, are consumed with greater gusto than any other. Dinner conversation ranged from the various modes of mayhem he and Ravn had mastered to the craft with which Aloysh-pandit arranged colored oils on the surface of still pools. Were it not for the fact that Ravn was dragging him into a civil war of which he wanted no part and in which he would likely find his doom, he would have found her an agreeable companion.

On the other hand, years before, she had been tasked to kill him if he failed his mission. A close relationship, an intimate relationship; but not a cuddly one. Olafsdottr had a most pleasant smile. But she would smile while she cut him down.

They left the refectory together and walked down the short hallway in their usual parade: Donovan to the fore, Olafsdottr behind with her teaser to the ready. She no longer held it shoved into his back, but neither had she relaxed to the point of shoving it into her holster. "But I suggest you are wrong, sweet," she said, continuing their conversation as if they had been amiable companions on a stroll. "The Roomie tradition of opera was much too bombastic. Their drama was too melo. The Nipny tradition was more spare, more elegant, more minimal."

The scarred man allowed the Pedant to hold up the other end of the conversation. "You misunderstand the criteria. Grand opera and Nō have not the same objectives. One may as well assail the lemon for lacking the sweet of sugar cane. Each may excel—but toward different ends. It is only the values we place on the ends themselves that make one means seem less than the other."

"Ah, but sweet, are not the weights we place upon our goals what matter most in the end?"

They had reached the T-intersection and had turned down the long stem of it. Donovan paused and said, "For me, the overthrow of the Names pales against one hour with my daughter in her home." When he closed his eyes, he saw Méarana's face before him, puzzled and hurt. He turned and faced his captor. "Make me one promise, Ravn."

Olafsdottr stopped a pace short of him and tilted her head, birdlike, to the side. "And what is that, my sweet?"

"Promise me that if I go with you, you will go to Dangchao afterward and tell Francine Thompson and her daughter Lucia why it was I never came."

"I am to walk into the enemy's lair on such a lark? You ask much of me, Donovan buigh."

Indeed, he was. He could see down the length of the corridor the blank wall where the secret panel must be. The expression "fish in a barrel" came to mind. Rigardo-ji would have a clear shot down the entire length of the corridor, all the way to the cargo lock at the end. No one in the corridor could escape, unless they made it to the ward room, or into the closet where he had first been kept.

And that included him. A steady eye might pick off the Confederal without also hitting her prisoner, but Donovan knew in that moment of clarity that the smuggler meant to kill them both.

"Let's go," Donovan said, turning to resume their trek.

Perversely, it was now Olafsdottr who held him back. "What is the hurry, Doonoovan? You ask me to venture into the heart of the Oold Planets to accost *a Hound*? From sooch a joorney even I may not return."

"Fair is fair, then. Isn't that what you're asking of me?"

"Ah, but I am not *asking*. Your condition is not a conditional."

Donovan could not take his eyes off the wall at the far end. He waited for the panel to open and death to emerge. "We can discuss this in my room," he said.

And still, like an ancient hero, ankle tied to a stake in the ground, Olafsdottr remained in the line of fire. "Ooh. Soo anxious! Do you have a trap led for me in your room? What cleverness have you been oop to?"

But then she noticed that his attention was fixed not upon her, but upon the far wall. She spun and aimed her teaser down the hallway. "What is it, sweet? What wickedness have you wrought?"

In turning away, she had turned her back on Donovan buigh. The Brute took charge of the scarred man's body and leapt for her. She buckled under his sudden weight and went to her belly and the breath woofed out of her. A moment, she lay still; and then she twitched and Donovan felt a burning tingle in his side.

And came to lying on the cramped bunk in the ward room. Olafsdottr sat, chin cupped in one hand, in one of the two soft chairs that gave the room its center. "Clever move, O best one. How you lulled me these past days! And had I lost my grip either on my teaser or my wits, success might have been yours. That would have been no good thing, either for me or for you."

She leaned forward and patted Donovan's cheek, and when he struggled to grab her arm he learned that he was strapped into the bunk. "You stay here some few day, I think. Review error of ways. Soon we enter Abyalon-Megranome Road. You no jog elbow."

After the Shadow had left, Donovan engaged in some experimental struggles, but Olafsdottr was a professional. He did not expect much to come of it, and was not disappointed when not much did.

"You did not want to see her killed," Donovan told himselves. "Why?"

The captive comes to love his captor, said the Silky Voice.

I don't love that stick, said the Brute.

𝔈𝔡𝔢𝔩𝔴𝔞𝔰𝔰𝔢𝔯 𝔭𝔯𝔬𝔪𝔦𝔰𝔢𝔡 𝔥𝔢 𝔴𝔬𝔲𝔩𝔡 𝔫𝔬𝔱 𝔤𝔬 𝔣𝔬𝔯 𝔞 𝔨𝔦𝔩𝔩, said the Pedant. 𝔇𝔦𝔡 𝔶𝔬𝔲 𝔫𝔬𝔱 𝔱𝔯𝔲𝔰𝔱 𝔥𝔦𝔪?

"And our lack of trust was justified," said the Fudir. "He didn't show."

<A different sort of betrayal than the one we feared . . . >

"Yes, why did he not show?" asked Donovan.

A) He lost his nerve, suggested the Sleuth. *B) We had the time or place mixed up. C) We were early. D) We were late. E) He couldn't find the weapon he planned on using. F) He found it, but it wasn't loaded. G) He . . .*

Shaddap, suggested the Brute.

It doesn't matter. Brute didn't want to see her killed. Why?

Who sez? Was me that *jumped* her.

No, you shoved her to the floor to knock her out of the line of fire.

"It wouldn't have worked," the Fudir told them. "Rigardo-ji would have kept on shooting. He would have shot us too, I think. I think he was planning to all along."

<I never did trust him.>

You never trust anyone, Child.

<I can't see where trusting has gotten us much so far.>

The young man in the chlamys said, *I didn't trust him, either. Something in his carriage, something in his expression.*

"What do you say, Pollyanna?" Donovan asked. "You always see the silver lining in every dark cloud."

The girl in the chiton was sitting on the floor next to the bunk. *And you see the dark cloud around every silver lining,* she said. *This will all work out. Wait and see.*

Donovan expected that the smuggler would return that night, using the secret panel through which he had originally entered, so Inner Child and the Brute kept watch through the scarred man's half-slit eyes and listened through his ears. Some explanation would be forthcoming for the failure to act as promised, but Donovan was no longer sure he was unhappy with that failure. Some instinct had urged the Brute to protect their captor. The Brute was not a keen thinker, but his instincts were sound.

He heard a clatter behind the wall and pressed his ear against the bulkhead to make it out more keenly. It came at intervals, distant at first, toward the rear of the ship; but it seemed to draw closer, come adjacent to him, and then pause. There was no sound for a time and the impression slowly grew within the heart of Donovan buigh that something lurked on the other side of the panel; and that this something sensed his presence.

Suddenly uneasy, Donovan pulled away from the panel as far as the straps would allow. He exhaled as softly as he could, made no move, no sound.

Moments dripped by.

Then there was a clattering by his head and a moment later intermittent impacts receding down the hidden passageway. The scarred man began to breathe normally. The sounds reminded the Silky Voice of a bouncing ball—if the ball were metallic and could hesitate from one bounce to the next.

A little later that evening, Inner Child heard the same sounds returning. He passed the sensations on to the Sleuth to puzzle over and continued to wait for the smuggler to appear.

But no one came to them that night, nor all the next day, nor the night after that.

He wondered if the smuggler had acted on his own after all. Maybe he had ambushed Ravn and taken control of the ship, and was content now to keep Donovan strapped into his bunk for the foreseeable future.

But on the third day, after the ship had entered Megranomic space and had begun the Newtonian crawl toward the Palisades Parkway, it was Ravn Olafsdottr who came to release him from his bonds. "Coome now, sweet," she said, "you moost be hoongry." She unlocked one hand, gave him the key, and stepped back.

"It's a psychological trick," the Fudir told her as he worked the key into the locks that held the remaining straps together. "That Alabaster accent is a comic's affectation. Most of us in the League have been conditioned to regard hooters as flighty. That's not exactly fair to the Alabastrines, but it helps if your adversary underestimates your wit."

"You very clever, friend. How transparent this unworthy one, that you see through her so!"

"And the Manjrin makes you seem sinister." Donovan, now loosened from his straps, stood up and rubbed his arms. Olafsdottr held out her hand and, after a moment, Donovan laid the key in it. "You didn't have to pull them so tight, you know."

"Yes," she said gravely. "I did."

"Anything interesting happen while I was tied up?"

Olafsdottr cocked her head nearly sideways. "Should something have?"

"Never mind." He stepped past her. "I'm hungry. Let's do lunch." He didn't wait to see if she followed, or if she held her teaser aimed at the small of his back.

The scarred man rustled his own lunch: daal and baked beans and sautéed mushrooms, with scrambled eggs and cold, fatty bacon drawn from the cold well in the pantry. Olafsdottr recoiled from this concoction when he brought it to the refectory.

"Why?" asked the Fudir. "How do you break your fast?"

Olafsdottr toyed with her teaser, remaining out of reach of her prisoner. "What any sensible one eats. A soft-boiled egg enthroned on a cup with its large end sheared off, a small plate of fruits of varied colors— green melon, yellow pineapple, white wintermelon— arranged as to best effect. A cup of pressed coffee thick enough to stand a spoon upright."

The Fudir regarded her curiously. "I would think espresso would be the last thing you would need. No wonder you always seem so wired. You should try Terran food someday."

She regarded his lunch with disfavor. "Perhaps. Someday."

"So, it's been a quiet couple of days?"

"With you bound in bunk, how could it be other?"

Well, said the Sleuth internally, *Rigardo-ji would not have taken her on by himself. He's lying doggo.*

As from a distant room, Inner Child heard the muffled sound that had bounced past the scarred man's head several times during his detention. A glance at the courier showed that she, too, heard.

"What's that noise?" the Fudir asked, twisting his head as if to locate it. "Something wrong with the ship? Maybe we ought to lay up for repairs here in Megranome."

Olafsdottr smiled slowly, held it for a moment, then allowed it to fade as slowly. "Always carping the diem, my sweet. Perhaps you have set something rolling about the ship to convince me to stop for repairs and so give you an opportunity to escape. There would be no such escape, but I will withhold the opportunity and save you the frustration."

"I did all this while I was tied up?" Donovan said.

"Nu-nu-nu, sweet. Great deeds await you on Henrietta. Tomorrow," she added with a sniff, "make a different meal. This one stinks."

But the *mal odour* lingered all day and the circulators could do nothing to dissipate it. By the next day's breakfast both Donovan and Olafsdottr had drawn the same conclusion, very nearly at the same time.

"Not your food," said Olafsdottr. "Stink come elsewhere."

Donovan wrinkled his nose. "There is something familiar about it."

"Agreed. But the nose is the most easily deceived of organs. It remembers well, but will not reveal those memories. Does not one of your shards have memory?"

Donovan was not sure how much Olafsdottr knew of his condition, but saw no reason to deny it. "The Pedant. But he remembers facts, not sensations."

The Confederal sniffed. "Perhaps that which broke

loose has caused something to burn out. Yet, it does not have the tang of burning."

"It has the smell of rot. Perhaps the protein vats have gone bad."

Olafsdottr viewed him with suspicion. "If you have sabotaged our food supply, it will be a long, hungry time to Henrietta. You very naughty boy, slip between the quanta of my notice."

"We could check the vats."

"We? I should let you near the vats?"

"Because, darling, you won't go check them yourself while leaving me free run of the ship."

The Confederal stood upright from her post at the doorway. "Could tie you up again, but too much bother. Put away breakfast things and come with me, and we see what new surprise you prepare."

The protein vats were hermetically sealed. In them grew mounds of flesh cloned from highly regarded ancestors known as "esteemed cells." The judicious metering of flavorings and odorants imparted the likeness and even the texture of poultry and pork, of fish and beef, of legume and root. "Like begets like," chemist-wallahs sang, and so, fed upon wastes, the "mother" deep in the heart of each vessel enrobed itself in tissues like unto itself, to be shaved off, harvested, pressed, pumped to the molder, and served.

The vat room was inboard of the alfven drivers and forward of the impulse cage. The space was cramped and pantry-cool. Despite the seals, odors slipped through the seams and joints and teased the nose with the rich, earthy scent of potato and carrot, with the iron aroma of beef, with the dank stench of fish.

Beneath it all the sweetish smell of something else.

The ship's architect had not supposed that pilots en route would have much reason to crawl around the vat room. Fresh bulk canisters were installed via external cargo doors at farmers' markets at the hoop stations. But neither was the room nonnegotiable, since a pilot might need on occasion to refasten a hose or hand-close a valve. Olafsdottr eased matters a bit by reducing the strength of the gravity grids in the vat room by two-thirds, but she still crowded close behind him.

The stink grew worse behind the fish vat, and this was not due entirely to the faux-catfish accumulating inside it. Squeezing between it and the neighboring legume vat, Donovan spied one of the smuggler's secret rooms, now wide open and lit. He paused in his contemplation to consider what he might tell his captor.

𝕶𝖓𝖔𝖜𝖑𝖊𝖉𝖌𝖊 𝖎𝖘 𝖕𝖔𝖜𝖊𝖗, said the Pedant. 𝕶𝖊𝖊𝖕 𝖘𝖊𝖈𝖗𝖊𝖙 𝖜𝖍𝖆𝖙 𝖜𝖊 𝖐𝖓𝖔𝖜.

On the other hand, said the Silky Voice, *there are tactical benefits to knowing that your opponent knows what you know.*

Ow, Silky! My head hurts.

It may need all of us together to get through this, said the young man in the chlamys. That right, Sleuth?

Some data are still lacking. Add the facts together and there is still a hole in the middle, but . . .

"Ya, but." The Terran withdrew from his position and sat under Olafsdottr's calculating gaze. "What is it, my sweet?" she said. "You can tell Ravn."

Donovan turned to her. "Follow me," he said, "but keep your eyes peeled for someone else. We're not alone on this ship."

"Ah. I had begun to wonder."

There was a torque wrench clipped to the fish vat for use in turning valves. Olafsdottr said nothing while he unfastened it, and that silent acquiescence to his arming was the loudest thing the Confederal had said so far.

"This is a smuggler's ship," the Fudir said, "and it's honeycombed with secret rooms, passages, and caches. When you hijacked it, the smuggler was aboard, drunk, in one of those rooms. Probably this one. He was afraid to act alone—"

"A man of much wisdom, then."

"So he solicited my help to retake the ship."

"And, of coorse, you tendered it. Ooh. I knew you had been a nooty buoy. What befell, then, seeing I am still captain of your fate?"

"He said he knew of a weapon aboard. Something the People of Foreganger were sending to assassinate the Molnar over a bit of piracy and massacre—"

Olafsdottr snorted. "The difference between the People's Navy and the Cynthian pirates is but the number and quality of the ships at their disposal. But say on."

"I was supposed to distract you, and he would shoot you from behind."

Donovan did not elaborate on that and waited to see how the Confederal would react.

Olafsdottr regarded him with the stillness of a serpent. The white of her eyes and teeth, so prominent against her coal-black skin, took on some of the seeming of ice. "So," she said at last, and patted him on the cheek. "You are a good buoy, after all. When all is said and done, and the struggle is ended, I will personally escort you home and see that you are buried with great honor." She gestured with her teaser. "Lead on."

Much became clear when Donovan slipped behind the vats and entered the secret room. It was a small room, but contained a chair and table as well as an open safe. The Fudir thought it might have been used as a sort of stateroom by smuggled personages.

I thought the smell was familiar, said the Silky Voice. The Brute and Inner Child immediately assumed guardian positions, listening at the ears, watching through the corners of the eyes.

Rigardo-ji Edelwasser lay sprawled on his back on the floor, arms splayed, mouth agape and bloody, as if he had been punched in the teeth by an iron fist. The wall behind the chair was spattered with blood, and bone, and bits of brain. On the table before the chair stood open a standard bushel-sized shipping container, and beside it a beautifully carved wooden chest, also open.

The chest was Peacock orangewood, from which skilled knifework had brought out vines and fruits and other figures. The interior was lined with silk over shaped foam dunnage, but it was not clear from the shape what it had once held.

Olafsdottr had crowded into the room behind Donovan and, like him, made no move to cotton her nose against the smell. "How long has he lain here?" she asked.

"By the odor and bloating, the Pedant says, four days."

Olafsdottr nodded slowly. "And now you know why he did not appear at the ambush. A good thing too, for I think he would have botched it."

Donovan turned and looked at her. "Why do you say that?"

She pointed to the empty box. "He came to get the weapon and managed to kill himself with it. Such mishandling does not lend confidence."

Donovan stared at the dead man. "I don't think it matters anymore."

"But it does, my sweet; for where is the weapon that once sat in this wonderful box?"

Donovan had not been paying attention to the kill space, but the Sleuth and others had been.

He was sitting in the chair when he picked it up, said the Sleuth. *It fired upon his mishandling, and he jerked back, then slid forward, feetfirst. The weapon would have dropped to the floor and perhaps rolled a bit. There is not much room here for it to roll very far; yet there is no sign of it. Conclusion: the weapon is self-mobile. Based on the dunnage in which it nestled, it would be the size of a ruggerball—the ellipsoidal kind used on Hawthorne Rose.*

Olafsdottr meanwhile had rolled the body aside, perhaps thinking the weapon underneath. What she found was a gaping wound in the back of the skull, as if that iron fist had punched its way out of the brain. "A bore hole through his head!" she said, bending over and looking through it. "Entry through the soft palate, up through the midbrain and the parietal lobe, and smashing out between the occipital and the parietal bones. What was this weapon that so badly backfired on him?"

"It was called the 'Frog Prince' on the shipping manifest."

Olafsdottr grinned. "Busy buoy! And what be the nature of this 'Frog Prince'?"

"We're not sure. But there are Terran legends," he said. "It was to be a trap for the Molnar." He looked again at the smuggler's body and the piercing wound through his head. "If I were you, and I saw it hopping about, I wouldn't try to kiss it."

Rigardo-ji was stupid, he decided. Like many petty scramblers, he could think from point A to point B, but not beyond it to point C. He had read between the lines and believed Foreganger's present to the Molnar was a vengeance for the massacre of the *Merry v Starinu*, but it had never occurred to the treacherous little beast that the weapon had been meant to kill its user.

"So," said Olafsdottr. " 'Tis loose." She looked about the room and went to the door to listen. Save for the normal susurrus and hum of the engines, the ship was quiet. The pork vat, out of sight of the doorway, hissed and a valve turned with a heavy clunk. The Confederal, already straining to hear sounds, jerked a little, though only a little, and her teaser moved fractionally. "But so long as we do not kiss this . . . Frog Prince . . . we need not fear it?"

Donovan shook his head. "I would not hope so

easily. It was designed to trick the Molnar into kissing it, but that trick would not have worked more than the once. It must have been designed, after the initial kiss, to seek out targets of opportunity in his stronghold—which to the People of Foreganger would mean anything on Cynthia that lived, man, woman, or child. It is the sort of boundless vengeance the People are famous for. Abyalon is more gently bred, and if word of this ever comes out, more than one national government there will fall. Meanwhile, we are in a pocket. We best back out and seal off the entry into the main part of the ship."

In the silence that followed, they heard the distant clang of a leaping object.

"*It must listen for sounds of life,*" the Sleuth whispered through the scarred man's lips, "*and then home in on them.* Quick," added the Brute. "And quiet."

It was a measure of the Confederal's concern that she turned her back on Donovan to leave the hidden room, and he with his knuckles white around a wrench. It was a measure of *his* concern that he took no advantage. One swipe, he thought, and I will see my daughter, after all. And Bridget ban.

You might see them, said the young man in the chlamys, but could you look them in their eyes?

He slipped out of the room close behind the Confederal, and they moved cautiously from behind the fish vat, pausing to listen at each step. They heard another spring, closer this time.

It must leap like a frog, the Sleuth deduced, *maintaining the metaphor.* A certain artist pride informed the death-techs of Foreganger.

"If we can close the door on it, we may breathe easier," whispered Olafsdottr. "His Highness may bounce around the hidden passageways to his mechanical heart's delight; but so long as he is confined there, we need not fear him."

"At least until he finds his way accidentally into the open part of the ship."

She turned to look at Donovan. "You are the cheerful one. How?"

"He may not know from doors, but he might strike a jamb-plate by dumb luck. Unless you can deactivate . . . No? Ah, well, it's a small ship, but there are too many conduits, chambers, channels, cable runs, hollow spaces; too many spaces, openings, gaps, apertures. Eventually, Froggie will find his way through."

A relief valve hissed and Donovan jerked, striking a standpipe with his wrench. The clang reverberated though the piping and, on its diminution, they heard the bounding sounds of the Frog Prince stop, then increase in frequency. It was no longer hunting a direction; it had found one. "**Quick**," he said, and pushed Olafsdottr on the rear.

They scrambled now, not bothering with silence. Donovan wondered if the Frog Prince would deduce from the sounds the direction they were headed and cut them off.

Olafsdottr reached the door and pulled herself through. The gravity grids on the other side were set to normal, so she stumbled, and momentarily blocked the exit. For an instant, Donovan wondered if she would slam the door in his face to ensure her own safety.

But it had never been her intent to destroy Donovan. And that explained his own earlier hesitations. Had she planned to kill him, he would have had no qualms about striking first. But her goal had been to deliver Donovan hale to Henrietta. That he was disinclined to go there and that whatever befell afterward was bound to be hazardous were not grounds enough to justify a cold-blooded killing.

Yer just outta practice, the Brute suggested.

"Hurry, sweet!" said Olafsdottr.

And to the left Inner Child saw his majesty, the Frog Prince.

A squat and ugly thing, like a toad, but gleaming of chrome, with great blue piston legs and adhesive grippers, large black-lens eyes, its deep-blue, black-spotted façade gore-spattered with Rigardo-ji's brains. It leapt atop a conduit three arm's lengths off facing the scarred man. Its mouth opened wide, and made a long, deep rippling sound.

The Silky Voice from her seat in the hypothalamus flooded the scarred man with adrenaline. Time itself seemed to slow.

Donovan knew that if he turned his back to run through the door, he would be a dead man. His only chance was to face it down. With a wrench. *It won't fire a projectile,* said the Sleuth. *Trust me.* And even the Sleuth's voice seemed sluggish and drawn out. *It will need to leap closer.*

As if on command, the Frog Prince leapt again, and landed on a primary lock valve. Its face bore the fatuous, evil smile of a frog. Once more, its lips opened wide, and inside its jaws, a coil of memory metal unwound and shot forth like a lance of steel. *Yes,* he heard the Sleuth say, *I thought as much. The metaphor is complete.*

Even under normal circumstances, the Brute had been trained to lightning-fast reflexes. With the boost the Silky Voice was providing, he could move faster still. He swung the wrench—as it seemed, through gelatin. The long, sharp tongue arced toward him.

The wrench connected, and knocked the reddened steel ribbon aside so that it penetrated like a nail into the side of the poultry vat. *That's how it killed the smuggler.* There had probably been an instruction: "Kiss to activate." Rigardo-ji had never had a chance. The steel ribbon would have uncoiled into his mouth and out the back of his head. Likely, he died without ever knowing he was dead.

The memory metal remembered and recoiled to its rest state. The Frog Prince leapt, pulled along by its own tongue. When it landed, it would tug itself loose and take another lick.

Donovan turned to the door.

And Olafsdottr was crowding in, blocking his escape.

His cry emerged as high-pitched as a bat's, so far into overdrive was he. Olafsdottr brushed him aside with her right arm. The Frog's tongue lanced again. She seized the ribbon with her left hand pushing it aside, as she had seized the flying shim during their workout, even as she fired the teaser with her right. She screamed.

"Serrated!" She released the tongue of steel, which with a lick swiped her across the side as it rewound.

But a teaser fires a coherent electromagnetic pulse. At certain settings and focuses, it can play havoc with a man's nervous system. Other settings can fry electronic devices. The Frog Prince flashed and sparked as the induced currents ran along its body and internal circuitry. Its head turned toward Donovan. The mouth opened . . .

. . . and smoke came out.

The Brute threw the wrench and it spun into the Frog's visual sensors, shattering them. But by then the bright blue of the Frog's body was fading with its power source. Donovan found the wrench and used it to beat the machine into scrap.

When Olafsdottr awoke, she was lying on a pallet in the infirmary. Both hands were encased in restoration gloves while regressed cells rebuilt the torn flesh and snapped bones. Her side, where the tongue had swiped it, was likewise bandaged. To inhale sent a stabbing pain through her.

Donovan sat by the pallet reading a book screen. He looked up when she moved.

"Rib?" she said.

He nodded. "Two. And a deep laceration. What possessed you to grab the tongue like that?"

"I thought only to knock it aside. I did not expect a saw blade." She raised the two gloves. "My hands?"

"The left one was badly sliced up. You must have grabbed at it with your right after you dropped the teaser."

"I promised Gidula I would deliver you in one piece to Henrietta. Could not let Froggie punch holes through you." She took another experimental breath. "I must praise your medical skills, sweet."

"The meshinospidal did all the work. I just zipped you in the basket and followed the instructions. The automatics took cell samples, regressed them, and applied them in the proper course."

"Ooh, but you had noo oobligation to deliver *me* whole. Or to deliver me at all. Foortunate, then . . ."

Donovan shrugged. "Look," he said, "can we drop the Alabaster accent? We're past that, I think."

"Fortunate, then," she said more quietly, "you spy Frog Prince in time; or both dead."

"Inner Child is paranoid. Makes a good sentry."

Olafsdottr sighed. "Must be very wonderful divide attentions so. I was told it had incapacitated you."

"It does have its drawbacks sometimes."

"How do you plan to explain the corpse to the Megranomese authorities?" she asked. "Or how you came by this ship?"

"It was his ship. He was giving us a ride. This *thing* broke out of its box. Missy, if between the two of us we can't concoct a story to fool a Megranomic *copper* we should both of us quit the Long Game."

Olafsdottr cocked her head sideways. "I thought you *had* quit."

"You know what I mean."

"Almost, you tempt me, sweet. But I am unaccustomed to asking for help."

Donovan grinned. "I'll teach you."

The answering smile was almost sad. "Sweet, between the two of us, we defeated a Foreganger killing machine. Tell me you are not the man we need for the struggle."

Donovan sat back so that his head rested upon the wall of the little infirmary. He closed his eyes and his breath slowly gusted from him. "I'm not the man you need."

"Ah, well, it would have been entertaining to watch developments. How long before we reach the Megranome way station?"

The scarred man shrugged. "The *'ospidal* had you in suspension for five days. We're out of Megranome space."

"Ah. You take me direct to Dangchao, then. Perhaps Bridget ban keep me in clean cage."

Donovan rose, wiped his palms on his trousers. "You sleep now, 'sweet.' Your hands are too badly cut up to pilot the ship. I don't have a certificate myself, except as a chartsman; but every chartsman is a pilot in training, and certificates are only for officials. We'll be on the Tightrope in another two days."

Olafsdottr struggled to sit up, winced at the pain, and slid back prone. "On the Tightrope?"

The scarred man, at the infirmary door, shrugged. "And don't ask us why, because there's not a single one of us knows the answer."

CENGJAM GAAFE: THE SECOND INTERROGATORY

So," says Bridget ban, low and drawn out, so that the sibilant slides like a hiss from between her lips, "it was no kidnapping, at all. He went with you of his own free will."

The Confederal shrugs and grins. "Not free. Cost great deal." Then, in Gaelactic, "And what is will, anyway? We are bounced about by the impacts of Fate and where we finally ricochet, *that* is where we fare. Whether we will to go that way or whether we simply will go that way is a question for metaphysicians, not for one so humble as I." She sips again at her coffee, which has grown tempered as she unwound her tale.

"Paint it as you like," the Hound replies. "He had control of the ship. He had the choice. To bring you here to me, or to proceed into the Confederacy."

"A false dichotomy," says Olafsdottr. "He did both; for here I am. The Fates weave cloth fine as silk."

Graceful Bintsaif stirs. "It seems clear to me," she announces. "Donovan's old loyalties to the Confederacy reasserted themselves, and he went to answer his masters' call."

The Shadow turns in her seat and smiles at the junior Hound. "It seems clear to you because you are young, if not . . ." Her eyes flick to the blazon she wears above her left breast. ". . . if not without some experience. As you grow older, matters become much less clear."

"Because eyes age and lose their focus."

"And that may be a good thing. Some things best not seen clearly. But what are these 'loyalties' you speak of that 'reasserted themselves' and drove him to the Confederacy? Are they incorporeal creatures that lurk inside Donovan's head—as his sundry selves do—awaiting opportunity to pounce and seize control of him? No, I think loyalties are things that a man expresses, not mysterious entities that express a man."

Méarana strikes a chord. "There was a tenth Donovan once," she remembers, "one he confronted and defeated, one that sought oblivion and death."

"Ooh, we all seek that, harper, though soome less willingly than oothers. Or perhaps I should say, we all find it in the end, whether we seek it or noot. For whether or noo we seek it, it surely does seek us."

The harper's fingers take the chords into a goltraí, a lament. "So, maybe the Tenth Donovan survived after all and, resurrected, compelled him to his doom."

Bridget ban snorts derision. "There was no compulsion, Lucy. You heard her. He chose to join them."

"Aye, Mother, I heard her. I dinna ken an I've heard the sooth. And in any case, he went to o'erthrow the Names, not to succor them. So whate'er loyalties impelled him, 'tis nae clear that they were loyalties to Those."

The Hound pours herself a fresh cup of coffee and replenishes that of Ravn Olafsdottr. "No, it is clear to me to whom his loyalty lay." She hands the courier the cup, and their eyes lock for a moment before the latter leans back and raises the fresh brew to her lips.

"But tell me," Bridget ban continues when Olafsdottr is once more set, "we of the League care mickle for Donovan buigh but muckle for the stirrings of the Confederation. Tell us more about this civil war you say roils the Shadows of the Names."

The Shadow flashes her mocking smile. "What should it matter to you whether a great edifice is fallen, save that when whole it once blustered and frightened your sleep? Is it not enough to know that, turned upon itself, it can spare no attentions for you?"

"When a building close by crumbles, the rubble may strike my own. Bad enough that your masters once sent raiders across the Rift to devil our borderlands. At least there then were Those from whom we could demand redress. But if you are coming apart, a thousand filibusters, a thousand mercenaries may now descend upon us. Bad enough, our own pirates. We'd rather not host yours."

The Shadow's face loses its smile. "Do not hope too fulsomely, Hound. Hope is the cruelest of virtues, for her betrayal strikes more deeply. What is underway is not bongkoy, but chóng jián, not disintegration but reconstruction."

"Are you sure," asks Bridget ban with a thin smile, "that it is not lam lam?"

The courier throws back her head and laughs, and even Graceful Bintsaif's stern façade wavers. Méarana plays an interrogatory note on her harp and asks her question with a glance.

"Ooh, your moother plays a foony jooke, yngling. We say 'lam' it means 'collapse.' But also with a change of tone 'sweet-talk' or 'coax.' She means to say that it was my sweet-talking of Doonoovan buigh that caused his resistance to collapse."

Méarana plays aimlessly. She has not yet found the right motifs for the tale. She has a bounding, rollicking, menacing melody for the Frog Prince, but she has not yet captured her father or his captor—or the lam lam.

"There is one thing I do not understand," says Graceful Bintsaif.

"Ooh, there is moor than woon, I'm thinking."

The junior Hound colors, but presses ahead. "Why did your rebels want Donovan buigh so badly? What is one more used-up, discarded agent among so many thousands fresher?"

"Many hands make light the work, but no one pair of hands lightens much. One may as well ask why we needed anyone at all, as in the limit the marginal assistance goes to zero. But . . ." Olafsdottr shrugs. ". . . I am but a simple Shadow. I am not told what I need not know."

But Méarana has the impression that the Ravn's duty had been more than mere courier work and that she regards a part of it at least a failure. Aye, a goltraí it would be for this opening section. And two melodies in counterpoint for Olafsdottr's theme, because for a certainty she had two purposes. But which had failed? The overt one of carrying Donovan into the storm? Or the covert one that remains as yet concealed?

"Now must I digress," says Olafsdottr, "and relate some while of such events as earlier befell; for our discord had been long a-building. Hear then while heroes in bold strife contend for twice-ten years among the homes of men."

III. HENRIETTA: THE DREAM OF AGAMEMNON

For far too long contentions lay abate
For what man dares to speak when all about
Are doubtful in their loyalties (or far too sure)?
The wrong word whispered in the wrong-sought
    ear
Is death. And death, though destination of us all,
Is none too dearly sought. Yet grievances do fall
In never-ending rain and drive bold men to shelter
    in
Overhangs of one another's confidence. So.
Is confidence betrayed! A body lies in backstreet
    Cambertown;
Another, crumpled on his hearthstones, whitely
    bled; a third
Bobs bayside in the Farnsworth Sea. Fair knife,
    garrote,
Or poison subtle laced within a tempting
    drink . . .
What cares the corpse by which device 'twas
    made?
More like by careless word was he betrayed.

*But slowly bonds are built and men learn where
    their trust
Lies safe, and lay clandestine plans. And deep
Within the Secret City, Those of Name do mark
That first fresh scent of fear.
And nameless dread on stealthy feet draws near.*

On scattered worlds were here and there strongholds held in rebel hands, strongholds made of discourse, not of stone. Such a redoubt might be an office, a department, an assignment, possessed of those oathbound for the overthrow of the regime. For this war sought not patches of land, but patches of command. Warriors did not storm beachheads, but subverted key positions, bureaus, jurisdictions; and an enemy might be isolated and surrounded by usurping the authority of his boss, by issuing a new procedure, or by infiltrating his department and undermining his efforts.

Not that there were no bodies. Wars want bodies. Quantity is a detail. The Glancer at the Dumold Fisc, known to all his friends as a keen outdoorsman, was found dead beside his fuel-depleted dūbuggi in the Great Pan of the Wúdãshwĕy Desert, "having brought insufficient potable water to last the crossing." This tragedy, suitably mourned by all and sincerely by some, meant that the oversight of the fisc passed to his deputy. And this meant in turn that Certain Expenditures made in the name of the rebellion passed unquestioned. This was neither the first nor the last death dealt retail in that quiet struggle. "The rats gnaw one another in the wainscoting," the boots muttered. As always, they preferred the wholesale.

An auditor here, a decoding room there, an intelligence office elsewhere—in such wise did the Revolution proceed—by promotion, transfer, and untimely passing. Worms were planted in soft wares, so that loyal men unquestioning went forth to do the biddings of their foes. The Protector of Western Sagzenau was shot down by his own bodyguard, acting in the firm belief that such were their orders from above—and who themselves died before the firing squad believing their executioners suborned.

It was the worst sort of civil war, for its primary weapon was deceit and its first casualty, trust.

The Shadows and agents who fought it carefully avoided the pitched battles and guerillas and street-by-street destruction that had marked earlier risings. But there is at least a kind of honesty in storming the barricades—and in defending them. One knows if nothing else where everyone stands. And a head that is "bloodied but yet unbowed" has a certain nobility of cast lacking in that head shaken in incomprehension over an unexpected demotion.

The game proceeded. Pieces shifted about a board composed of stars—threatening here, checking there, protecting elsewhere a pawn or knight. Complexity built upon complexity, intricacies difficult at times for even the players to comprehend. Key pieces were lost. Positions were abandoned. Identities fatally revealed. Or kept! (Grizzlywald Hupp died because his cover identity had been marked for death by a comrade. Even secret wars have friendly fire.)

But what began in grim anticipation had grown to smell more of desperation—or at least of impatience.

After twice ten years, even the most eager of rebels might find his enthusiasm thinning, and a certain hunger for results had begun to inform their thoughts.

And so those who must never meet in person had decided that they must meet in person. They had chosen for this purpose the outpost of Henrietta in the remote border province of Qien-tuq. They gathered there from across the CCW: from Dao Chetty and the Century Suns, from Big Dog and the Groom's Britches, from Hasselbard and Paladin, from worlds of legend and ancient renown. And while they could not hope to meet entirely in secret, they hoped at least to meet where no one paid much attention.

Henrietta was the sort of world that had betrayed the promise of her youth. The lushness of her terraformation imbues the visitor with awe at the powers of the old Commonwealth of Suns—or would have, had Henrietta visitors to awe. Her verdant hillsides ache for the plow, her splendid vistas for the well-sited villa. Her broad, gleaming rivers want earnest industrious traffic and even more earnest fishermen. By rights, the planet should have been thickly settled centuries since.

But she sits hard by the border with the Peripheral League, and her strategic value is too great to pimp herself as a tempting prize. She dare not be too wealthy, too prosperous, too desirable, lest she invite attack—by the pirates of the Hadramoo, if by no one else. Yet here and there stand ancient ruins, tumbled reminders that there had once been a different age, when no borders ran through the worlds of men.

Like a promising young woman who has settled

for a lesser beau, Henrietta has been rimmed in steel and not in verdure. Grim men stand guard along the walls of the world. Fortresses orbit o'erhead, and burrow deep within her vales. Corvettes hold station at the Visser hoops of her roads, even the narrow, minor stream known as the Tightrope.

Of course, no one attacks. No one has ever attacked; and the thought that the sprawling, barely United League of the Periphery could muster enough common purpose to do so has grown every year less likely. But the pretense that they might still do so serves a purpose, and the garrison acts as garrisons always have when bored in their duties. They are far enough from Dao Chetty to feel the slack in their tethers. The natives of Henrietta, heirs to obsolete traditions, find the boots of the garrison heavy on their necks; but they cannot remember a time when those soles did not rest there, and most have forgotten that it had ever been otherwise.

The garrison, for its part, knows to both apply the pressure and withhold the worst. What fool kills the cow he milks? All told, the garrison commander has told his staff, it was nice to lie doggo in a corner and be forgotten by those in power.

And so a certain unease grew in the heart of Swoswai Mashdasan as he reviewed the Ten-day Reports. A visitor from off-world named Egg Mennerhem had been accosted by two ratings on groundside leave from WŠ *Gentle Caress*. Touristas being targets of opportunity, they had pressed of him a donation to the Astral Shore Leave Benevolent Fund and, in the ensuing discussion, each had broken an arm. Boots did not always get the better of these little extortions, but they usually did at two to one. That made Mennerhem a Person of Interest.

MILINTEL was set to watch the tourista and reported back the curious fact that he took none of the day tours to the Commonwealth Ruins in the nearby Gyorjyet Narrows, the only conceivable reason why a tourista might come to Riettiesburg in the first place, but he remained idly content in the Grand Khyan Hotel.

That was bad enough. But it was as the first raindrop before a storm. Others followed in a quickening drizzle, arriving by ones and twos, never overtly acknowledging one another, but congregating as if by accident here and there—in the hotel lobbies, in the restaurants, casually on the street corners and in the parks. They came by packet and they came by liner and they came by monoship. Mashdasan's agents watched—and the touristas grinned and watched MILINTEL watching them.

The conclusion was soon inescapable.

They were gathering.

Dawshoo Yishohrann waited until he was certain that everyone who was coming to Henrietta had come. If the absence of some of his allies, indeed of some of his staunchest allies, disturbed him, he gave no sign to the others. He was affable at meals, engaging in his conversations, suitably grave at the reports delivered in face time. Those missing had undoubtedly excellent reasons. Death, perhaps; or, like Olafsdottr, a special assignment. In the meantime, he showed his teeth to everyone and gave reassuring shoulder claps to the more disheartened. Dawshoo was wide shouldered and possessed a hooked nose of impressive scope, so that he was known quietly as "the Beak." Some called him arrogant; others called him less arrogant than he had a right to be. His enemies said that self-interest was his guiding principle, but his friends pointed out that he had risked and lost both wealth and position to lead the rebellion. He was a marked man; and a dead one if the Long Knife ever found its mark.

For his own reassurance, the Beak sought the company of Gidula. Whether the old man had any other name, Dawshoo did not know. The name had resonances of torture in one of the ancient tongues of men, so it may have been an office-name and, as the office had consumed the man, so the name had consumed his identity. But any random combination of phonemes could find kin in some old language, and office-names were less common in the Confederacy than among the Peripherals. In any case, Gidula had grown old in a service little known for longevity. If that did not mark him wise, it at least marked him nimble.

The two met by prearrangement on the terrace of a small restaurant in the Skimkhorn district of Riettiesburg. The kitchen boasted the cuisine of the Century Suns, though it was an empty boast. Perhaps at some remote time, a Centurion had been assigned to Henrietta and had afterward received permission to remain. If so, his family recipes had suffered over the generations. Dawshoo was a native of Alpha, the Big Sun, and knew whereof he spoke.

Still, a home-cooked meal was a home-cooked meal. Dawshoo arrived first and was amused to see how the locals shrank a bit from his presence, as if they were ants, and he a drop of pesticide. Evening had fallen and the terrace was ablaze with tiki, their guttering flames casting dancing shadows upon the flagstone patio and obscuring the vista of the half-barren heavens above. The tikis, at least, were a genuine touch, and for a moment they stirred in Dawshoo a long-dormant homesickness for the warm surf of the Enameled Isles on a world he no longer called home.

Gidula approached silently and without announcing himself. His shouldered hair and shovel beard were pure white, which made darkness no longer his friend. He took the seat opposite Dawshoo and touched the menu to activate it. For several long moments he studied the selections, as if his choice would be the most momentous decision of a long and distinguished career. Dawshoo said nothing, had said nothing, not even in greeting. He took great comfort from Gidula's advice, though it would never do to acknowledge that.

"Many eyes caress us," Gidula said without looking up from the screen.

"We are strangers in a neighborhood eatery. Strangers are never welcome."

"With good reason," Gidula said dryly. He raised his head. "Overcome by a fit of nostalgia, were you?"

Dawshoo bobbed his head toward the menu. "For the savors of my youth? No. But have you sampled the *local* cuisine? They boil the taste out of everything."

"What do you recommend, First Speaker?"

"Fasting. But from this menu . . . If they have faithfully executed it, the Darling Lamb was always a favorite of mine. Much depends on the chutneys they have used. The same herbs grown in different soils often bear small resemblance one to the other."

Gidula nodded. "I bow to your superior wisdom in such matters." He touched the screen, made his choices, and Dawshoo—as the host—transmitted the order to the kitchen.

"A human servant will bring it out. A nice touch, no? One might even suppose the place to be of the upper cuts."

The Shadow tossed his head. The white hair bobbed. "The greater the gap, the greater the effort to close it." He shaded his eyes and squinted through the flickering tikis toward the night sky. "Why the torches?"

"A custom on my homeworld. I was born in the cities; but on some of the isles they use such devices, both for lighting and to repel insects . . . But this place is too bleak and cold for them. It wants bonfires and mulled wine; not dancing torches and fruited rum." He held up his preprandial drink.

Gidula gave it a brief grimace. He himself never poisoned his wits. "It is bleak and cold because it is their winter season here in the southern hemisphere. Call another meeting in the springtime. I am told it is quite delightful. The young women wear colorful wildflowers wound into circlets in their hair. There.

That's the Perseus Arm, just rising over the hills. You can see it through the goat willows."

Dawshoo twisted a little in his seat. "Yes. So it is. The League stars."

"Do you think she's found him?"

First Speaker shrugged. "It was a cast of the dice. If she has, that may solve one problem. If not, that would solve another."

"And if she never comes back at all?"

"A third."

"A superb galaxy, then, where whatever befalls solves one problem or another."

Dawshoo straightened in his chair. "Small problems are easily solved. The greater ones linger. I fear many comrades are losing heart."

"I think perhaps just the opposite," Gidula answered. "The great problems are more easily solved, while the small ones remain stones in our shoes. The struggle *has* been a long one. Enthusiasm by its nature burns hot and fast. Yet, there may be a simple solution."

A human waiter had brought their meals and the two fell silent while they were presented and suitable solicitations and compliments were exchanged.

"He does not really wish my opinion on this travesty," Dawshoo said when the waiter was out of earshot. "These provincials ought not attempt the cuisine of the Triangle worlds unless they have some skill at pulling it off." He took a bite of his perch.

Gidula smiled and cut into his lamb. "It is the taste of your youth you recall, Beak. Should Fate take you once more home, I dare say you would find the cuisine there as disappointing."

Dawshoo snorted, and the two ate in silence for a time. "All right, Gidula," First Speaker said after a number of chews. "You intend to make me ask and, while the night is pleasant enough to be worth extending, there is too much yet awaiting my attention. How do you recommend dealing with the loss of heart?"

"Say rather 'impatience,'" the other reminded him. "Their enthusiasm wanes because they are eager. A paradox. But the answer is not to deal with the symptom, the ennui; but with the cause, the impatience. Strike now. An all-out assault on the Secret City. Hold nothing back."

Dawshoo placed his fork carefully on the table. "We would be crushed," he said flatly.

"Would we? We have been gnawing at the extremities for twice-ten years. Surely that has impaired their capabilities. Key men have been assassinated or suborned; key intelligence and communication posts lie secretly in our hands. And is it not better that our efforts be crushed than that they sputter out ignominiously?"

"Padaborn's Rising was crushed," First Speaker observed. "Are you so eager to end as he did?"

"Padaborn was betrayed. And in some ways he did not fare too terribly. You told us yourself: The game is worth the candle."

Dawshoo squinted at the sky against the glare of the torches. "We shall see." When he lowered his gaze once more, Gidula was gone and the lamb barely touched. Dawshoo Yishohrann sighed and, reaching across the table, gathered the lamb unto himself and chewed upon it thoughtfully.

They congregated the next morning in a large meeting space provided by the hotel. There were thirty of them, many known to one another only by reputation. Some had met. A few had worked together in pairings. Perhaps, Dawshoo thought, some were surprised to see who else had shown up; or perhaps they were surprised at who had not.

It was a well-lit room, with a dais on which Dawshoo sat with Gidula on his right and Oschous Dee Karnatika on his left. The Triumvirate, some had called them during the anonymous phase of the conspiracy, when it had not been safe to use names; when no man knew more than two others. Through ka-owèn, any man might be brought to betray another, and the rebellion had been built in water-tight compartments, lest loose lips sink it.

Down the center of the room ran a table around which sat the Ten, or at least most of them. Domino Tight was not present. The others leaned against the walls or perched upon sideboards in various attitudes, perhaps understanding only now their place in the scheme of things. Conversation filled the room like a swarm of bees.

Little Jacques the Dwarf completed his circuit of the room and nodded to Dawshoo, holding up four fingers. He had found and neutralized four devices. First Speaker had expected MILINTEL to bug the room, but the thoroughness surprised him. Swoswai Mashdasan must be uneasy at this unwonted gathering in his jurisdiction—for by now he had surely realized the cut of men involved.

Dawshoo leaned toward Gidula and whispered, "I think I will test their mettle before I press your notion." Then he stood, stilling the idle conversations. "Deadly Ones," he said formally. They pressed forward to hear him better, sensing a cusp in their affairs: the physical nature of the meeting, the grave demeanor on the faces of the Triumvirate.

"Comrades," he added more gently. "For twenty years we have struggled against greater numbers and greater guile, and *Those* who held the Secret City hold it still. Brave friends have died; and strangers you knew only by their deeds. And still no end heaves in sight. What lives, what honors we had before we took up the cause lie ruined and neglected. We have come so far into the woods, comrades, that but two paths lie before us. The first . . ." And here he paused artfully to enhance the tension. "The first is to fold our tents, dissolve our oaths, and salvage what we can from the debacle."

A small smile played across his lips. Gidula and Oschous stared at him openmouthed. In the rear of the room, a man shrugged. Another threw his stylus to the table and closed his note screen with a snap. One of the couriers sitting perched along the windowsill slid to the floor, clapped a comrade on the shoulder in farewell, and strode to the door. A second followed her. Someone said, "Well, we had a good run of it," loud enough for everyone to hear.

With glances both furtive and calculating, they made their way to the doors. More followed. Then two of the Ten stood. Appalled, Dawshoo counted half the room on its feet.

Then Dee Karnatika stood. "Cowards!" he bellowed.

Heads turned at the cry. Hands flew to scabbards. Those at the door paused. Egg Mennerhem called back. "No cowards have come this far," he said. "No coward would ever have started."

Oschous tossed his head. "What man fears the past? Its hazards are dead and gone. What matter if it's two years or twenty? We know what they looked like, those old familiar years. What you hazarded then has no more power to harm. It's the new years, the stranger years, that inspire dread."

"There's a proverb," said Egg, "about straws and camel backs."

"Aye. Any man who's shouldered twenty years has a right to be proud of his burden—and is right to wonder if the twenty-first might break him. But he's less right, having twenty and facing one, than that same man earlier having one and facing twenty. You've come this far. Why not farther?" He suddenly grinned and rubbed his ear. "By the Fates, we're all dead men anyway. Quitting now would hardly make us lively."

"Dee Karnatika's right," said Big Jacques Delamond, one of the Ten. Some said he was two of the Ten, so large was he. He rose now, like a mountain uplifted by colliding continents. "We've come through too much to balk at going through a little more."

"I never said I balked," Egg replied. "The Beak did." He looked about, uncertain. Some of those who had stood to go had returned to their seats. "I'll see it through—if I see a chance."

"Happy, I am," said Dawshoo in a voice that commanded everyone's attention. "Happy, I am to see Egg Mennerhem of two minds about our enterprise. It would be wrong if all our Egg were in one basket."

The room broke into laughter, and Mennerhem flushed. A Shadow nearby slapped him on the back. Dawshoo gestured for silence and when he had it, he filled it with his words.

"Happy, I said, and happy, I am. Egg, you and I see the same two paths. You want to see a chance of success if we press on. But do you see a chance of success if we give up? Don't suppose that we can call an armistice with the Secret City and everything will be as it was before. We are all dead men walking, as brother Oschous said." He threw an arm around Dee Karnatika's shoulders. "And any man defying death with me is my brother. You too, Egg. All of you here. Not a one of you has been backward in our cause. So do not think that the Names will forgive everything, and kiss us on the cheeks. More likely, they would ram 'the gay barb' up between those cheeks. Those they know of, they will kill. Those they know not, they will track down and then they will kill. In the end, it is all the same."

Big Jacques made a fist and struck the table. "Press on, then!"

"No," said Dawshoo.

And that silenced everyone. Oschous sat slowly.

Egg lowered himself to the floor, where he squatted cross-legged. Big Jacques looked left and right at the Ten and resumed his seat. "What then?" he asked in a voice like an earthquake.

"I said there were two paths," said Dawshoo Yishohrann. "But we can blaze a third. We do not merely press on. *We break through!* We have been fighting our colleagues, the ones who remained slaves to the regime. The time has come to attack the Names themselves, to lay siege to the Secret City. Victory, or death!" He spread his arms wide. Grand gambles required grand words and grand gestures.

There was a moment of silence. Then Big Jacques struck the table once more and the table, big as it was, shuddered.

"Victory, or death!"

The cry was taken up around the room, by a few at first, then by all. Some, Dawshoo noted, called on victory; but others, and by no means the fewer, called on death.

After the meeting, they broke into small groups and each group discussed what would be needed for the planned offensive. Dawshoo, Oschous, and Gidula circulated among them, collecting and collating their ideas, encouraging their thinking. "Don't stop with the obvious," Oschous told them. "The mad ideas are the best."

When they broke for lunch, Dawshoo excused himself and crossed town, where he stealthed into the governor's compound by *an unexpected route* and waited in Mashdasan's office until the swoswai returned from his own lunch. The governor, when he saw the Shadow occupying his desk, hesitated an instant at the door. Then he allowed the door to slide closed behind him and hung his cap casually on the hat tree. Dawshoo admired the sangfroid. Whatever their cognitive shortfalls, the boots did not lack for bravery.

"Well?" the swoswai said. He stood, awkwardly, before his own desk. He did not waste time blustering or asking for identification. He knew what he faced.

"Stop trying to listen."

Mashdasan thrust chin and chest forward. "You don't think we'd learn anything?"

"On the contrary, I am very much afraid that you might." Dawshoo paused, then added, "You ought to fear that, too. The man who knows things makes of himself a target for all. One side may destroy him to silence what the other side would destroy him to hear. What man is so foolish as to place his generative organ in the buzz saw? Wiser, he is to know nothing."

The swoswai's hand had moved protectively at Dawshoo's pithy image, but he checked the motion. "I could order this planet destroyed, and all of you with it," he said. Now came the bluster. He was compelled to say something of the sort, Dawshoo knew, because he knew he was afraid and did not want to know that.

Dawshoo shrugged. "And I could order you destroyed. It would last longer and hurt more, and it would certainly be less impersonal. But I bear you no ill will, Swoswai. I would regard that passage no more happily than you, and so, we both having the same objective, some accommodation might be reached."

The governor swallowed. "Some may ask later why I did not listen. I have my duties."

He was answered by a guileless smile. "Perhaps you did not suspect who we were."

"Then I would have been a blind man."

"Then perhaps your devices were detected and disabled. No one can fault you for being bested by the likes of us. We found all four this morning."

The swoswai blinked. Then he nodded. "Perhaps we will continue to hide them and you will continue to find them."

Dawshoo understood his meaning. The motions would be gone through, but the military would restrain themselves. He rose from behind the governor's desk and, as he circled it to the right, the swoswai edged around to the left. Seated once more in his proper place, Mashdasan seemed to grow more confident. "I will have my men show you out," he said, reaching for the summoner.

But Dawshoo demurred. "Don't trouble yourself. I will leave the way I came." As he faded toward the door, Mashdasan bent over his reports. "Oh, one thing," the governor added just before the Shadow touched the door plate. He looked up from the desk. "We only planted three."

In the afternoon, the group meetings produced success trees and idea boxes. The trees detailed the sequences of contingent events required to ensure a successful operation. The boxes listed on their stubs the essential features an operation must possess—facilities, assets, materials, time lines, and so forth—and along the rows multiple alternatives for each. Dawshoo turned copies of these over to Oschous and Gidula, who would generate random combinations of alternatives as a way of seeding their own creativity.

"Nothing too pedestrian," he warned them. "A coup is as much an art form as it is a decapitation. Future generations should admire the craft of our blow, and not merely the cause in which it was struck. Besides, anything too ordinary has already been anticipated. Our erstwhile colleagues will have analyzed the failure modes of their defenses. We must identify some unexpected weakness; some blind spot in their foresight."

When Oschous Dee Karnatika smiled he resembled a fox. He belonged to that race of men whose faces bore a fine, red, downy fur. The magicians of the old Commonwealth had in their pride toyed with the genes of men; and what they had learned before consequence brought them low was that genes were like a dangling mobile. If you jiggled one of them, others jiggled in response, and often in surprising and undesired ways. Dee Karnatika's ancestors had been engineered for enhanced cleverness and—on the broad average—successfully so. The price had been paid in face fuzz and protruding lower facial process, so that their fellow men recognized them immediately as the clever sort and responded with increased wariness. So does yin excite its yang.

"Gidula and me, we'll work the problem separately. Then score each of our plans against the goals and objectives and hybridize what we can. We may go several rounds before we come up with something invulnerable. Do you want a plan before we leave the planet?"

"A fisherman impatient catches naught. Hasten slowly, my friend."

The Fox struck his breast in salute and left the meeting room, leaving Dawshoo with Gidula. A few moments passed in silence. Then the old man said, "Oschous is a clever man. Far more clever than I. He will devise a good plan."

"So will you. His will be clever; yours will be wise. The child born of their mating will be the superior to both." First Speaker paused and looked away. "How clever is he, do you think?"

Gidula hesitated and cocked his head. "Is there a problem?"

"Mashdasan told me that MILINTEL planted but three bugs."

"Ah." The old man tugged on his beard. "And we found four."

"Yes. Who planted the fourth bug?"

"Mashdasan. He lied. He wanted to upset you."

"If so, a point for him. But it seems more clever than his wont. What if he spoke truly?"

"I could visit him tonight and learn."

Dawshoo shook his head. "No. We have a truce, an understanding. If we break it, the garrison will take revenge. They have not our talent for retail mayhem, but for wholesale they do well enough."

"You think perhaps an agent-in-place is here on Henrietta and we were misfortunate enough to meet here in his lap?"

"That, or a colleague of ours still embraces the Names."

"Twenty years is a long time for undercover work. Pretend too long and . . . can it remain pretense?" Gidula thought about the matter and walked to the window, where he looked out over the harbor. Gulls shrieked over the naval craft and pleasure boats. "If a Deadly One had planted the fourth bug," he said finally, "would Little Jacques have found it so easily?"

"You think we were meant to find it."

Gidula nodded and Dawshoo scowled. "We should have swept the room yesterday, then we could have discussed this at dinner last night."

"Perhaps the intention was to sow uncertainty in our hearts."

"Ha! That's like hauling dirt to a Terran ghetto. Uncertainty is nothing we have in short supply. Yes, Little Jacques, what is it?"

The Shadow had appeared by the meeting room door. He was a small man and could fit into spaces a normal man might not. His ancestors had once been called pygmies, but there was something in him of the dwarf, as well. And no natural pygmies had been so pale.

"Message for you, Beak," he said, extending a packet.

Dawshoo detested the nickname, but he tolerated its use by his companions lest he appear haughty. He glanced at the seal and saw it came from SkyPort

Rietta. He broke it open and removed the flimsy, read it, and smiled.

"It's Olafsdottr," he told Gidula. "She's brought us a present."

The old Shadow pursed his lips. "So. The long shot pays off."

"Maybe. I need to inspect the goods first."

Little Jacques smiled. "I love opening presents."

CENGJAM GAAFE: THE THIRD INTERROGATORY

Méarana plucks a diminished seventh on her harp. "So," she says. "The extra bug was 'the discord note.'"

"How nice to hear of the enemy," Graceful Bintsaif adds, "picking themselves apart."

Bridget ban says nothing, but sips her coffee and watches the Shadow through lowered lids. Méarana plays a goltraí, something sad but hopeful. She uses her sky-voice, so that the keening appears to emanate from a far corner of the sitting room. Olafsdottr glances briefly in that direction before realizing the trick, then listens for a time in silence.

Bintsaif, finding no reaction to her jibe, shrugs and settles back and the Shadow, as if sensing that motion, turns abruptly toward her and jabs a finger in her direction. The junior Hound flinches, but only a little. Olafsdottr grins. "Do not be too happy, turtle egg," she says, "oover the misfortune of oothers." Then switching to Manjrin, she adds, "Fates deplore happiness. Seek always balance."

"Is that why Dawshoo took such a desperate

gamble?" Bridget ban asks. "By courting disaster, did he hope the Fates would award him success?"

"Never good, gamble with Fates. They load dice. You have never been married, have you? Any of you."

A moment of silence ensues. No one speaks.

"Ooh, it is a chancy thing at best, this marriage thing; and one ill-advised for those in our profession. It is a deep union, I am told; deeper than pair-bond contracts, for it is a mingling of the hearts and not only a meeting of the minds. It has a sort of life of its own; and so may have a sort of death. It is a fragile thing—a spark in a blustery wind—and wants constant vigil to keep alight. Yet, even with the best of wills, even with a common intent, it does not always survive. It is always sad," she says, lifting once more her coffee to her lips, "to see what began in hope to end in strife."

When she sets it down again, her face is more sober than at any time since entering Clanthompson Hall, not excepting the moment when she had found two guns and a knife aimed at her heart. "Our confraternity is closely knit. More so, I think, than your Kennel. We trace our 'ancestry' through those who taught us. The students of a common master count themselves as brothers. We know our teacher's teacher, and his before. We train and practice together in the Abattoir, deep within the Lion's Mouth. In this struggle that now consumes us, *I have killed my brother.* So, Graceful Bintsaif, do not rejoice that he chose one path and I another. For I do not."

She turns once more to face the junior Hound. "Do not celebrate the failure of hope, even if it be the hopes of your enemies. The Confederation bore much fruit, and some of it was bitter and some of it was sour; but it salvaged much that was good from the wreckage of the Commonwealth, and there were times in our history that will shine whenever men gather and sing of the past. Even when your dog has gone mad and you must put it down, you still recall the bounding puppy that you raised."

Méarana notices her mother's grimace. Bridget ban too had once owned a dog and had carried out that dread and terrible service. The harper wonders if Olafsdottr knows that and has used the imagery to a purpose.

"I recognize perhaps half of the agents your tale has mentioned," the Hound says. "Oschous and Dawshoo, I do not know; but of the others, I have fought two, and thought one no longer quick. Do you have the names of all?"

"No."

"Would you tell me if you did?"

"No."

"I could compel your telling."

"No."

Bridget ban had leaned forward as she pressed her guest. Now she leans back again into her chair, and sets her coffee cup aside. "The Two Jacques were in it for the game when I knew them, though I encountered only the Dwarf. They would serve any master, could they but test their lives against their skills. But Gidula struck me as a faithful servant of the Names. What turned *him* to treason?"

The Shadow retreats behind her grin, spreads her

hands in ignorance. "Who can say what stone on life's path sent them stumbling off?"

"And you. The Shadow we knew a case of years ago did not chafe under Those of Name. What stone lay in your own path? That, you can surely say."

Méarana awaits an answer, but she does not think it forthcoming. The Shadow will tell her tale in her own way, and not to the tempo her host would set.

Olafsdottr lifts her cup. "My coffee has grown cold," she says.

Bridget ban leans forward again. "I want to know," she says implacably, "why devoted servants of long-time tyranny turn against their masters."

The Confederal Shadow smiles. "And that kenning's grasp, would not we all. And in the course embrace the tyrants' fall."

IV. HENRIETTA: THE SECOND COUNTER-ARGUMENT

While iron hands hold tight the leash,
    obedience is less command
Than 'tis constraint. What chance is there to turn
    and bite?
What fate impends, but clammy death? Fatality,
    the common taint,
So why the knife provoke? Better far to suss the
    wind and wait.
Yet time does worry all and loosens tight-drawn
    bands. Housebroke,
Sheep all bleat in dazed confusion, unaware of
    shepherds' dampened fury.
But sheepdogs' eyes do track, and sense their
    chance. While leash-bound, sweet;
Slip sour when once they feel the slack.
                    Tentative, they prance and sniff
The figure comatose, not quite sure the fearful
    thing is dead,
Or playing only possum so to learn which trusted
    men their fealty would toss.
What stays that first hard bite but awe? The thing
    has lasted all this long

That mere continuation pleads its case,
And none can vision what might take its place.

Olafsdottr and the scarred man landed by shuttle at Port Rietta, just ahead of a winter storm. They left *Sèan Beta* in orbit, to be cleaned and refitted in the Navy Yards and taken into the Service. The scars of Olafsdottr had healed well during the transit, though her smile had taken on a subtle lopsidedness that she found roguish.

Donovan was less well pleased. He had conducted his abductor to her destination; but her ends were not his own, and he had been dissuaded from turning right about to heigh for the League only by the impossibility of that prospect. The entry into Henrietta Roads had been facilitated by Olafsdottr's particular identity signal, her "fu." Leaving would invite fleet action.

"Don't suppose I've joined you," he muttered as the two of them stood waiting on an open platform for a rail pod at the Port Terminus. Sullen, gray clouds were piling up like dirty laundry in the western sky, and Donovan clapped his arms around himself. "Buy me a snow cloak, would you? I didn't get a chance to pack before I left."

"The pods will be heated and the trip into Riettie-center will not take long."

Donovan shivered dramatically. "What I did for you, you owe me least a cloak."

Olafsdottr checked their queue number and the ready-board, and sighed concession. "This way." They left the pod platform, losing their place in line, and retraced their steps to the concourse of shops immediately inside the terminal. "There's a shuvan high-guy right over here," she told him.

"An autovendor? Isn't there a custom tailor? If I'm going to be kidnapped, I'll be kidnapped in style."

"No," said Olafsdottr, "you won't. The tong will give you later whatever you truly need."

Donovan snorted. "Oh, good. I didn't know what I truly needed; so I'm glad of some strangers to tell me. But at least you offered to give me some tongue."

Olafsdottr scowled. "I do not understand your humors, Donovan."

"Tongue. There's an ancient Terran language that . . ."

Olafsdottr stopped dead and pulled Donovan aside from the flow of pedestrian traffic. "Listen to me, Donovan," she whispered. "Do not present yourself as a Terran here, ever. Terrans are jidawn, 'regulated people.' Do you understand? It is not here like in your Periphery. Terrans have not the respect and honor they have out there." Olafsdottr overrode Donovan's bitter laugh. "Do you understand?"

The scarred man pulled his arm from her grip. "Sure. The good news is: I'm out of the frying pan. I take it the 'tong' is your little group."

"It means 'a Togethering.' "

"So the earwig tells me." Donovan tapped the device nestled in his right ear. "But I imagine there are lots of Togethers for all sorts of purposes. If I had to guess—and my Confederal is rusty—I'd guess 'Gaagjawn tong būpun.' Revolution-together-partner."

Olafsdottr hissed and pressed him against the wall

of the confectioner's shop. "Fool! Some things must never speak aloud."

"Must make for lively craic. If you think I jabber too much, maybe you should just send me back home."

The Shadow released him. "Are swifter means to silence thoughtless lips. You are wanted here, but not wanted *so* much that we risk all."

Donovan decided that he had pushed her as far as he might safely do, and followed silently while she sought out the kiosk for temporary weather clothing. He made a great show of selecting the size, color, and cut of the snowcloak.

Two boots stood in front of a nearby Approved Books kiosk. They were dressed for downside leave: loose, burgundy silks and black trousers, with their ship's medallions pinned above their right breasts. They went uncovered, and made no effort to hide the fact that they were staring at Donovan and Olafsdottr.

The dispenser delivered the cloak and Donovan pulled it out and shook it straight. "Ravn?"

"Yes, I see them. I was told during the crawl-down that they like to shake down dyowaqs—what you call 'touristas'—for detachables."

"Do we call the cops?"

Olafsdottr laughed. "Those *are* the cops. Not those two, I mean. But Henrietta is under martial law. So . . . Listen, Donovan, I am not supposed to be on Henrietta; and you are not even supposed to be in the Confederation. So this must not come to the attentions of the swoswai, the military governor."

"No cops," the Fudir agreed. "Suits me. But I thought your boss had an understanding with the governor."

"He does. Those two don't. They're probably only just down-planet."

The scarred man scratched his hair, replaced his skull cap. "Then this is what we call a learning moment."

Olafsdottr fastened her collar and waited while Donovan swirled his cloak about him. "We could simply pay them," she said.

Donovan held up his right palm. "My implant is loaded up with Gladiola Bills of Exchange. You think they'll take those?"

"Ah. I see the problem. That's why you had me pay for your cloak. Funny the things we sometimes overlook."

"*I* didn't overlook it. Chain up. Here they come."

The two boots strolled over with exaggerated casualness and planted themselves directly in their path. Other travelers in the concourse swerved around the little group like a stream around a rock. A few shot worried glances as they passed; most simply tucked their heads down and pretended not to see.

"Ha, dyowaq," said the one on the left, a young, beefy man with a tonsure of blond hair. "Welcome a Henrietta. We collecting donations a the Distressed Spaceman's Benevolent Fund, help out shipmates down a they luck." He addressed Donovan because those who bought temporary weather clothing at the autovendors were typically off-planet touristas unprepared for the season.

"Fund balance real low," added the second boot, an older, wiry man who reminded Donovan of a rat terrier. His medallion had chief's bars on it.

The scarred man waited patiently, and there was something about the patience of the scarred man that induced hesitation in others. The two boots shifted foot to foot and looked to Donovan's companion.

And if there were anything in the Spiral Arm more daunting than the patience of Donovan buigh, it was the smile of Ravn Olafsdottr.

The beefy one took a step back. "Law shí! Deadly Ones. Chief, remember what Tsali and Chim-bo told us when they coming back a leave?"

"Tsali say they go-gone."

"Ooh, not all at once," said Ravn. "Some may remain. Tie up loose ends. You pardon, we not introduce selves."

The two boots grunted and made awkward attempts to hide their name tags behind folded arms. "Jin, sure, wakay."

"Wait," said Donovan. "You not want donation?"

"Not needful. So sorry a bother you." They began to back away.

"We insist. My fund transfer from off-planet not yet arrive, but my companion happy pay for both."

Olafsdottr shot him an annoyed glance, but extended her hand. The boots flinched and stared at it, as if it had transformed into a flame lance. "The Mouth much grateful for protection boots give against League," she said. "Your pay, never enough. Allow me show gratitude."

A moment more they hesitated, then the chief

reached out slowly and shook her hand. In theory the two palm implants could have interfaced by wireless, but direct contact was both more secure and regarded by custom as more sincere. The chief's eyes glazed for a moment as his balance updated, then he gasped. "Ladyship being most generous!"

Further expressions of politeness followed before the two boots withdrew and retreated down the concourse.

"To seek other prey, no doubt," Donovan said.

"The strong take what they can," Olafsdottr reminded him, "and the weak suffer what they must. First you didn't want to pay; then you did," she said. "Why bother? We had them sheeped."

"Yeah, and that's why. We backed them down with no more than a shady look. They would have taken their humiliation out on the next citizen they ran into."

"That would be the next citizen's problem, not ours. You have a funny way of not getting noticed." She glanced at her ticket. "Hurry. We may still catch our pod."

But they returned to the transit platform just in time to see the Rettiecenter pod slide down the rail.

"Aren't those things supposed to be silent?" Donovan asked her above the squealing of metal and ceramic.

Olafsdottr ignored him and once more entered their destination on the demand-board. They received a new queue number in return. This they turned over to the pod starter, who inserted them into the line for Rettiecenter. "Sure you're going to pod out this time?" he asked sarcastically. When they made no answer, he added, "I hadda send the first one out empty."

"I weep," said Olafsdottr.

Pods arrived at two-minute intervals so the wait was not long before the starter announced, "Riettiecenter pod next. Queue numbers fifty-three through sixty-two. Yah, that's inclusive, lady. Pod sliding in. Stand back behind the stripe."

The gleaming silver ellipsoid flashed a bright red symbol on its nose, a stylized city skyline indicating its destination in the city center. Gull wings popped open along its length to reveal two-seat compartments, enough for twelve. Olafsdottr secured one of these for herself and the scarred man.

<Why did the earlier pod leave empty?> said Inner Child.

Depends on how many are waiting in line for a destination, deduced the Sleuth. *Fifteen minutes ago, there were just the two of us, so the dispatcher sent down a double. We weren't there when it arrived. When these other people showed up, he had to order a twelver. They probably use base-twelve arithmetic here, like in the Old Planets across the Border.*

Show-off, said the Brute.

The doors closed, the pod seized the magnetic field, and they shot down the rail fast enough so that Donovan was pushed back into the cushions. Olafsdottr grinned at him. "Woory not. Pods stop more slowly than they start."

The pod settled into a steady velocity. In the compartment ahead of them, visible through the plex at head level, a young man and woman had begun to kiss as soon as the gull wings had closed. Now, she turned about and straddled her companion, unfastening the bolero jacket she wore. Donovan imagined her companion unfastening much else below the sill level. He glanced at the clock. They had time. Looking up, the woman saw Donovan grinning and, with a scowl, slapped the plex to opaque it.

"Ah, yoong loov," Olafsdottr said with a smile.

"Don't get ideas."

Olafsdottr snuggled in her seat and said nothing while the scenery flickered past. Parklands gave way to manufactories. Ground argosies wound along the truck-ways below the pod rail, containers joining into strings and shuttling toward the city. Residential villas and sporting fields began to appear. The pod-string passed over a pentagonal field on which three teams struggled against one another before a modest crowd.

Olafsdottr broke the silence. "Overthrow of tyranny worthy goal."

"Only if the outcome is net improvement. We've been over this already, Ravn. It's a big Spiral Arm, and tyrants move at a discount. I'll overthrow them, each and all, if they get in my way. Otherwise . . ." He shrugged. "It's not my job."

"Perhaps Dawshoo can persuade you."

Donovan folded his arms. "He can try."

Olafsdottr laid a hand on his shoulder. "Noo, noo, noo, my sweet. I did not mean he would *persuade* you. We want your help, not your submission. He will—"

The pod underwent a sudden, brief lateral acceleration. From the compartment ahead, they heard the sound of the lovers tumbling to the floor.

"<What was that?>" Inner Child asked through the scarred man's lips.

"Switching rails, I think," said Olafsdottr. She touched the screen set into the forward wall and called on a system map, upon which she traced the Riettie-center Line with a finger. "We have been shunted to the Bayside Line," she decided.

"Why? Are we in the wrong pod, after all?"

Olafsdottr cupped her hands around her eyes and stared out the side window. She could see the city-bound magrail curve away to the left, toward the towers that marked the town center. "There is a plume of smoke," she said. "There may be a fire near the rail."

A speaker grill in the compartment came to life and a cheerful voice announced that all pods headed into the city center had been diverted to Bayside, "due to an accident. If you disembark at Heroes' Plaza, a swift-tram will be waiting to take you to the center. Be advised that all blocks from Jester to Commonplace and from Fourth to Sixth have been interdicted on upper and middle levels while our heroic municipal services deal handily with the problem. Bottom level is open for traffic. If your final destination is within the cordon, you will need a pass from the wardens stationed at the apexes."

"The pod platform is in the center of the cordon," said Olafsdottr, examining the system map. "And the Hotel Grand Khyan is at Fifth and Commonplace."

Donovan grunted. "Meeting still on?"

Olafsdottr said nothing, but continued to stare out the side window while the pod slid along the shoreline. The scarred man turned to the right-hand window, but the scenery in that direction was less interesting: a few pleasure craft snatched the wind across Biscuit Bay, a foil-freighter skated on its hydroplane down the channel toward the open ocean. Dolphins danced ahead of the sailboats.

His kidnapper said, "Donovan, if you would not join us . . ." She hesitated before continuing. "Perhaps, you might not show yourself healed. If they think your mind impaired, they may not want you."

The scarred man tore his gaze from the bay. He removed his skull cap and scratched at his scars. "More likely, they would kill me for being useless. A tiger does not change his stripes simply because he fights other tigers."

"Doonoovan," she said, adopting once more the playful Alabaster accent. "Troost me oon thees metter. Better for you to play mind-cripple."

The Bayside rail passed the dockyard end of Flannelmouth Boulevard, and awarded them with a brief glimpse down the great, wide diagonal that bisected Riettiesburg. At the far end, black smoke billowed from the Riettiecenter pod station on the top level above the Hunterfield Traffic Star. Lime-yellow suppressor trucks sprayed the platform with foam and water. Then the pod was past Flannelmouth and only the blank façade of warehouses stared back at them. The grill announced, "Heroes' Plaza" and the retards kicked in, slowing the pod's progress.

<Remember what Teddy used to say?>

That can't be good, recalled the Pedant.

A coincidence? the Silky Voice wondered.

I've done some calculations, the Sleuth told them. *If we assume that the fire broke out after we left Riettieport Terminal, but before we reached the rail point for the Bayside diversion, then it must have happened about the time our original pod reached the station empty. The conclusion is elementary.*

<Someone blew up our pod.>

Fudir, said the Silky Voice suddenly, *why did you insist on buying a snow cloak?*

"I just wanted to mess with Ravn's head," the Fudir murmured. "Maybe Inner Child had a premonition . . ."

<No. Random changes in speed and direction come natural to me.>

That sounds squirrelly, kid.

There was no room in the compartment for a third person, but Pollyanna was sitting beside him. Don't worry, she told them all. There may be an opportunity in this.

Which we won't seize by "not worrying," girly-girl.

He noticed Ravn smiling indulgently. "Very good, sweet," she said. "Act distracted. Converse with selves. Not too much, but enough." She turned back to the window and the plume rising now behind the shorefront high-risers around Heroes' Plaza. She looked worried, and Donovan remembered that civil wars often have two sides.

The scarred man sat in the bar called Apothete, three blocks east and one block below the now quiescent flames of the Riettiecenter fire. The bar was a dark room with cleverly hidden lamps designed to flicker like torchlight and tables set in niches in masonry walls. Within the dimness, and thanks to a trick of the bowl, the uisce glowed as molten gold. At least the people of Henrietta—or at least the people of the Lower City Center—knew the proper way to serve the uisce; although here the bowls were beaten metal, not ceramic, and had little pedestals on which they perched.

The meeting had been hastily arranged, the venue chosen at random. Two magpies, apprentices to the Deadly Ones, guarded the niche within which they sat.

"Hello, my sweet darling," the Fudir told the bowl, or rather its contents. He used a dialect that his ear-wig told him was spoken on Heller Connat that was kissing cousin to the Gaelactic of the Periphery. Then, using a different voice, Donovan chided himself, "A drunk loves his creature."

Across the table from him, Dawshoo Yishohrann sampled a mug of red beer and replaced it softly on the table. His face was still as stone. He exchanged glances with Gidula, and then with Ravn Olafsdottr. The latter shrugged. "This is as I foond him."

Gidula reached across and slapped Donovan on the cheek. It was not an attack, but neither was it gentle. "Pay attention, can you?" the Deadly One said. "Your eyes wander all over."

"Each piece of his mind wishes to see," Ravn volunteered, "and so, jostling for the power of sight, the eyes jostle in response."

"I would not mind half so much," Dawshoo

muttered, "if they would but jostle in sync. Donovan! Do you understand what the situation is?"

The Fudir took a bold swallow of the uisce. "Course, I do," he cackled, wiping his mouth with the sleeve of his blouse. "You Shadows are fighting each other. Want no part of it, me."

Dawshoo shook his head. "Did the Names take your balls as well as your mind?" Then, to Gidula, he said, "I did not expect much. The last message we had from Billy Chins said Donovan was falling apart."

"Billy Chins was a traitor and a liar," Gidula answered. "I thought he exaggerated, for his own reasons."

"Look," Donovan said, allowing some of Inner Child's fear to show. "Tell me what you want me to do. I'll tell you why I can't do it and then we're done, and I can go home."

Dawshoo spoke to Ravn. "Discard him." He began to rise.

"Wait," said Gidula.

The Beak turned to him. "Would you lean on this broken reed?"

"He may serve, even in this impaired state; otherwise I would not have suggested the play. Certainly, Those fear so, or their agents would not have bombed the pod station."

Dawshoo glowered into his beer for a moment, took a hard swallow, and set it aside half-consumed. He coupled his hands into a ball on the table and with evident reluctance sought out Donovan's wandering eyes. "We need you to infiltrate the Secret City and assassinate the Secret Name."

The eyes stilled momentarily as each and all of him froze at the prospect. "Heh! Which of us is the madman here?"

"This war," said Gidula, "has gone on long enough. Past time to bring it to an end."

"But why us?" the scarred man asked. "A task like this wants the finest lock picks, not a rusty old hammer."

Dawshoo seemed inclined to agree, but Gidula smiled, though his teeth barely showed. "Two reasons, and they are the same."

A magpie stuck his head in the niche. "Oschous is here," he said and stepped aside to admit the third member of the cell. Olafsdottr made room for him on the bench.

"What news?" Dawshoo asked him.

"It was a bomb," he confirmed. "The boots are bees from a struck hive. Citizen casualties were heavy, and the civic administrator stood up on his hind legs and demanded answers from the swoswai. MILSEC and MILPOL are everywhere, questioning everyone, stopping and searching everyone, but to no effect. My guess: a human detonator. MILSEC won't find him because he's a pink mist in the air above the station. The swoswai dare not pursue either us or our foes; but neither may he be seen as not acting at all. Thus, the security kabuki. But the sooner we are all off-planet, the better . . ."

"Aye," said Gidula. "The attempt today shows that the loyalists are closing in. We must push the effort to the utmost. Strike quickly, or we will be struck."

Dawshoo sighed. "I chose this world because it is

out of the way, but when so many knew to come here, perhaps it was inevitable that it be so many plus one."

Oschous hooked a thumb at Donovan. "Is this *him*?"

"Yes, this is Donovan," Olafsdottr said.

The Fox turned to Donovan and tapped his forehead with the side of his fist. "It is an honor to meet you at last."

Donovan did not need to act confused. "Honor? We've done nothing yet."

"He has forgotten," Dawshoo told the newcomer. "*Those* took the memory from him."

"Ah. Then how do you expect him to . . . ?"

"His memory may return," said Gidula. "Or you may concoct another scheme. Or . . ."

"Or the horse may learn to sing?"

The Old One smiled. "Or that. But his mere name may be enough."

Oschous pursed his lips before nodding. "Possible." He did not sound as if the possibility were high.

The Fudir sighed. "Me-fella acetanan. Poor ignorant-man. You-fella Gidula say two reasons why rusty hammer for delicate job."

Gidula's lip curled again. "No need for the Terran jabber. First of all, you were an inspiration to millions when you led the earlier uprising, and you may be so again."

"What!" Donovan nearly spilled his bowl and stood from the bench.

Olafsdottr put a hand on his arm. "You have forgotten even that? 'The lamp that was lit has been lit again'? 'The names that were not forgotten have been remembered'? Do these bold slogans not ring in your ears?"

"You led the last holdouts atop the Education Ministry," Gidula insisted. "And then, when all was lost, came within a hair's-breadth of escape, save that you were betrayed by one of your own comrades."

Those dreams we had on Gatmander, said the Pedant. *They were memories unlocked by Teddy's drug! If I dig, I can find them again! I know it!*

Oh! To remember! cried the Silky Voice.

The scarred man's mouth worked, but no words emerged. Slowly, he resumed his seat. "But then," he managed at last.

Gidula leaned across the table. "Yes." The word was almost a hiss. "Yes. You were found on the riverbank, on the *eastern* bank, miles from the Education Ministry."

"Which means," said Dawshoo, "that you knew a secret way out of the Secret City."

"Appropriate that there be one," murmured Ravn.

"And a secret way out," said Oschous, "may be a secret way in."

"That is the second reason we need the rusty hammer," Gidula said. "If you lead a team of assassins into the Secret City, we can cut the head off the snake." He smiled a little at that. "Cut the head off the snake," he said again. "Your name will live forever."

The scarred man sank back in his seat, overcome by his contending emotions.

★ ★ ★

The Brute *wanted* this.

★ ★ ★

The Sleuth saw it as a game, an intellectual exercise.

★ ★ ★

The Pedant wanted to recover lost memories.

★ ★ ★

But Inner Child was terrified,

★ ★ ★

the Silky Voice doubtful,

★ ★ ★

and neither Donovan

★ ★ ★

nor the Fudir saw any gain to be had.

★ ★ ★

"My name would live forever?" the Fudir said. "That sounds far too posthumous. If it's to be one or the other, I'd rather the name die and the rest of me live." He cackled, picked up the uisce bowl, but it trembled so that he could barely sip from it.

"Indeed." Olafsdottr smiled. "Posthumous fame is something few enjoy."

Gidula scowled at her, but Donovan almost choked and the uisce burned his throat. He set the bowl down so hard that it nearly toppled. "What name is it," he croaked, "that would live forever?"

"Do not speak it aloud," Dawshoo cautioned him. "Not until the time is ripe and we rally the masses."

"Geshler Padaborn," said Gidula.

Donovan heard Ravn suck in her breath, and realized that it was a revelation to her, too. Otherwise, she might have used it as an argument during the slide down the Tightrope. He could feel Pedant digging and digging. But . . . nothing surfaced. All memories had been cauterized.

"Padaborn," he whispered, as if the sound of the name on his own lips might resurrect some sense of identity. But it was the name of a stranger.

"An inspiration to us all," said Gidula. "When the others learn you have returned, their morale will soar."

"You owe it to the men you once led," Oschous added, "to lead them once more—and their sons and daughters with them."

"Do we?" Donovan said. "We have no recollection of being Padaborn; no desire to pick up his fallen torch."

Dawshoo smacked the table. "I never thought this play too promising, and the promise grows less. A man is the sum total of his deeds. If this Donovan buigh does not remember that Padaborn, he will not remember how he escaped the Secret City. Olafsdottr?"

The ebony Shadow cocked her head. "Yes, First Speaker?"

Dawshoo jerked his head at Donovan and shrugged.

"Hold," said Gidula. "Rofort once wrote that 'A house is a pile of blocks, but not only a pile of blocks. When the house is torn down, the blocks remain, but where has the house gone?'"

"We haven't time for your philosophy," Dawshoo said impatiently. "We leave for Ashbanal tonight. Manlius awaits us there."

"The house of Padaborn has been demolished," Gidula said. "But perhaps some blocks remain. He need not remember himself in order to remember his deeds. And all we need is the remembrance of one deed particular."

Oschous grinned. "You're a clever one, Gidula. Or you're a fatuous old fool. We're as likely to hear wisdom from the one as the other. What say, Dawshoo? We'll take him with us. Something familiar may jog a memory or two."

Dawshoo rose. "It's your play, Gidula. Take it as far as you can without risking us all."

"Will you start the whisper campaign?"

"If I do, you had best deliver Padaborn. If not *the* Padaborn, at least *a* Padaborn. Train him up, if you must." He watched Donovan drain the uisce bowl. "And if you can."

With that, he departed. One of the magpies left with him.

Gidula too prepared to leave. To Olafsdottr, he said, "Be sure he arrives at Port Rietta before the departure deadline. Keep the boots off his neck. Are you coming, Oschous?"

The third Triumvir shook his massive head. "I think I'll stay with our hero."

Gidula shrugged. "As you will."

After Gidula had left with the other magpie, Oschous shifted to the other side of the table so he could sit facing Donovan and Olafsdottr. He leaned back against the partition and lifted his feet to the table, linking his hands behind his head. His smile heightened his foxlike appearance. "So, Gesh," he said. "What are we to do with you?"

The scarred man shrugged. "Send me home? I doubt we can be of much use to you."

But Oschous shook his head. "That's not what we do with things of 'not much use.' You should be grateful to Gidula, you know. He saved your life—twice—this past hour."

The Fudir grunted. "Tell me again the difference between your lot and Those."

The Dog head smiled broadly. "'It takes all kinds to make a world,' an ancient prophet said. People are like those gas molecules the scientisticals jabber of. They go about in every direction and so the whole body of them goes nowhere in particular. To have enough people move in the same direction you can't wait until they do it for the same reasons. Afterward—if there is an afterward—there will be a sorting out. And Friend Donovan?" He stopped smiling. "I think you'll be a lot more useful than you realize."

CENGJAM GAAFE: THE FOURTH INTERROGATORY

A faint band of red has cut the throat of night and bleeds across the eastern horizon. Bridget ban studies this herald through the bay window. Her hand reaches involuntarily to her right breast, where the Badge of Night is placed, before she remembers that she is not in uniform. Her daughter and her subordinate watch in equal wonder, for to gaze out the window she has turned her back on the Confederal Shadow.

Olafsdottr, for her part, pays this no apparent mind, and selects delicately from a tray of finger sandwiches that Mr. Wladislaw has unobtrusively conducted into the room. Behind her, the Shadow hears the creak of Graceful Bintsaif's jaws and smiles. The long tense night is poised to yield a daylight no shorter or relaxed.

Méarana plays a melody tangled and unresolved. It is neither geantraí nor goltraí but, like the meeting in the pit of Apothete, it searches for its boundaries, for its resolutions. It hungers for the progressions that will grace it with either triumph or tragedy. Much depends, she tells herself, on whether her father is dead or not. But she tells herself this at such a deep level that she is herself barely conscious of the thought. Donovan had told her once that Confederal Shadows are past masters at the arts of torture, and she has no choice now but to believe him. For Olafsdottr has been torturing her since the story's inception—by withholding that one particular facet of it, the only one that matters. The entire mode of the song depends upon that one fact; and so the Ravn's silence on that point can have no other purpose than to keep the harper balanced on the knife's edge.

Yet Olafsdottr is telling the story and not her father. Absence is also a fact, of sorts. And it may be that it needs no elaboration.

Méarana glances at Bridget ban just at the moment her mother turns away from the window. Does Olafsdottr's coy silence torture her mother, as well? Does the uncertainty gnaw at her, too? Does she ache—as Méarana aches—to reach down the Confederal's throat and drag the words forth by main force?

If so, neither her face nor bearing betrays her. Perhaps nothing can break a wall built against twenty-four years' resentment. Yet Méarana had spent a long, hard journey with Donovan and found him not the man of her mother's memories. He had been both more and less than the tale told of him, and so, more or less, a man.

The silence breaks when Olafsdottr wipes her hands on her pants and says, "One drawback of the 'invitashoon for cooffee'—it leads of necessity to anoother invitation; or to at least a request."

Bridget ban snorts brief amusement. "I will go with you."

Olafsdottr ducks her head. "Please, is there to be noo privacy for even my moost intimate mooments? In my coolture . . ."

"You are not in your culture. Here, we think nothing of going together. Graceful Bintsaif, you will stand guard at the door. Alert Mr. Tenbottles that our guest is on the move."

Méarana chuckles and, when her mother and the other Hound glance her way, she says, strumming an arpeggio on her strings, "Is she such a poor storyteller that she would leave before her climax?"

"Why assume her purpose is storytelling?" says Bridget ban. "She may have come only to gain access to this building; in which case, the less she sees of it, the better. Perhaps, I should have a chamber pot brought in."

Olafsdottr cringes at this. "With my complexion you cannot see me blush, but I cannot bear the thought of pot-squatting."

"Ravn," says Bridget ban, "ye hae nae blushed ower muckle in yer entire life."

"Oh, how little you know! I was born on the Groom's Britches—the race you call Alabastrine is common there—and attitudes ingrained in childhood the adult cannot easily ignore."

"Naetheless," Bridget ban says with a wave of her teaser.

Her prisoner sighs and leaves the room bracketed between the two Hounds. When they are gone, Méarana laughs out loud and plays a little passage on her harp.

"Miss?" says Mr. Wladislaw with a cock of the head. Ever attentive, he has seized the moment to tidy up the library.

"Oh, nothing, Toby. An' I bethought me the ainly one who could play anither."

"I don't understand, miss." He picks up the sandwich tray and waits to see if clarification is forthcoming.

"Hae ye e'er seen an instrument try to speil the harper e'en while the harper tries to speil the instrument?"

This is not clarification. He smiles politely, responds, "No, miss, an' I hae no," and he beats a hasty retreat.

"Regarding the explosion," Bridget ban says, when all have been refreshed and have resumed their respective positions, "who knew that Donovan was to be on that pod?"

"The pod starter," Méarana suggests.

The other three women laugh. "No, darling," says Bridget ban. "He would have known they *missed* their pod and would have passed along the new pod number."

"The boots, then. Their humiliation festered, so they called a colleague in the city and . . ."

"Noo, noo, noo, Little Lucy," says Olafdottr, once more comforted on the sofa. "They not know first pod, only second. But man *watching* pod platform may note our queue number, and having transmit this, he depart."

"That was a mistake," Graceful Bintsaif comments. "He should have waited and confirmed that you had in fact entered the pod."

The Shadow shrugs. "Even enemy make mistakes. May theirs be worse than ours. But best place observe ready-board in queue itself. Break queue draw attention, as we did. Perhaps," she continues in lilting Gaelactic, "the man was after knowing Padaborn by sight, and feared that Padaborn would recognize him in turn if he lingered or drew attention to himself."

"I think he waited," says Graceful Bintsaif. "But he waited at Riettiecenter. He was the bomber."

Bridget ban tosses her red hair. "Then he could have detonated himself at SkyPort. Why wait, if he were certain of his target then? He was not tender of bystanders." She considers a moment before murmuring, "By their fruits ye shall know them."

Olafsdottr spreads her hands. "Oschous consider play from all angle, and all as he say. But one aspect bother me."

"You mean," says Méarana, "aside from narrowly escaping an assassination?"

"Ooh, that boother me less than *noot* escaping."

Bridget ban steeples her fingers under her chin. "Style." The other two professionals nod.

"Shadows usually more subtle with message they deliver," the Confederal says. "Bomb artistically dissatisfying. Our people minimalist."

"Aye," says Bridget ban. "There was no need to shout. And that means . . ."

". . . message meant for someone else."

Méarana is incredulous. "You mean their pod was targeted randomly?"

Olafsdottr shakes her head. "Ooh, noothing randoom. All is Fates. You know proverb: 'Two birdies, one stone'? Donovan and I, we first birdie. Big noise for second."

"So, who was the second birdie?" asks Bridget ban.

Olafsdottr spreads her arms wide. "Maybe swoswai—caution him against choosing sides. Maybe Triumvirs—show their secrets known. Oschous no such fool that this escape him. Of all of us, some say, he is best. So joins he us to fare with our reluctant guest."

V. ASHBANAL: A GATHERING OF SHADOWS

Inbound toward the suns of men we slid,
The old Home Stars from which we once set
    forth,
Which saw gone days of glory burn and fade
To embers and to ashes raked and cold.
"Bright suns shining in the memories of men,"
Worlds from sterile stone and rock long wrested,
Whereon the scattered assets of our strength
Struggled with the foe and waited word:
Those few we sought who might essay assault
On Secret City. Bold men and subtle, sufficient
For the task which Oschous limned for our
    endeavor
When once we should gain entry. But Donovan,
    the key,
Stayed silent, the mem'ry lost amidst the shards
Of he who once he was. Or—remembered, but
    withheld?
What lies engendered in such jangled minds
As his? He, having cause a-lack to join our stock,
Might fain keep peace, and so evade the lock.

The Confederation names its Krasnikov tubes after rivers, finding the analogy to flowing streams more apt. From Henrietta, Oschous followed the Gong Halys into New Anatole, and thence by the Mekong past St. Khambong before joining the Great Ganga and the stately voyage into Ashbanal.

On this latter world awaited Manlius Metataxis, who had gone thither to settle an old score. Many were the motives that drove men into our ranks, O harper; and for Manlius those had been the oldest in all the worlds: jealousy over a woman. Kelly Stapellaufer had been a colleague—a "sister" under the rules of the Abattoir, and so forbidden to him. But in the course of several missions, they had become entangled, and Shadow Prime had dispatched Epri Gunjinshow, his second-best student, to separate them. This, he had done in the old-fashioned way: by seducing Kelly to himself. Manlius might have tolerated her kidnapping, her imprisonment, or even her assassination, but not the theft of her heart, and not by Prime's second-best.

Donovan was granted the liberties of Oschous's ship, but those liberties were few in any case. It was a large and sprawling vessel. Nestled in a planet's arms, she might resemble more a castle than a means of flight. There were rooms for exercise, for zazen, for torture, for relaxation, for dining. There were even places where Donovan could enjoy the illusion of solitude. But he was not so foolish as to suppose that any move of his was unobserved, that any word he spoke expired unheard, or that any text or entertainment he consulted passed unremarked. The smuggler's ship had been retrofitted in haste and there had been inadvertent pockets of privacy, but *Black Horse* was Oschous's personal vessel and was permeated with his intentions.

Eight magpies crewed her, standing alternate watches on the old naval pattern. They wore black body stockings—shenmats—that left only their faces bare. After a day on the crawl up Henrietta, Donovan confirmed that there was always one magpie in his line of sight. This caused him some unease, for there was an ancient Terran fable by which a magpie at one's window was a foreboding of death.

During the transit, Oschous sought by sundry means to quicken Donovan's memory, calling him habitually by the name Padaborn, or more familiarly as Gesh. He supplied the summary reports on Padaborn's Rising, both the official and the unredacted versions, and praised him for his deeds therein. There was even a bootleg partisim—a "participative simulation"—produced before the Names had decided that the Rising had never happened, and had obliterated all references to it. But even when he reenacted the role of Padaborn himself, Donovan's memory came back dry. The simulation was deficient. Most of the rebels had perished and so their deeds were sheer guesswork.

Oschous tried altered states, three times with Donovan's consent, twice surreptitiously. But Donovan's fragmented mind frustrated every effort. Whether drugs, hypnosis, or dhyāna, some part of him remained unaffected, so that he was never entirely in flight.

"We could have told you," the Fudir said in the meditation room after one such session. "We spent twenty years drinking uisce in the Bar on Jehovah, and hardly got a buzz on. We're like a ship with airtight compartments. Drug or hypnotize one personality, and another remains untouched." Only once, he remembered, had he ever been affected in his entirety; but this he did not mention. Whatever the Wildman's potion had been, it was unknown to him.

He and Oschous arose from the mat and bowed to each other. "Small wonder then Those smashed you," Oschous suggested. "As a broken vessel, you've formidable resistance to the Question. Whole, who could say? There is always kaowèn," he added in a meditative frame. "It has oft reaped unexpected returns."

Donovan's scalp prickled. "I'm not holding out deliberately," he ventured.

Oschous waved a hand. "I know, I know. That's why I've not used it. A man who knows things can be brought to confess them. But a man who knows nothing can also be brought to confess. At some point he would desire more than life itself to tell me what I ask. It need not be the truth; it need only bring him surcease. On such information, we might proceed confidently to our doom."

"Then why employ kaowèn at all?"

Oschous's ruddy eyebrows climbed his forehead. "But I told you. If a man does know the truth, the confession would be genuine. Really, Gesh, we don't pith a man on whim, wondering if he *might* know something. That would be barbaric. We only employ kaowèn if we already know that he possesses the knowledge we want."

"Considerate of you."

"The sort of men we question don't merit consideration. Well, perhaps you and I will have better luck next time. We'll try a different school of meditation. Perhaps that of Gundilap. Memories are holograms. They can never be entirely eradicated. It's simply a matter of finding the right fragment and reflecting upon it from the right angle."

"There is a third possibility," said Donovan. "I might not remember how Padaborn escaped because I'm not Padaborn."

"I hope for your sake that you're wrong," the Shadow said gravely. "But I don't think there's any mistake. What Those did to Padaborn they didn't do to many." He bowed. "Go in peace, Gesh."

Donovan opened the door to the corridor, and Ravn was suddenly in his face, shouting, "Run!"

Donovan started and cried, "Down!"

Ravn fell to laughing at this splendid joke and after pacifying the somewhat nettled Donovan and sending him off, she and Oschous pondered the involuntary response he had made and wondered at its significance.

"The Question was in his mind," Oschous said. "When Padaborn ran at the last, he ran down."

But Ravn was unimpressed. "He was last seen on a rooftop. In what other direction could he have run?"

Donovan, for his part, as he made his way to the suite he had been provided, wondered at Oschous's own revelation. *So,* said the Sleuth, *there are others like us.*

Ashbanal was a fourth-generation world lying in the district called the Karnatika, a cluster of worlds interlocked by a web of short, fast roads known as the Oaks. One of these planets was said to be Oschous's home world, but he would not say which, nor even whether it was truly said. "When a man enters the Lion's Mouth," he told Donovan during the crawl down-system, "his old self dies and with him all old ties. 'The Abattoir is my home,' we say, 'and its Shadows are my family.'"

Ashbanal had been settled at various removes from Elria, Dunlemor, Habberstap, and New Krakas. Her Desolate Ocean had held few of those elementary prokaryotes from which life built itself, and the ancient terraforming arks had known no easy time in her quickening. Now, however, three continents lay verdant with old growth forest, save near the bays and inlets where the skimmer-boats put in and atop the mesas set aside for the ballistic shuttles. The fourth continent either had failed of terraformation or else had been reserved by the ancient Commonwealth world-planners for mining and extraction, for it was pitted worse than the oldest shield-moon, and giant molecular sieves crawled its surface and minced, swallowed, and sorted its native ores.

The port on the moon Neb'Qaysar was known as "the Anemone" for the many umbilicals by which the ships attached themselves. Leaving four magpies to secure the ship, Oschous led them through the tunnels inside the moon to the Inbound Customs gate and the drop ports.

The boots who inspected their documents seemed amused. "Have fun donn dere," said the inbound section chief in a guttural Sconsite accent. "Bott doan cut no sheep t'roats, mindja."

Dee Karnatika cocked his head in interest.

The boots were military, feared enough by the commoners, but the chief grew uncomfortable under that cock of interest. He grimaced, tugged at his collar. "Just a lotta youse guys coming by lately, aina."

Oschous had not identified himself as a "Deadly One," but neither was he traveling "under the radar," and it was neither surprising nor bothersome that the boots had pinged him. There is an aura projected by those whose profession is death. "Just passing through," he said. "I've no official business on Ashbanal."

The chief glanced at Olafsdottr, who wagged a thumb at Oschous. "I'm with him."

He looked at Donovan.

The Fudir handed over travel documents no less impressive than the official sort despite being crafted only lately during the slide from Henrietta. "I was heading this way," he said, "and they gave me a ride." Which was close enough to the truth to have a nodding acquaintance with it.

That elicited another shrug. "Hey, our swoswai, he ain't no dumb mutt. Youse make twenty-four come by here so far. Do whatcha gotta do, but try not to spook da sheep."

As they passed through the gate, the magpies exchanged glances with the boots. There was on the one hand the disdain of a skilled craftsman for a common workman and on the other the resentment of a laborer for the professional.

They filed into a groundside shuttle past the ranks of commoners who had been evicted from it to make way for the Shadow and his entourage. The former passengers stood with eyes downcast, though a few glowered in sidelong glances. Donovan sensed an undercurrent of ill feeling toward the Lion's Mouth by both the military and the commons. In the League, the Hounds were often glamorized by entertainers and admired by the masses; but in the Confederation, the Deadly Ones were only feared. That might work up to a point, but admiration could inspire men to follow, while by fear they could only be driven.

Oschous and Ravn took two seats in the last row and indicated that Donovan should sit in front of them. The four magpies spaced themselves about the cabin: one by the entry, one by the hatchway to the pilot's cabin, and two in reserve. Once they had settled in, the copilot walked through the cabin checking that everyone had his safety harness fastened. "We drop hard and we drop fast," he said by way of explanation.

<But the typical result of a malfunction,> said Inner Child <would be atmospheric incineration. Which would make the safety harness a bit irrelevant.>

Hey, said the Brute, we may end up as cinders; but at least we'll burn up securely fastened to our seats. This did not comfort Inner Child one whit.

Oschous leaned forward and tapped Donovan on the shoulder. "Stop muttering to yourself and pay attention. Here's the situation. Manlius tracked Epri to Ashbanal and threw down a pasdarm challenge. Epri cannot leave the planet without fighting Manlius. Everyone has agreed to it."

𝔓𝔞𝔰 𝔡'𝔞𝔯𝔪𝔢𝔰, said the Pedant. 𝔉𝔯𝔬𝔪 𝔞𝔫 𝔬𝔩𝔡 𝔗𝔢𝔯𝔯𝔞𝔫 𝔱𝔬𝔫𝔤𝔲𝔢, 𝔪𝔢𝔞𝔫𝔦𝔫𝔤 "𝔞 𝔭𝔞𝔰𝔰𝔞𝔤𝔢 𝔬𝔣 𝔞𝔯𝔪𝔰." 𝔍𝔱 𝔦𝔰 𝔞 𝔰𝔬𝔯𝔱 𝔬𝔣 𝔦𝔪-𝔭𝔯𝔬𝔪𝔭𝔱𝔲 𝔱𝔬𝔲𝔯𝔫𝔞𝔪𝔢𝔫𝔱, 𝔬𝔯 𝔧𝔬𝔲𝔰𝔱. 𝔍𝔱 𝔦𝔰 𝔞 𝔠𝔲𝔰𝔱𝔬𝔪 𝔣𝔞𝔯 𝔬𝔩𝔡𝔢𝔯 𝔱𝔥𝔞𝔫 𝔱𝔥𝔢 𝔠𝔬𝔪𝔪𝔬𝔫𝔴𝔢𝔞𝔩𝔱𝔥 𝔦𝔱𝔰𝔢𝔩𝔣.

Oh, shaddap, Pedant.

"*You* agreed," said Donovan. "*We're* here under duress."

"Listen, Padaborn! All the Lion's Mouth would keep this struggle of ours sub rosa. Open battle would catch the attention of the military and draw in the boots. We've no desire to see pitched battles, bombardments, planets blistered. The League would seize advantage and nip at our border worlds. That bomb on Henrietta was conspicuous enough. We must contain this quarrel of ours, lest worse befall."

"It's not my quarrel, either," Donovan said. "Don't expect me to take part." He turned and faced forward just as the shuttle's engines kicked in, killing her forward velocity and dropping her toward the planet.

"I wouldn't want you in it," Oschous told him. "Not with the state your mind is in. I can't risk losing you yet. I swear, I don't know why Gidula had such hopes."

The shuttle put them down at Shallumsar, the capital; and the high-speed bullet took them to Nimway, a medium-sized city in the province of Willit Small. There, Oschous placed Donovan in a room of the Hotel Axhlã on the rotting edge of the city and in the charge of one of his magpies.

Ravn patted him on the cheek before she left with the others for the Isle of Tears. "The magpie will see to your needs," she assured him. "Doon't kill him and he woon't kill you. You are an honored guest and—when once you remember who you are—a leader in our stroogle."

"You're motivating my amnesia," the Fudir muttered.

Then Ravn and Oschous were out the door and down the drop well, where they exited on Grandmother Street, magpies first, forming a triangular cordon, then Oschous, then the Ravn. It was evening already and the world's sun, called Avgar, glowered behind the towers of Margash Nimway on the farther side of the Gennel River. They wore black or violet shenmats dotted with silver tears. Saving Ravn, they wore on their arms red brassards with the black horse of Dee Karnatika. Ravn's black brassard bore the stylized white comet of Gidula. From their belts and webbing depended a variety of useful devices. Oschous consulted one of these and said, "The arbor is north," and they turned right up Grandmother toward an abandoned automill.

They drifted like shades conjured prematurely by the sunset, moving swiftly and with an economy of motion. Few were the Ashbanalis about—dusk was not a friend in this quarter of the city—and those by chance encountered gave the Deadly Ones a wide and sudden berth. One man alone stood his ground and, from the gathering gloom on the corner of Grandmother and Beryl, he watched them as a jackal does a passing pride of lions.

"Above," Ravn whispered to Oschous.

"I saw," he answered. He consulted his locator once more, but did not change direction.

Above them another Shadow swung on a tzanwire from the balcony of an apartment building to the pylon supporting the Beryl Street Elevated. There, he—or she—paused to reel in the wire and watch like a spider from the web of support struts while Oschous and his party passed below. Rebel? Loyalist? One of the dwindling band of neutrals attracted by the pasdarm? Ravn did not know, but the back of her neck prickled as she passed beneath the Elevated. There was a Truce supposed; but the amity within the Lion's Mouth was long sacrificed on the altar of Manlius's lusts, and the Truce of a pasdarm seemed a frail reed on which incautiously to lean.

Oschous made a sign and pointed, and Ravn and the magpies turned their attention to a figure lurking in a doorway, his own magpies arrayed about him in a checkerboard defense: Dawshoo, who had been sucked in half against his will to the rebellion against Those of Name.

Not that it mattered in the end. Willing or not; eager or reluctant; motives venal or noble. If you cast the die, the price of life was victory. Ravn noted how drawn Dawshoo had grown since she had first known him, a lifetime ago on Dungri's World when she had been a magpie herself. The Life took it out of one, even under the best of circumstances—and circumstances these past twenty years had not been the best.

"The arbor has been set up in there," whispered Dawshoo, nodding toward the abandoned factory. "It's agreed. The rest of us keep our distance. Prime said . . ." He hesitated, licked his lips. "Prime said that this will settle the quarrel. If Manlius wins, Prime will call off his fighters. If Epri wins, I'm to do the same."

Oschous stiffened. "Was it for Manlius's pride then that we sold our oaths?"

"Manlius is my brother-in-arms. I could not stand by while Prime crushed him."

"And one thing led to another," murmured Ravn. "From mighty acorns feeble oaks do grow."

Dawshoo shot her a look. "Your lips move, but I hear Gidula's voice."

"And if Epri kills your brother?" demanded Oschous through tightened jaws. "Do we throw aside twenty years of struggle and subversion? Our brothers who have died—and those whom we've killed?"

There was another presence with them: a tall figure cloaked in dun and like Dawshoo wearing the ceremonial skull cap of a senior Shadow. Ekadrina Sèanmazy leaned upon a walking staff as tall as she. Her grin matched that of the skull that crowned her. "As would we," she told the rebels. "And ours is da bitter side of da wager, since we fought to protect da Names dat you have fought to tear down." She spoke in a broad Kotyzarmayan accent that clipped her consonants and hardened the endings of her words. Her final S's hissed; her initial ones buzzed.

Oschous reared back. "We are the true servants of the Confederation . . ."

Ekadrina waved dismissal. "Believe your own propaganda, Karnatika, at your own risk. I told Prime diss was a bad play; but de infighting among us tears his heart and diss can make an end of him, de strife. He cares less upon what terms we make de peace den dat we make him." In the peculiar dialect of Noytáyshlawn, even abstractions demanded sex.

Gidula had come silently among them, and took the opportunity to scoff. "Will Prime join us in our struggle against Those of Name when Manlius prevails? Tell us another story. You are more entertaining than most."

Ekadrina threw her cloak across her shoulder. She wore, underneath, a fine mesh of spun dispersal armor, and a belt and bandoliers well hung with weaponry. "Da Names can care for demselves," she said, and added slyly, and not without a certain reserve, "Dere's word dat some are abroad."

Dawshoo started visibly. If the commons and the boots walked in fear of the Shadows, even the Shadows feared Those of Name. "They've left the Secret City?"

"Some. Maybe. What confines Dem? Remember da rumor years ago dat one once fled to da Periphery?" She grinned once more and turned away. "And now, if you will excuse me, I must see to my idiot brudder."

When the leader of the loyalist Shadows had gone, Oschous sucked in his breath, expelled it, looked to

Dawshoo. "So. There is an agreement. But will they abide by it?"

Ravn asked the better question. "Will *we*?"

The building complex had once housed an automill and the floorway was gridded by the lumpish bulks of gutted mill frames. The omni-tooling was long gone, of course, along with the robots—sold off when the mill went under—and most of the fittings had been harvested by the departing owners and then gleaned by scavengers. What remained was as a pencil sketch to a fine painting in oils. Large portions of the roof had blown away in this storm or that over the intervening years. Rust had claimed those metals capable of it; corrosion had tarnished the rest; rot had eaten into its timbers. Only the ceramics and plastics remained unmarked by the years, beyond a patina of grime and the assault of optimistic molds.

The exposed skeleton served as perches for the gathering of Shadows, though one might search twice to assure oneself that they were there. They embraced their namesakes cast by the setting sun, seemed indeed to be extensions of them, and their motions appeared no more than the natural elongations of the evening.

The interior had been decorated in gray with touches of gold and silver. A great banner of deep violet hung from the central rafter bearing a single silver tear in its field. Flanking it were two others: a sky-blue banner with a white dove and a forest-green banner with a yellow lily. The mons of the combatants, Manlius and Epri. A third banner hung to the side, one that Ravn did not recognize: bloodred with a white cross of the sort called "Maltese."

"The Riff of Ashbanal," Gildula told her as he followed her into the arbor. "He is to be judge of the kill. After all, it's his planet."

Among the spawn of the Abattoir, those Shadows assigned to police a single planet were held in some esteem by those who carried roving commissions. A roving commission usually meant singular assignments and particular targets, in and out, been and gone. A single planet might seem insignificant against the sprawl of the Spiral Arm, but it was large enough when a riff and his magpies must see to the apprehension of criminals, the punishment of treasons, the suppression of dissent, and the purging of corrupt officials, day in and day out. Riffs were marathoners among the sprinting Shadows.

A loggia had been cleared and a fountain set up from which a punch spiced with licorice and rum flowed across a bed of cleansing stones. Near the fountain, three of the Riff's magpies played light music on lute, tambour, and viol. Personally played music on antique instruments! Shadows and their magpies stood about deep in conversation and laughter, enmities in abeyance, old friendships briefly renewed, orders and brotherhoods conferring on their particular concerns. Ravn paused to fill a cup. The cups were of frangible ceramic, purple to match the pasdarm flag, and bore the teardrop pattern.

"I've attended pasdarms," said a magpie at the fountain, "where dozens of banners o'erhung the kill space, and the duels ran all day and through the night." He wore the taiji of Ekadrina Sèanmazy, yin encircling yang encircling yin, and a numeral that marked him third in her following. He glanced at Ravn's unnumbered brassard, but made no comment, and sipped his own drink. Yesterday, they might have been sent to kill each other. And tomorrow they might yet be. But for today, there was a Truce, and they were brothers in an ancient rite. "I've seen Shadows die in mock-combat," he confided, "but this is the first I've been where the chapters read à outrance."

"The fight will be no different," Ravn told him, "only shorter. Dispersal armor is forbidden. And a purposed kill looks much the same as the accidental sort."

Above them, Gidula's comet banner unfurled on the sidelines, drawing the eyes of Magpie Three Sèanmazy. "The Old One," he whispered. "'Tis a grand show, is it not?" His eyes roamed the banners on high, naming them, reciting their own famous passages at arms. "There! Lime, a lion. That's Aynia Farer, and . . . yellow, two crows! Phoythaw Bhatvik, Ekadrina's adviser. Crimson, a black horse. Oschous Dee Karnatika himself! Oh, there are great names here today . . . Did you witness the pasdarm, O Deadly One," her chance companion asked, moist-eyed, "where the Hatborden fought Billy Chins? That was on Whitefield, Tobruk's Sun. Aye! Was there e'er such noble courage shown? E'er such skill shown in gunplay or the knife? At the end of it, they exchanged their personal sidearms and pledged to fight again, when next the Fates allowed, though they never did. The entire set was taken to the Abattoir and displayed for a year and a day in the temple." A sip from the spiced rum. "I hope he dies well."

Ravn Olafsdottr did not ask him which combatant he expected to die. "The great game of the beautiful life," she murmured. She emptied her cup, placed it upended on the sideboard, as was the custom, and prepared to leave for a perch in the rafters. But Magpie Three Sèanmazy held her arm, a gesture in other contexts potentially fatal.

"I didn't catch that."

"The great game of the beautiful life," she said. "Why do you think we wear silver tears on our shenmats when we attend these affairs? Why do you think we decorate the kill space so gaily and discuss so avidly the art with which a stroke or a shot or a move was made? It is because within this space, within the 'squared circle,' *it all has meaning*. There is closure. There are rules, and within those rules the better warrior wins. Outside the arbor, it is not so orderly, not so pretty. Death is never according to the rules, and never the reward only of the less proficient. Much of the time, there is never even a reason; only a moment of carelessness. No one will stop to record our last brave words. Our final enemy will walk away and leave us to bleed out in some back alley. Or some natural disaster will fell us, and no one will ever know. The Hatborden died in an aftershock on Jasmine during the cleanup; and Billy Chins disappeared in the League, and none know where or why."

The magpie had colored under these words. "Then why do you continue in the service?"

Olafsdottr shrugged. "It's what I do."

"When your final enemy leaves you to bleed out," he said, "pray that it be a Hound and not a brother Shadow."

Ravn made a sign against Fate. "May it be so, save that the Hound lies bleeding."

That lightened the other's countenance. The Shadows might be in civil war among themselves, but they could agree about their enemies across the Rift of stars. "Well said, sister!" And they parted on a more amicable note.

Ravn studied the banners hanging in the dead air of the ruin. She thought about raising her own, but as she was presently attached to Gidula's section, that would be unseemly.

On her way into the rafters, she caught up with Gidula. "He grew angry," the Old One said, "because he knew you spoke truth."

She did not ask him how he had overheard her conversation. "Truth has oft that effect." Ravn reached up and hauled herself onto an angle brace, where she nestled. Around her, others found perches and vantage points. Some deployed recorders of various sorts. Both combatants were highly rated, and the contest promised to be instructive as well as entertaining.

Directly forward, across the kill space, the one-time management offices had been broken open into a sort of balcony and decorated as the Isle of Tears. From it deployed the banner of Shadow Prime, the only banner in the Lion's Mouth that was plain black, without icon or adornment. Prime stood above it, pretending a sort of neutrality, Father of the Lion's Mouth, Judge of the Abattoir, benign mentor to all here present—but whose sentiments were subtly known: a loyalist by long indoctrination and by special affection for both Epri and Ekadrina. His hair was grayer and his face more drawn than when last Ravn had seen him.

And what if his two favored students had chosen the other path? Ravn wondered. What if they had gone into rebellion? Would Prime, from love of them, have rallied the whole of the Lion's Mouth to the overthrow of the Names? Did his loyalty lie with the Names or with his "children"?

And there, a flash of white in the darkness beside him, the "pale princess" Kelly Stapellaufer, whose all too plastic affections had started the whole chain of events. The only one present garbed in white, her banner alone was not flown. Deprived in this venue of her own identity, she was simply "the Lady of the Secret Island" for whose affections the two Shadows would contest.

Of the three Deadly Ones caught up in the wretched affair, Ravn Olafsdottr found no sympathy for any of them, least of all for Kelly. Manlius had let his rod rule his mind. One day it would kill him; for a man cannot be a Shadow and harbor affections. Epri had at least been following orders when he broke them up, though in following those orders he had committed the same crime. But it seemed to Ravn that Kelly Stapellaufer had seduced first one, then the other, and so, whatever other motives had since accumulated, had brought the Lion's Mouth down into this quiet, desperate civil war.

"What say you?" asked Gidula, who had come silently to Ravn's side. He had followed her gaze and found the object of it. "Which does she truly prefer? Did she resent Manlius's attentions from the beginning and use Epri to exact a vengeance on him? Or, once Epri's captive, did she find her cupid in convenience?"

Ravn affected disinterest. "She no longer matters. All of their grievances have been tumbled under a milliard others. She was the spark, not the explosion. This fight will settle nothing."

"You think Prime will not honor the chapters?"

"Does the dynamite care if the match that lit its fuse has been extinguished?" Her teeth showed briefly in the night. But then Ravn realized that she was talking to empty space. Absently, she fingered his sigil on her brassard and waited. The Old One had strange humors. In the watching crowd she saw taijis, doves, lilies, and other mons and arms and logos.

Poder Stoop, the Riff of Ashbanal, stepped forward into the open space on the floor below. Poder wore a white surcoat with a red sash to mark him as the Judge of the Kill. So far as Olafsdottr knew, he was neutral in the war. Whoever won would need order maintained on Ashbanal, and that meant a riff and his deputies.

Beside him stood Epri Gunjinshow and Manlius Metataxis and two of the Riff's magpies. All but Epri bore grim countenances. Epri smiled and waved to supporters in the audience. He did not turn to look at

Kelly. Both combatants wore ceremonial golden shackles around their ankles as a sign that they were bound to fight each other. Manlius, it was said, had pledged not to eat sitting down until he had slain his foe. Ravn did not know what pledges Epri had made, but she was certain they were every bit as extravagant.

It would not be fair to say that silence fell, for the gathered Shadows had made little in the way of sound. But the silence deepened when the Riff raised his staff horizontally above his head.

"Honored Father." He bowed low toward Shadow Prime. Then, over the network that encompassed the arbor he said to the assembly, "Deadly Ones, hear me. These are the chapters of the Pasdarm of the Isle of Tears. It has been agreed, each and several, that the matter of Manlius Metataxis and Epri Gunjinshow will be settled after the ancient traditions of our Guild. Despite the rulin' of the Courts d'Umbrae that both Manlius and Epri have equally transgressed our Laws and that the slate was therefore wiped clean between them, our two brothers have persisted in their feud, and in doin' so have sown dissension in our ranks. An' this dissension bein' the greater evil," the Riff continued, "our Father and our senior brothers—Dawshoo Yishohrann and Ekadrina Sèanmazy—have sponsored this-here pasdarm." He allowed his gaze to travel around the impromptu gallery while a light patter of applause and tapping of roof beams rattled the old building.

"Heh," whispered Gidula. "He wishes no doubt as to where the blame lies, does he?"

A plague on both your houses. "He straddles the fence," Ravn told her section leader. "Matters always seem different from the gallery than they do in the blood and the sand."

Gidula smiled. "A neutral, yes, but is he a loyalist neutral or a rebel neutral? I wonder if he realizes that the time for safe neutrality is passing . . ."

On the floor, Poder had finished the by-laws and intoned the ritual preface. "Brothers! À outrance! To the blood an' to the bone!" Then he struck the floor of the automill sharply with his staff of office and the boom reechoed through the empty caverns of the building. The Lady of the Isle of Tears threw a single black rose from the catwalk. The Riff's magpies struck the golden shackles from the fighters' ankles and led their charges to their randomly-chosen starting points on the factory floor.

"Best we illuminate ourselves," Gidula whispered, "lest one combatant or the other mistake us for his opponent."

Ravn flipped her night goggles into place and, as she did so, noticed others throughout the building flickering into the pale green glow that marked them as spectators. Golden beams of light sprang up, resembling ropes or fences and marking the bounds of the kill space. She glanced once more at the roost where Prime had stood and noticed that the Lady had vanished, unable perhaps to watch her lover slain. Whichever of the two that might be.

On the old manufacturing floor, neither Epri nor Manlius was such a fool as to step forward. No one emerged victor from a joust of Shadows by offering himself as a target. From her perch high above, however, Ravn was able to pick out both men as they moved cautiously behind cover of the rusting hulks of machinery probing for each other's location. Their starting positions had by chance been set in the same quadrant of the space, and not terribly far from each other. Ravn wondered if the Riff, hoping for a quick end, had rigged the draw. If so, the play had failed, for the two were unknowingly moving away from each other. Suppressed amusement rippled through the gallery.

Manlius was the larger of the two, supple and well muscled. He moved like a panther. If it came to close combat, the advantage would be his. Epri was more slender, more graceful—a dancer—and owned the clearer eye. At longer distance, where aim outweighed strength, he would hold the edge. The Riff had chosen the venue well. The combination of obstacles and lines of sight gave both men a play to their advantage.

"I will enjoy your dissection, Epri," Manlius called out.

And Epri whipped a shot with his tickler in the direction of the voice.

Mentally, Ravn deducted a point from both men's score. There had been no wagering permitted on this pasdarm, since it had not been joined for sport; but she had made her own bets with herself. Manlius should not have wasted breath taunting his opponent. And Epri's hasty shot showed him nervous and on edge. The likelihood that Manlius would be anywhere in the vicinity of his voice was small to the point of vanishing.

And to a man wearing the proper night filters, as Manlius certainly was, the small spark of the tickler's discharge marked Epri's location as surely as Manlius's voice had not.

Clever. She notched Manlius up half a point. Dawshoo's brother did not fire at the spot thus revealed, because it was improbable that Epri had remained in it. But he worked his way closer to where he thought Epri had gone. The best way to track a quarry was to follow his mind, to go to where he would be and not to where he had been.

The combat proceeded as delicately as a ballet, and like a ballet it remained on point. Both Shadows floated silently from cover to cover, seeking always that advantageous position above and behind the opponent. Manlius stalked Epri, moving closer each time to his opponent's shifting location. Epri evaded, probing with exploratory fire, circling the perimeter of the kill space. The opening gambits, as always, probed for the other's position and sought out his strategy; but the spectators waited expectantly for the endgame, when Manlius's greater strength would prevail—and made quiet side bets whether Epri would pot him before that could happen.

Epri threw an I-ball on a high arc and its spinning cameras sent an image of the kill space to him, stabilized and integrated by his suit's processors. It must have caught Manlius's location, because Epri hurled a multibomb in that direction. Its explosion jarred, even through the ear filters everyone wore. Secondary munitions seared the five places Manlius might have leapt to—but Manlius had run to a sixth.

"He ought to try the Spider," said a magpie who perched nearby and wore the two crows of Phoythaw Bhatvik. "Let the slut come to him."

Ravn made no reply. When Shadow stalked Shadow, setting up a sniper's nest was suicide. Your opponent would more likely locate your nest before crossing its lines of fire.

Early on, Manlius had strewn "crispies" in one of the intersections. This eventually paid off when Epri passed through the intersection and stepped on them. Passive munitions were forbidden by the chapters, but Manlius had set crispies only for the distinctive crunching sound they made when stepped upon. He had naturally logged the location into one of his hand-bombs and let fly when he heard the signal. But Epri at the first crunch had fled down an aisle picked at random and leaped to one side, and atop one of the machines.

Ravn deducted points from both: Epri for being so incautious as to tread upon such an obvious alarm; Manlius for placing it at an intersection. Had he placed the crispies in the middle of an aisle, Epri would have had fewer escape routes and he could have more easily bracketed them. Of course, in a pasdarm à outrance, one could win on points and still lie dead at the end.

A splinter of shrapnel had found Epri's calf as he pulled himself up and over the machine. The assembly roared, "Blood!" Though the blood was minor and once the shrapnel had been pulled out, the shen-mat closed up the wound. Ravn deducted further points because at the roar, Manlius had paused to preen, and so lost the initiative.

The second time Epri tried the trick with the I-ball, Manlius shot it from the air on the fly, earning an appreciative murmur from even Epri's partisans. Then Manlius rolled his own I-balls down the aisles of the factory floor, one after the other, grasping the layout of the kill space from a more pedestrian angle. They were harder to pot on the roll, but also less panoramic in their harvested images. Epri deduced from the several paths of the balls the intersection from which they had been rolled; but before he could home in on it, Manlius had gone.

And so it continued, as patiently as a chess match. Now and then, the combatants caught sight of one another and guns would snap and knives or whistle-trees would fly. More often, indirect fire sought out grid squares where the opponent might lurk. Once, a cry from the sidelines indicated that a spectator had been slow to move from the line of fire. Manlius grinned at the sound, and at first Ravn wondered at his misplaced glee.

But then she saw what Manlius had noticed. The shifting spectators, illuminated as they were, gave him a vector by which to locate his foe! For those directly in the line of fire would drift off to either side, leaving a space devoid of lights. If he drew a line between himself and that bull's-eye in the gallery, he would find Epri somewhere along it.

Manlius closed the distance on cat's feet before

Epri should notice the similar gap in Manlius's six and realize its significance. He reached an old gutted machine and swung to its top as if weightless, plucking a throwing star from his belt. The crowd sucked in its breath and Epri, crouching below Manlius, heard the intake and, though not understanding its precise significance, pulled a dazer from its scabbard and peered around the corner of the next machine.

But this was a personal grudge and feelings ran high. Manlius paused a moment to savor his victory and in that savor lost the sauce.

A voice cried out, "Epri! Your seven!"

Manlius let fly—and Epri rolled aside, loosing behind him a hasty dazer bolt. The star skittered along the composite flooring, clattering into the darkness. Sparks danced along the seams of the machine on which Manlius had lately poised.

"Who called out?" demanded Dawshoo in the darkness. "A violation!"

Manlius had launched himself after Epri, unwilling to surrender his advantage at close quarter combat; but Epri avoided his grip and completed a double roll. His dazer came up and Manlius kicked it loose from his grasp. Epri backed away swiftly, scrabbling at his belt for another weapon, but Manlius whirled a back-camel kick into the side of Epri's head.

The loyalist dropped, stunned, and Manlius seized a rusted steel bar from the machine beside him and brought it down sharply to impale his enemy to the floor.

And Epri wasn't there.

The steel bar struck the floor with a *clang*, and

Manlius released it and spun defensively, expecting a riposte. But there was no sign of his opponent. The spectators began to murmur from their perches.

Ravn scanned the kill space, but Epri was simply . . . gone. "I saw him," said a Shadow on her right. "And then I didn't." Ravn's goggles picked out a taiji on her brassard. Ekadrina's section.

As she cast her mind back, it seemed to Ravn that, at the very instant when Manlius was poised to impale Epri, the world had hesitated, as if time had been spliced and a moment snipped out. But in that lost and extra moment, Ravn remembered a ghost of movement, like the swirl of a cloak in the darkness. And then Epri had been gone.

A confusion of voices roiled the old mill. She heard Dee Karnatika declare that Epri had forfeit. Dawshoo claimed victory for Manlius. Beside her on the rafter, Ekadrina's courier stroked the butt of her teaser. Perturbed, Ravn backed away into the recesses of the roof struts. This was not right. Something—she knew not what—was seriously awry. A prudent man he might be, and more prone to settle disputes with clever stratagems or distant assassinations, but Epri was no such coward as to desert the field.

Another Shadow crouched to her left on the same beam as she, panting heavily with excitement and peering with bright eyes at the commotion on the shop floor, where Dawshoo and Manlius argued with Ekadrina and Shadow Prime. She heard Dawshoo call on Prime to honor their bargain.

A distraction.

She suddenly knew that the argument on the floor

was a distraction, intended to fix everyone's attention. She looked across, up, down, right, left.

And the Shadow on her left was not panting from excitement, but from exertion. It was Epri. After escaping Manlius's death-stroke (somehow!) he had hidden himself the only way possible: by making himself more visible. He had turned on his running lights and joined the spectators, trusting to darkness and unexamined assumptions for his concealment.

Down below, Oschous Dee Karnatika scanned the galleries. He seemed to be counting spectators.

Epri specialized in the long shot. At this distance, his marksmanship was deadly and three quick shots would pot Manlius, Dawshoo, and Oschous and virtually decapitate the rebellion.

Peace at last within the Lion's Mouth, after twenty years of Shadow War.

Epri held a dazer double-handed, crouched to fire from the kneeling position. Ravn's hand dropped to her belt and came away with a stiletto. She threw it side-wristed and impaled Epri's right hand just as he fired into the press on the floor.

Cries broke out below. Manlius! Manlius is down! Treachery! No, a legitimate play! Ambush! No, Manlius quit too soon; the pasdarm was still on!

It was not, Ravn knew. The chapters of the pasdarm gave the players wide latitude; but hiding oneself among the spectators was not one of them. Epri had been forfeit the moment he had climbed into the girders, but if Manlius were slain, the technicality would hardly matter.

Epri had meanwhile yanked the stiletto from his

hand and backhanded it at Ravn. But she had expected the move and had already ducked aside, snatching the knife from the air as it passed and dousing her running lights with the other hand.

Epri might be second-best, but Ravn knew he was far above her own class. The prudent thing to do was flee and link up with Gidula or Oschous. She was clambering up the strut before the thought was formed and Epri, firing at her left-handed, missed. Someone else in the galleries fired back, perhaps on general principles.

Fighting had broken out on the floor and in the galleries. Oschous and other rebellious Shadows had returned fire to the locus from which the treacherous shot had come. Then some loyalists, perhaps thinking that the rebels were attacking the gallery, had joined in. The rebels were now pinned down near the middle of the kill space, taking fire from all sides, but protected by their own magpies and allied Shadows among the spectators. One was a former neutral, pushed to take sides by the treachery. Ekadrina and Prime had withdrawn to cover, but both were holding fire and Ekadrina was arguing with Prime. Dawshoo crouched over Manlius, shielding him while he fired at loyalists pinned down behind a conveyor head. A magpie fell from the rafters to strike one of the milling machines and then roll bonelessly over its side. Oschous had Dawshoo's back, snapping orders over his link, and directing a counterattack. Coherent light flashed here and there among the girders, made visible by the dust raised by the tumult. Projectiles whined and snapped off girders.

Ravn fired her tzan-wire at an overhead beam and even as it fastened itself she swung across the cavernous open space to land beside the Riff of Ashbanal, who had taken refuge with his magpies behind a stack of corroded drums. He had his teaser out, but had yet to fire it.

The Riff had not achieved his position through mere politics. A fell fighter in any league, he swung his staff left-handed and nearly knocked Ravn off her footing. But she danced a little away from him, holding both hands to the side weaponless, and blurted, "Appeal the Truce, master! You are neutral and this is your bailiwick. They will listen to you."

"Will they? Small weight my word has had 'fore now."

"Habits die hard. Your brassard yet commands respect. Call on Oschous and Ekadrina to act as your deputies. There has been dishonor on our House." She told him of Epri's foul.

Stoop studied Ravn for a long moment, during which two more magpies died.

"Quickly," Ravn urged him, "before there are too many bodies for a Truce to overlook."

The Riff nodded and opened his link. "Deadly Ones!" And his voice echoed across the ruined factory. "There is a Truce in play! That Truce was violated most foully, and charges will be laid at the Courts d'Umbrae on Dao Chetty. Ekadrina Sèanmazy! Oschous Dee Karnatika! I *demand an' require* you to enforce the Peace!" He turned and gave Ravn a twisted smile. "Now let's see how much respect this ol' badge still commands," he said quietly. He stepped from concealment, banging the floor of the kill space three times with his staff.

Silence spread in a pool around him and one by one the combatants stilled. Oschous came to stand beside the Riff and a moment later Ekadrina joined him. Poder holstered his weapon, and took a breath.

"Metataxis?" he said.

"A wound," Oschous replied. "The shot went wild."

"Den it was not my brudder who fired," said Ekadrina. "Epri does not miss."

"He does if my stiletto impales his hand," Ravn said. "He hid himself among the spectators, on the beam beside me. I fouled his aim."

"I don't believe dat!"

"It was a foul, Sèanmazy," said the Riff. "The bolt came from the rafters. A violation of the chapters and of the agreement reached beforehand between Dawshoo and our Prime."

"Compared to foul deeds already done," the Long Tall One said, "what matters such a peccadillo?"

"Manlius is the winner," Oschous said. "By our agreement . . ."

"Da fight was 'to da blood and to da bone,'" Ekadrina shot back. "I demand habeas corpus. Where is Epri's body? Widdout it, where is da victory?"

Oschous bristled, but the Riff held up his hand. "I'm the Judge of the Kill." Then, in a louder voice, over the links, "Deadly Ones! Hear my rulin'. Manlius Metataxis does not win the pasdarm because he took no bone from Epri Gunjinshow. But neither does Epri win, for though he took blood of Manlius, he took no bone; and the blood was taken by foul. I declare this-here pasdarm null an' void!" He banged the floor with his staff. "I demand an' require all concerned to leave this place in peace, the Peace to extend from here to the coopers." That meant no fighting anywhere in the Ashbanal system.

"Brave words, Riff!" shouted a voice from the darkness. "But how will you enforce it?"

The Riff's own magpies had gathered around him, and exchanged the uneasy glances of neutrals. Then Oschous spoke up. "I will."

Ekadrina was less than a beat behind. "And I!" And she held up her own staff horizontal above her head.

Poder Stoop cocked an eyebrow at Ravn Olafsdottr, and the Ravn shrugged. "They are enemies," she said for no other ear, "but honorable."

The Riff closed his eyes for a moment and sighed. "That's the worst of it, ain't it? Right there. That men of honor find honor has driven them to opposin' sides. If they were corrupt, we could settle all this with a well-cut deal."

Later, as the friends and enemies of the slain and injured carried out their useful duties, Ravn Olafsdottr and two of Oschous's magpies turned over a teardrop body that had fallen from the rafters when a "mourning star" had found his throat. The Ravn noted that the cruelty of the Fates had handed her the corpse of Magpie Three Sèanmazy. She paused in her labor and stared at his contorted face. So surprised he seemed. He could not credit what had happened to him even as it happened. She bent and closed his eyes for him.

Oschous stood nearby with Sèanmazy herself, who regarded her magpie without expression. "I hope he died well," was all she said before turning away.

Oschous leaned to Ravn. "What is it?" he asked.

Ravn Olafsdottr gestured to the limp and empty corpse. "Tell me it meant something," she said. "Tell me it mattered."

"It mattered to him."

"It was supposed to stay in bounds."

"What was?"

"Death. It's how we face Him. We convince ourselves with these plays that, when we want to, we can contain Him. Here. Within the squared circle. Did he die well? He died stupidly, as a bystander to another's quarrel. And as a consequence of his own side's treachery."

"All the more reason," Oschous assured her, "that we overthrow their regime."

But Ravn turned away and bent over the body. "Sleep well, Deadly One." She spoke the formula and bestowed the kiss on the cold and torn lips. He would be carried back to the Abattoir along with the others in Prime's ship, mulched in the Rose Garden, his name plaqued on the Cöng Sung, the Wall of Honor, but the treachery of this day's actions would taint the magpie's death, and few would come to honor him. There was no death worse than a forgotten one, but none were very good.

Oschous said nothing until she had turned away. "And now the mystery," he said.

The Riff's people were tearing down the arbor, smashing the fountain. The musicians would break their instruments, and Epri's banner, torn from its hooks, would be burned when the building was torched.

Olafsdottr did not ask what the mystery was. Epri had vanished in plain sight of two score onlookers. If there were another, deeper mystery, she did not want to hear it. For Ekadrina Sèanmazy had given them the answer, in their converse before the fight; and Ravn had detected in the Long Tall One's confident eyes the selfsame horror she felt in herself.

The Names were loose.

CENGJAM GAAFE: THE FIFTH INTERROGATORY

With the breaking of the true dawn, Mr. Wladislaw introduces a breakfast cart into the sitting room. There are eggs gently boiled and mounted on thrones, a haggard sausage, sautéed mushrooms, and a porridge of oatmeal. Olafsdottr selects an egg at random and regards the giant sausage with considerable suspicion.

"You will pardon us," says Bridget ban, "if we restrict the carving of it to Mr. Wladislaw."

Olafsdottr grins. "No knives too close to poor Ravn. Afraid, perhaps, she cut self? Well, small individual sausages might be used to poison me; but from this monster, we shall each and all safely eat."

Méarana hands an egg cutter to the Shadow, who looks at it curiously until the harper demonstrates how to use it to snip off the small end of the egg.

"Ooh . . . You oopen your eggs from the small end," she says. "No woonder matters pass ill between your League and my Coonfederation."

There is apparent humor in the remark, but the nature of it eludes her captors. "The eggs at least are sufficient size," she continues in Gaelactic. "On the

Groom's Britches, we have eggs the size of grapes, which are eaten whole. The hens have been cultured with various foods to impart diverse flavors to the eggs. They are accounted a delicacy."

"Och," says Bridget ban with a straight face, "our eggs too are the size of our grapes."

Ravn blinks, then decides to smile.

"And was Fa—was Donovan still in his hotel room," Méarana asks, "when you and Oschous returned from the pasdarm?"

"Ooh, surely! He was no man's fool. Where on the planet could he have gone?"

The Terran Corner, Méarana thinks, but she does not say it aloud. Perhaps there are no such corners in the Confederation.

"One thing bothers me," says Graceful Bintsaif.

"Ah! One thing oonly! How wise you must be!"

The junior Hound has learned to brush off the jibes. "Epri was there; and then he was not. That offends my sense of seamlessness. The world is not that abrupt."

Bridget ban nods. "Inattentive blindness," she suggests.

"Yes," answers Olafsdottr in Confederal Manjrin. "Ancient wisdom, before even time of Commonwealth. Fix attention on one thing—not see others. Gorilla dance through, you not see." Then, switching back to the Gaelactic, "Sure, I may have been the only one there who noticed the faltering of time, but I saw nothing else beside."

"I dinnae hawp it!" Méarana exclaims. "Some

gomeral can walk right athwart yer line o' sight and ye dinnae see them? That's gae glaikit!"

Bridget ban sweeps her hair back. "Believe me, darling. 'Tis possible. The conditions must be right— the kill space was dark, the spectators fixated on the combatants—but the ancients demonstrated 'inattentive blindness' under looser conditions than that. The trick lies in knowing how to induce it in others. To 'cloud men's minds,' as the saying has it." To the Ravn, she adds, "I take it there are few Shadows who own that ability."

For the first time since she has entered Clanthompson Hall, the serenity of Ravn Olafsdottr falters. "I would have said 'none.' But the Names do. The Names have that power."

Méarana shudders. "There was a Name on Ashbanal? I thought they never left the Secret City!"

"Not often," says Olafsdottr, "and never happily when they do. It is said that one once left the Confederation entirely."

"Then," says Bridget ban, leaning forward, "one of Them intervened—either to save Epri or to assassinate Manlius. Or both."

But Olafsdottr shakes her head and, interestingly, Graceful Bintsaif does as well.

"No, Cu," says the junior Hound. "Had that been the intent, why not ensure that Manlius was killed within the rules of the . . . the pasdarm? Dawshoo had pledged to end the rebellion if Manlius fell."

"You grow in wisdom, child," Ravn tells her. "Pasdarm settle nothing. And why Dawshoo agree?

Motive of Prime, I grasp. *But why Dawshoo?* One thing only I see accomplish."

Bridget ban snips the end off her egg. "Aye," she says. "Some of ye were forced to show yourselves openly."

Méarana plays an intricate and unresolved chord progression on her harp. One hand picks out a lively *geantraí* fit to sketch a joust of Shadows while the other hand plays in counterpoint a *goltraí* to suggest the lurking Name and, overall, the tragic nature of the whole affair. She sings a bit too, using sky-voice and ground-voice to simulate two singers at two points in the room. But she does not feel the conflict, she does not feel the story in her heart the way she felt the story of the Dancer. The players are too remote, too strange, too unfamiliar. Only her father, under guard in the hotel room, unaware of the events in the "arbor," his well-being subject to the whims of his captors, only he wants to live through her strings.

And Olafsdottr. She has begun to resolve, a little, in the music. She has begun to live in the mind of Méarana Swiftfingers.

"Why do you call it an 'arbor'?" she asks. "An arbor is an artful arrangement of trees."

"I do not know, young harper. It is only what it has always been called. The arrangement of trees, we call a *kjumuq*. But," and she turns to the Hound, "a Name on the wing explains much. The bomb at the Riettiecenter monorail. Now, he swoops Epri to save at the very point of his defeat. Come, attend! To Fair Yuts'ga next, uneased in mind and very much perplexed."

VI. TOWARD YUTS'GA: THE THIRD COUNTER-ARGUMENT

From Ashbanal departed, Yuts'ga bound,
We forward pressed. Or did we flee,
From that ill-vanishing by which
The sly Epri did whisk away?
Harper! Know what doubts devoured us!
As rats do creep through walls and drains,
Their fortunes sought through quiet stealth, to
    gnaw
At power, become in one fell mirrored moment
Those self-same rats 'tween mazes run
At others' whims. Had Those wit of our intent?
Or did Those their own ends pursue,
Worldines crossing ours by wondrous chance
Entwined in doubts we plied the streams of space.
Uncertainty our load, at hell-bent pace.

Oschous was a clever man, and one bewonted to subtle plays and deep deceptions. But why a Name had intervened to save Epri, he did not fathom. He threw the subject on the table at dinner, the first evening on the crawl.

One of the magpies brought into the dining room

a gravity cart piled high with food, for not merely the six magpies off-duty, but also Ravn, Donovan, and the injured Manlius and four of *his* magpies were gathered around the broad table. The injury to Metataxis had been a serious one—burns to the shoulder and upper arm and induction shock to his nervous system—but the autoclinic was healing him up nicely. His right arm was immobilized and he had to spend two hours a day in the tank. He had a slight tendency to slur his speech. But he would grow more hale as time passed on. Meanwhile, his ship was coupled to Oschous's own, and he guested in *Black Horse.*

"Perhaps they have a mission," Ravn suggested, "one for Epri alone to perform, and his untimely death would have hindered it."

"I think," Manlius said, rubbing his shoulder absently, "Those just like that misborn git. Prime's pet, is what he is." He stood at the table, his oath as yet undischarged. Oschous had lightened the gravity as a courtesy.

Donovan pursed his lips. "Is deep affection then among Their qualities?"

"Epri *is* a loyalist," one of the magpies suggested.

"Where the Names are concerned," said Donovan, "loyalty runs but one direction."

"Then Epri's salvation," Oschous concluded, "was the means, and not the end. The Name did not intervene to save Epri, but saved Epri to . . . ?"

". . . to intervene," said Donovan. "What was actually accomplished by the deed?"

"I was almost killed," said Manlius. "If not for Ravn's timely deed . . ." He raised a pine-liquor to his savior and drank the implied toast.

But Oschous shook his head. "Had your death been intended, the meal before you would now languish unenjoyed. What Name having taken pains to place a sniper would take no pains to ensure that sniper's success?"

"Some neutrals were outraged by the foul," Ravn suggested, "and have joined the rebellion. Some honorable loyalists may have drifted toward neutrality."

But again, the Fox dismissed the idea. "Beyond those actually present, few will believe Epri's fell deed. Propaganda, they'll call it. Faith overcomes all rumors of fact."

"So," said Donovan, "what is left but the one sure, concrete result of the act? *Your war will go on.* There was a danger of peace breaking out; and your Name's intervention—the very *manner* of that intervention—ensured that it would not."

"Yes," said Manlius, tasting the possibility. "Prime had pledged to bring the rest of the Lion's Mouth over to the rebellion once I had defeated Epri. The Names could not risk that."

"Then why not simply ensure your death?" Oschous asked. "Dawshoo was pledged to *end* the rebellion if you lost." His brow furrowed at that and for a moment he resembled wolf more than fox. "Instead, matters muddle as before."

"Those have always liked to 'stir the pot,'" Donovan said. "Perhaps your twenty-year war amuses them."

"Ngok!" cried Manlius as a magpie set a platter on the table directly before him. "What are these slops, Oschous Dee!"

"Hmm? Oh, a bit of thaklam rasam," the Fox told him. "It's a tomato soup I'm fond of. Those are hoddawgs with zorgrot. And that plate is banana-flower curry."

Manlius grunted. "Smells Terran to me. Who knew bananas had flowers!" He indicated to his chief magpie that he should dish out the more familiar foods: a stew of snakes, snails, chicken feet, and duck tongues in a ginger sauce, and small plates of taro puffs in spiderweb pastry.

"Oh, the Terrans may be venal and untrustworthy," Oschous said, "but that doesn't mean they can't cook." He ladled out a bowl of the rasam and, with a cautionary frown, passed it across the table to Donovan, who sniffed it.

"Ha!" said Manlius. "Smell bothers you, too? Don't blame you."

The Pedant stirred the scarred man's memories. 𝔚𝔥𝔞𝔱 𝔦𝔰 𝔦𝔱, 𝔖𝔦𝔩𝔨𝔶? 𝔍'𝔪 𝔫𝔬 𝔤𝔬𝔬𝔡 𝔞𝔱 𝔰𝔢𝔫𝔰𝔬𝔯𝔶 𝔪𝔢𝔪𝔬𝔯𝔦𝔢𝔰, 𝔟𝔲𝔱 𝔱𝔥𝔢𝔯𝔢'𝔰 𝔰𝔬𝔪𝔢𝔱𝔥𝔦𝔫𝔤 𝔣𝔞𝔪𝔦𝔩𝔦𝔞𝔯 𝔦𝔫 𝔱𝔥𝔢 𝔰𝔱𝔦𝔫𝔨.

The coriander! the Silky Voice exclaimed.

"Grows no place else but Terra," the Fudir muttered.

𝔍 𝔨𝔫𝔢𝔴 𝔦𝔱 𝔴𝔞𝔰 𝔣𝔞𝔪𝔦𝔩𝔦𝔞𝔯. 𝔅𝔲𝔱 𝔦𝔱 𝔤𝔯𝔬𝔴𝔰 𝔞𝔩𝔰𝔬 𝔞𝔱𝔬𝔭 𝔱𝔥𝔢 𝔒𝔬𝔯𝔞𝔥 𝔐𝔢𝔰𝔞 𝔬𝔫 𝔈𝔫𝔧𝔯𝔲𝔫.

But, the Sleuth added, *Oschous has no access to Enjrun. So unless it grows on other Confederal worlds . . .*

"The spice in this soup came from Terra herself."

He sniffed again the aroma, this time more deeply, trying to imagine fields of waving coriander bushes, although he was none too sure if coriander grew on bushes. It was a spice that had grown legendary by its absence among the Terrans of the Diaspora.

<Oschous has a purpose in serving us this,> warned Inner Child.

"Yes," agreed Donovan. "But what?"

This inner conversation, punctuated by a few comments sotto voce, took no more than moments; but moments were enough to draw Manlius's attention.

The wounded man regarded Donovan with a profound uncertainty, then cocked his head at Oschous. "So this is the great Geshler Padaborn. His name in the struggle is worth a hundred ordinary shenmats. It will rally a great many waverers to our cause. Or it was supposed to." He again glanced doubtfully at Donovan, plucked a "phoenix talon" from the stew and sucked the meat off it.

"You know," he told the table, "I never made it to that final battle. My section got orders to join the forces besieging Padaborn, but the orders came too late, and there were delays assembling . . . Foot-dragging by our section-leader, some said. Perhaps he favored Padaborn. We never knew, and he disappeared afterward. If we all had had that Circuit thing the Peripherals have nowadays, the word would've come in time and . . . I don't know. Back then, I thought Padaborn was a black traitor and a disgrace to the Lion's Mouth. Now . . . I don't know. Maybe he was just 'ahead of the curve.'" He turned once more to

Donovan. "If my brothers and I had been there, you'd've never escaped."

Donovan shrugged. "I don't even know if *I* was there."

Manlius sat back in his chair and sucked on his teeth. "I was going to say, Oschous, that Padaborn's banner would tip the balance. But that was Padaborn-that-was. This ramshackle wreck . . ." A cock of his head toward the wreck. "You can hear the broken gears grinding against one another. I fear you've brought us damaged goods. Does Ekadrina know he's back? I'm not sure I'd put this thing up against her. His mind is broken."

The scarred man cackled. "Who is Ekadrina?"

Oschous smiled. "The one who broke it."

That elicited a short silence, but one wide enough for the scarred man's thoughts to fall into it. Inner Child trembled; the Brute growled revenge. The Sleuth pointed out that Ekadrina might know the identity of others like himself. <Why?> cried the Child. <Who cares if there are others?>

But a young man in a chlamys stood beside him. The ancient garment was open up the right side, showing him naked underneath. His face was Donovan's, but as Donovan had been in the blush of his youth. He placed a hand on the scarred man's shoulder. For brotherhood, he said.

Or seemed to. The sundered parts of Donovan's mind wondered why this young man and the young girl in the chiton were the only shards that manifested as visual hallucinations.

"Let's not forget," the Fudir muttered, "that we

were going to Dangchao Waypoint. There's business there that wants doing."

"Does he always talk to himself?" Manlius asked his host.

"Gidula has hopes for him," said Ravn.

Manlius turned to her. "It was Gidula, your master, who told Dawshoo this war would take ten years," he pointed out.

"And so it has," said Oschous. "Twice."

Manlius blinked, then threw his head back in a great guffaw, and slapped the table with his left hand. "Oh, that's a good 'un, Oschous. Have you told the Old One?"

"Gidula cracks his own jests," Dee Karnatika said. "He doesn't need mine."

"Yeah. I'd watch myself around him, too. He may be old, but who knows the plays better?"

"It is because he is master of plays," Ravn pointed out, "that he succeeds in growing old."

Manlius grunted. "I take nothing from him. His exploits are legendary. I studied them when I was schooled. Our common goal makes allies of us all."

"Well said," Oschous told him. He raised a flagon of wine and the others at the table did as well. After a moment, Donovan aped them. "The Downfall of the Names!" Oschous said, and the others murmured concurrence; but Donovan noticed variation in the enthusiasms with which they did so. There were a few faint hearts among Manlius's magpies.

And neither Oschous nor Ravn regards Manlius highly, the young man said. Surely, you have noticed. It is in their bodies and in their voices. They are

"Hail, Comrade" aloud; but it is only necessity that has driven them together. They hold his actions with Kelly to be contemptible.

"I don't know," the Fudir temporized. "I rather like the idea of Shadows in love."

While Donovan was thus distracted, Manlius pressed him on how he would lead them all into the Secret City.

"I don't know," he snapped. "I haven't said I'd join you!"

"What would it take to convince you?" Oschous asked mildly.

"If I get steamed up enough!"

Manlius frowned. "'Steamed up' . . . ?"

"A Terran expression," Donovan told him.

"That's not important," Oschous said. "Gesh is simply unsure that in his present state he can be of any use to us."

That was not precisely the source of Donovan's reservations, but it would do for use among his present companions. Getting tangled in the secret war among the Confederal Shadows was a ticket to the knacker's block, in his opinion.

Privately, he wondered more whether the *others* would be of any use to *him*, either in staying alive or in gaining home. It was a tribute to their skills that the rebellion had lasted twenty years, for based on what he had seen so far, he would not have given them twenty weeks. They were an unlikely band of brothers. Manlius had fallen into rebellion because he had fallen into love, and while that might ring brightly in song, it dulled on closer inspection. A man driven by desire might be driven in whichever direction his member pointed. Ravn, on the other hand, showed genuine distress over the state to which the Lion's Mouth had fallen, but remained a reluctant rebel obedient to Gidula's orders. Remove Gidula from the equation and in which direction would she turn? And Oschous and Manlius both harbored doubts over Gidula on account of his age. He had not gotten a "read" on Dawshoo yet, but noted that he had been conspicuously absent from the conversation of his fellows.

Inner Child shivered. He was alone, and deep within the Confederation, without friends and uncertain of his allies, and every day farther from his daughter and Bridget ban.

After dinner, Oschous dismissed his staff, sending two magpies to relieve the watch, granting the others liberty. Manlius returned to the autoclinic for another healing session and his own magpies went with him or back to his own ship, *Fell Swoop*. Ravn Olafsdottr lingered, but Oschous waited her out and, after an uneasy glance at her charge, she too departed.

The scarred man cackled across the dinner table. "Alone at last." And he essayed a Terran expression. "The bull's in your court, Oschous Dee. Start waving your cape."

If the idiom confused Karnatika, he gave no sign of it. Instead his lips quirked in a brief and frosty smile, and he retrieved a bottle of spirits from the sideboard. "My people will want to clear the dishes," he said, "and I do hate getting in their way. You'll be coming to my room directly. There's something I want to show you. But first, a question. Neither appeals to revenge nor appeals to vanity have moved you to join us."

Inner Child came alert. <Ah! Here comes a third appeal.>

Donovan chose his words with care. "Those who wiped my memory and broke my mind did a very professional job. Without memory, vengeance is a theory; without memory, past glories are tales told in books. Neither the great deeds you claim I wrought nor the tortures I once suffered live within me. It is like a numbed tooth. There is nothing there." He accepted a glass of the liqueur, waited until Oschous had poured and sipped from the same bottle, then tasted the drink and found it to smack of apples. "But Oschous Dee . . . that I am disinclined to join this feckless rebellion does not mark a lack of sympathy. I would disclose the secret way if I could remember it, even if I don't crawl down there with you myself. But in practice, pride and glory really mean death and gore."

Oschous finished his drink in a swift toss. But he did not set his glass down, turning it instead in his hand. "You object to death and gore?"

"Well, to death and gore *and losing*. Winning makes it easier to turn over the memorial glass."

"Death may be preferable betimes to life itself," Oschous said, looking off a little to the side.

"I'll believe that when I hear it from someone with firsthand experience of both."

"A life spent cringing on your knees is no life at all."

"Finely spoken, Oschous Dee. But how long did you serve the Names before you finally stood upright?"

The Shadow rose from the table. "Bring your glass." He had his own and the bottle in his hands. "Don't be too harsh on us, Gesh," he said as they proceeded down the hallway toward his suite. "Before he would risk all, a man must see some small hope of success. The revolution comes when the iron grip has just relaxed. When it is tightly held, none dare."

"There's a lesson in that . . ."

"Know when to strike?"

"No. Never relax your grip."

Oschous glanced over his shoulder. "Windhook Keopisenichok attacked and burned a district governor's station on Basilònway fifty standard years ago. It was one of those small local rebellions that people sing about in pubs and wine-stoops when the nights grow long and the fire turns to embers and they don't know too many of the details. *Bold Windhook drew a line and cried 'Nay more!'* It really is a rousing song, but the line was drawn less from a love of justice than in the hope of liquidating his debts. Madness and desperation drove him. The ashes of the station were still hot when the boots leveled the entire township. Most of the townies hadn't been in on it. In fact, most of them had opposed Windhook, called him a lunatic. But it didn't matter. They all died. And Windhook wasn't even in the township at the time. It's funny. The over-governor could imagine arson and rebellion, but he could not imagine that a man might leave his licensed township."

"I'm sure the townies found it hilarious. Is there a point to the story?"

"Only this: Many a heart may yearn for justice, or retribution, or simple relief, but still play the obedient servant *because the price of failure is too great*. A man might put up with much if the alternative is putting up with worse. That's the secret of government, my friend: To know how far into the mud you can grind people before they find rebellion worth the play. The over-governor and his cronies misjudged this, and the Names sent their Shadows to discipline them. What fool torments the cow he means to milk? It only sours the cream. Here we are."

They had arrived at a portal at the end of a long corridor. Oschous spoke some private words to the doorway, and it slid open to admit them to his quarters. This proved to be a set of rooms sparely done and set at three-quarters standard gravity. Objets d'art stood about the main room on pedestals and in niches, lit to best effect by concealed lamps. Most were relics of Confederal worlds, but the Pedant recognized some pieces originating in the Periphery: a steinwurf dating from the Dark Age on Friesing's World; an ancient circuit board, burnt and smashed, under a glassine bell jar; a transparent hand made of thin cellulose wrappings and raised in a defiant gesture. 𝔅𝔶 𝔱𝔥𝔢 𝔇𝔦𝔢 𝔅𝔬𝔩𝔡 𝔰𝔠𝔲𝔩𝔭𝔱𝔯𝔢𝔰𝔰 𝔅𝔬𝔬𝔰𝔦𝔢 𝔟𝔞𝔫 𝔓𝔢𝔱𝔯𝔞, the Pedant said. 𝔓𝔞𝔯𝔱 𝔬𝔣 𝔥𝔢𝔯 𝔰𝔢𝔯𝔦𝔢𝔰 𝔐𝔞𝔫𝔲𝔞𝔩 𝔏𝔞𝔟𝔬𝔯.

"And worth a decorous ducat, that," the Fudir added.

Oschous heard and cocked his head at the circuit board. "That, too. It's Valencian work. Came from the wreck of the Grand Fleet in the Second Valency-Ramage War. It was touched by greatness."

Donovan said nothing. If greatness had lain anywhere, it had lain with the Ramagers, who had destroyed the fleet. But perhaps that was what Oschous had meant by "touched" by greatness.

Souvenirs, the Sleuth decided. *A memento of each world where he has performed feats.*

But not mementoes of the feats themselves, the Silky Voice added. *Interesting.*

The floor was laid of hardwood and tile and dressed in carpets woven into intricate geometric patterns. Reading chairs with screens, game tables with projection stages, workstations with racks of bubbles and sticks. The arrangement seemed at first haphazard, the room somehow both too open and too cluttered. But on closer inspection, the furnishings proved less the obstacle course they seemed. Pathways were always clear and straight; frequently used objects, always within arm's reach.

Donovan considered what this said about the man whose unwilling guest he was. A man subtle and disciplined. A careful man.

"Very nice," he murmured, since some comment seemed expected of him.

"It pleases," the Shadow remarked.

"Whatever happened to him?"

"Hmm?"

"Windhook Keopisenichok. He was out of town when the boots retaliated."

"Oh. He'd fled into the Fetch-a-bun Hills right after burning the governor's station. He was a madman, but not so mad as to stick around. The townies would've lynched him if nothing else, poor devils. *They* knew the penalty for illegal rebellion. He'd recruited a few likeminded folk—the desperate and feckless—and remained at large for the next five years, mostly raiding and robbing from the very people he was supposedly bent on liberating."

"If you are trying to recruit me with inspirational tales," Donovan said, "I'd suggest you build a better repertoire. 'Illegal rebellion . . .' Is there another sort?"

Oschous nodded. "Surely. Bring your glass with you." He led him to the rear of the suite. "Windhook's mistake," he said as Donovan followed, "was that he struck too low and too openly from too narrow a base. A district governor? A station house? Pfaugh! What did he imagine he would accomplish by smashing a giant's little toe?"

"And what was Geshler's mistake?"

Oschous glanced over his shoulder. "Pretty much the same, though he did strike higher. He was too impatient. He should've worked sub rosa, built a wider network of supporters; and he should not have struck openly. Seizing the public buildings in the capital made him a sitting duck."

"Better a duck on the wing? But it might be that like the sacral kings of old, he hoped the gesture would inspire others to action."

"A foolish hope."

"Was it? Nearly half the Lion's Mouth have now risen up. Perhaps Padaborn was more successful than you credit. Not every seed germinates overnight."

They had stopped before a blank wall and, because Donovan did not suppose this a particularly final destination, he was not surprised when Oschous spoke and a secret door opened on a small chamber paneled in sweetwood.

"By the way, let me congratulate you," Oschous said before leading the scarred man inside. "Your performance has been excellent so far, but you are not nearly as disintegrated as you pretend."

Donovan hesitated only fractionally. "No, not really."

"Why the act, then?"

"If I failed to meet your expectations, you would send me back to the Periphery."

"You can see how well that worked. A tool ought not pretend to uselessness. If you'd been just another Shadow recruited into the struggle, we'd've discarded you that first night, in the alley behind the bar called Apothete. There's a ravine there . . . But the name of Geshler Padaborn was worth something, even if the man no longer was."

Donovan sighed. "And now . . ."

"And now I have some matters to ponder privately. Who else knows?"

"Ravn, of course."

"Of course. Based on the reports we had had, I had opposed bringing you back. I expected very little from you."

"And now?"

"I expect a little more." With his teeth, he pulled the cork from the bottle and spat it to the side. "Here. This is the fenny." He filled both glasses, raised his, and waited for Donovan to do the same.

"To the blue skies and the green hills," he said. "To all that was and all that yet might be."

A terrible silence formed between them, into which the Fudir finally spoke the countersign:

"To the Taj and the Wall and the Mount of Many Faces,

"That Terra, long a province, be her own world once again."

Oschous tossed back his fenny and Donovan watched to make sure he swallowed before he did the same. "So," he said in the Tongue when both glasses had been emptied, "thou art of the Brotherhood?"

"Aye and all. And I swear that what we say will be said only here and only now. May I never see Green Terra if I lie."

"How, brother, rose a Terran so high in ranks Confederal, being that the Folk suffer much on this hither side of the Rift?"

"By nosuch else means than the lie of silence. I speak Manjrin with no-but accent. I speak nogot-nothing of Herself. The man who joineth the Abattoir loseth his past."

"A thing convenient in this wise."

Oschous nodded. "Even so. I will now tell thee a thing so that thou mayest join with us at last. This is the thing. The Brotherhood will in this rebellion support us, and the payment be much of a such, no-but less than Terra free, and autonomous in Her own affairs. And with the right of all Terrans to return there to live their lives."

Donovan swallowed and, within the confines of his heart, the Fudir wept. The young girl in the chiton sang. But Inner Child came alert, and the young man in the chlamys remained silent.

Oschous inserted a rod key into the wall. A tabernacle swung open and from it he removed a casket. This he placed on a small sweetwood table in the center of the little room. The opened lid revealed a few scoopfuls of dirt.

Donovan stared at the dirt in silence; then he lifted his gaze to his host and the question in his eyes never reached his lips.

"Aye," said Oschous. "The soil of Terra Herself."

The Fudir extended a hand, hesitated; but Oschous nodded, and he touched the dirt.

Perhaps it is true that the accidents of dirt are the same everywhere, that a scoopful of Dao Chetty or of High Tara would own similar moisture, similar texture, similar chemicals. But the substance was surely different. This dirt was *earth* in a way that no other dirt could be.

The scarred man had few sentiments. Behind the cynical exterior with which he faced the world was a cynical interior. His tears and smiles and anger were mostly constructed for effect. But the tightness in his throat was genuine. It came from none of his nine personalities, but from his body, directly from the soil into his blood.

"The Brotherhood will join the rebellion?" he said when he could trust his voice again.

"Not openly. Many who travel with us would part company if they thought this matter Terran. The negotiations are delicate and private. Neither Dawshoo nor Gidula know of them, and thou wilt not tell them so. But, 'aye and all.' They will be in it." He let that sink in before adding, "And you, Donovan buigh, Geshler Padaborn . . . If not for vengeance and not for pride, perhaps for the liberation of the Mother World."

The Fudir nodded dumbly. "Aye," he heard himself say. "Aye and all."

"Ah, well said, Gesh!" Oschous exchanged arm-grips with him. "Well said."

Slowly, reluctantly, Donovan broke contact with the dirt in the casket, and Oschous closed the lid and restored it to the hidden tabernacle in the hidden room. Donovan said nothing while he did. That Oschous Dee Karnatika had lied to him he was certain. But the nature of the lie so far eluded him.

CENGJAM GAAFE: THE SIXTH INTERROGATORY

So," says Bridget ban, leaning not toward the now-silent Shadow but toward her daughter, "he threw in with them after all." There is a mix of triumph and satisfaction in her voice that Méarana does not care for. Her mother had the finest intuition in the Periphery, but sometimes she leapt to conclusions. That was well enough when the conclusion was on the other side of a chasm—who can cross a chasm in small, careful steps?—but sometimes it was simply irritating.

She strikes her chords sharply, a jarring dissonance. "Did he? He had grave doubts that Oschous had told him the truth, or at least the whole truth."

"Then where," Bridget ban asks with a sweep of her arm, "is he? Leaving the Confederation cannot be impossible, given that *that* has made it here."

That sits on the sofa and grins without comment.

Deft fingers wrest a defiant tune from the strings. "Sometimes, when you are going through hell, there is only one thing you can do."

Her mother cocks her head. "And what is that?"

"Keep going."

Graceful Bintsaif says nothing. She senses that there is a different debate underway than merely whether Donovan joined the Revolution. She puts an apple to her lips, but her eyes never leave the Shadow. Her right hand strokes the butt of her teaser. She has not yet refastened the snap. Sunlight slashes through the blinds of the bay window and strikes the carpeting like the burn lines of a light cannon.

"When a man is in stress," says Bridget ban, "he runs to his beloved."

"He was cooming here when I diverted him."

Bridget ban tosses a fleeting look toward Méarana before turning to the Shadow. "So you say. He thought he left something here. But his greatest love has always been Terra. And that is the apple which finally tempted him to bite."

Graceful Bintsaif glances self-consciously at the apple in her hand and quietly lays it aside. She thinks about moving her chair before the sun is directly in her eyes.

"I think, Mother," says the harper, "that he had a greater love. Or one that with nurture might become so."

"You?"

"We did go on a faring . . ." The harper hesitates and looks to the Confederal and decides against offering details. "All things have their final causes. We did go on a faring together, and were you not at the end of it?"

Bridget ban snorts derision. "And you at the beginning. When did he realize that you were his daughter?"

"Sooner, I think, than you have."

Oh, that brings silence to the room! Bridget ban's face turns marble; Graceful Bintsaif's wary. Ravn Olafsdottr claps her hands and rubs them together. "I loove family reunions!"

After a moment, Méarana begins again to play with her harp, trying one theme, then another.

Finally, Bridget ban says, but as if to herself, "It matters not what he wist. The siren sang, and he has gone off with her." She does not look at Ravn Olafsdottr when she says this, though her eyes search out every other quarter of the room.

"Ah, Mother, ye're a fool. Ye hae e'er been his end, even when he knew it not himself. If he maun topple an empire and free a world to make his way here, why, he'll do it."

Olafsdottr raises her brows. "You think he can break an empire?"

Méarana strikes a gay chord. "He has a habit of breaking things." But she does not explain.

Bridget ban has recovered her aplomb. She smoothes her blouse, tosses her hair, and nods toward Ravn. "Then, why is he not here? If this could come, why not that?"

The Confederal smiles broadly. "I coom to that part shoortly."

Méarana misses a string, creates a discord. "He's deid, isnae he?" she says without looking up. "An' ye've come by here tae torture us wi' the news."

Olafsdottr's eyes soften fractionally. "Ah, why would I wish to torture you, yngling? For who else here would feel pain at such a tiding? Only you and I."

Bridget ban mutters, "Ha!" But Méarana stares at the Shadow. "You?"

Her mother answers for her. "You forgot, did you? Donovan made his choice well before—when he might have turned back *with her* but did not. She saved him from the Frog Prince; and he nursed her afterward. There's a bonding in that. But never forget this . . ." And she pointed toward the Shadow as if toward an inanimate object. "They ne'er do aught by chance. Every word she's spoken since coming, every gesture of her body, even her choice to chant her story like a skald, has been to a purpose. Everything has an end, you said? Aye, an' 'tis true, or Nature would not follow laws. You say that you and I are the end that the Fudir pursues? Ask yourself, then, what is Ravn Olafsdottr's end?"

The Shadow chuckles into the silence. "A nameless grave, moost like. But coome, my friends, this tale regards me noot. Let's leap ahead to Yuts'ga, there to find deceit and ambush foul, where in her darkened alleys Shadows—and worse—do prowl."

VII. YUTS'GA: A ROLE, IN THE HAY

Yuts'ga, whose star, once spied from Earth
In nameless twinkle, whose seas once swam
With proto-life prolific, joined in metazoan joy,
Her skies well crossed by many streams,
*   convulsed*
At times by strife to seize them, has now in gentle
*   peace*
Reposed these slumb'rous years, to dream . . . of
*   what?*
Here too, a crucial bottleneck where messages
Must criss and cross their way among the stars,
A place where proper hands may stay or speed
Intelligence sore-needed elsewhere by the foe.
And so have Shadows dimmed Fair Yuts'ga
To gather all into that fatal commonwealth
In which we all find membership. In stealth
To play the game upon the razor's edge;
Life sweetly-dreamed along the borderlands of
*   death.*

Yuts'ga was known once as Second Earth; but that
was in the Commonwealth's palmy days, when

comparisons to Terra were made openly and with pride. She bulked larger than the Homeworld, tugged a bit more than bones or muscles liked, and spun more slowly. She owned a moon too, which they called "Djut Long Dji," which meant "second moon" in some ancient tongue of Terra; but their grandchildren's grandchildren wondered why it was called "second" if there was only one and the name eventually collapsed into Tchudlon.

She was a large moon as such things go, and it was a rare thing for a small planet to have a large moon; but she was not so large as Luna, and so was less of a pestle to Yuts'ga's mortar. The seas were stirred by moderate tides; life was ground, but not so finely as on Earth.

Still, life was life. It was more than the prokaryote cryptolife that was the fruit of most worlds' groanings; more than the lichens that had graced the downy cheeks of Dao Chetty. Her vast world-sea was called the Wriggling Ocean because there were—by the gods!—*worms* burrowing in the ooze. Who knew what might next be found?

The answer, as it turned out, was nothing; and as world after barren world followed, men ceased to care. Worms? They vanished under the bioload of the terraforming arks. An easy job, the old captains said. Yuts'ga had done half their work already. They stroked her seas and quickened her with fish and insects and smiling crocodiles, graced the land with pine trees and waving grasses and fragrant rhododendrons. They did remember to save a few of those ur-worms, and studied them closely and found them much like Terran acoels; but they did not let them get in the way of things. There was work to do! A galaxy to conquer!

Much later, the world was called "Tikantam," which meant "the sensible horizon," because her star was the farthest of the Commonwealth suns plucked by eye from the skies of Terra. But it was not too long after that men ceased to care what could or could not be seen from Terra. There were convulsions, wars, cleansings. In the end, as epigones reconnected their ancestors' bones hoping that they might once more live, the older name was rediscovered and she became Yuts'ga once more.

Somewhere along the way, they lost the worms.

Yuts'ga was now a moderately prosperous world, dimly aware that she had once been important. But importance was gathered now into the Secret City like pretty baubles into a raven's nest, and the Yutsgars hunkered down and did as they were told. Now and then, the plates trembled and the sea floor turned over and the night breezes brought the stench of the ooze onto the land. "Worm weather," the Yutsgars called it, though no one remembered why.

Cambertown was the largest city in the Arwadhy District and the site of Number Three Spaceport, and several Confederation Sector Offices. The people there spoke a dialect that was a mixture of the old Taṇṭamiž lingua franca and the cant of the Zhõgwó, who had held the Mandate of the Heavens before the Vraddy. Consequently, they spoke Manjrin in an antique manner that otherworlders found alternately charming and exasperating. Definite articles were nowhere to be found; "is" and "have" lurked in elliptical constructions; and parts of speech oft jammed together into a single word. They would serve you up a word, and then start decorating it like a Festal Tree, adding markers for voice, tense, aspect, person, and sometimes just for the hell of it, negation, so that after you thought you had grasped the gist of it after all, it was turned at the very end all topsy-turvy on you. "Of course, you help ing do will I—*not*" was a favorite punch line on scores of nearby worlds.

The Mountain Dragon Inn stood on Fishbound Street in the Seventh District of Cambertown, just off the Ring Road. There were no mountains in the surrounding countryside; and even dragons were more rumored than seen, so where the name came from no one knew. It was justly famed for its own brew: Bartholomew Black.

Domino Tight was a small man, well formed of countenance. His hair curled in tight, black ringlets; his lips curled in perpetual good humor. A good man to drink with; a good man to sport with. During one assassination, he had reduced his target to helpless laughter while in the very act of killing him. "Screams of laughter," he liked to say when he told the story on himself, which was often enough that it had grown tedious.

He had settled himself into a companionable silence in a booth near the inn's rear exit with a schooner of Bartholomew Black. But a Shadow like Domino Tight does not wait for no purpose. He waits for signs and portents. He was on Yuts'ga to move the Talker of the Yutsgar Nexus. Once that unfortunate was cleared away, the Third Undersecretary for Information could take charge of the Interstellar Comm Clearance Center, and message packets entering the Sector on their way to Dao Chetty would thereafter be inspected, censored, and cleared by the Revolution. But while the Talker was a dead man walking, he was under the protection of the loyalist Shadow, Pendragon Jones; and so he might yet walk a little farther.

It was a matter of insertion between Pendragon Jones and the Talker. Domino Tight had narrowed the search to Cambertown and had scattered his magpies to scour the city for signs.

From time to time, young men and women garbed in the current fashions of the Arwadhy drifted into the Mountain Dragon, some for a "pint o' th' Black," others for the free lunch, but still others to drop a word or two in the ear of Domino Tight. Pendragon's magpies had been spotted here, there, moving thus. The Shadow collected these words and pricked them off on a chart he kept on his pocket screen. The screen pondered vectors and applied algorithms of the mathematical art, searching for the barycenter of the motions, for at that centroid would, like mistress spider, lurk Pendragon Jones.

Among those lifting "pints" in the Dragon were three of Domino Tight's magpies—Two, Five, and Fourteen—forming a cordon. There was also a man at the bar who reminded Domino Tight of steel wool. He did not grow hair so much as bristles, and the eyes above the thin mustache were a deadly topaz. Domino Tight wondered if he might be in the Life and crooked a finger at Two, who shook her head at the question.

"Not one of Pendragon's men," she murmured when called to his side. "We've pegged them all. A courier for someone else, maybe, just passing through."

Or a local thug—a mover, a scrambler, or whatever they called their petty criminals in Cambertown. He sat on a bar stool and drank his Black and seemed to pay no mind to the comings and goings of magpies, by which Domino Tight knew he was paying very keen attention indeed.

The rear door to the Mountain Dragon creaked open and Domino Tight released the safety catch on the teaser he held unholstered in his lap. As he was a bilaterian, like many Shadows, his left hand oft worked independently of his right.

The light from the wall lamps blotted out and the entry to the booth was eclipsed by a presence. Domino Tight reengaged the safety catch. "G'day, Jacques. When did you blow in?"

"Since three days," said Big Jacques, finding a bench to sit upon, which he angled to take in the room. "You be a hard man to track down, Domino Tight."

"I should be an impossible man to track down," he answered. "What brings you?"

Big Jacques rumbled. One always knew when he was about to essay a joke, for he laughed peremptorily at his own wit. "Why, my ship done brought me." Then, unable to contain himself, he slapped the table, causing the accouterments to dance. Domino Tight snatched his schooner up before it could topple, and returned a smile as broad as the humor.

There is a stereotype held in the minds of most, even of those moderately keen, of an inverse relationship between the size of the body and the size of the mind. Big Jacques knew that and played to the stereotype. The duller his opponents believed him, the greater the edge he had in playing them.

"We missed you at the facemeet on Henrietta," Jacques added. "You shoulda seen it. Dawshoo told us the Cause was lost and we should just give up. I think he said that so we'd all cry up nay. You shoulda seen old Gidula's face! And Dawshoo's too, when half the room started to walk out."

"Hunh. Dawshoo's a galah." Domino Tight took a pull from his schooner while Jacques signaled to the tavern-keeper for a drink of his own. "I'm going to guess," Tight said when he put the schooner down, "that Oschous rallied the troops."

"Oh, he did, for sure. That face of his would have gone white if it hadn't been all covered with red fuzz. Dawshoo oughta watch his back. There may be some discussion on who should lead us, once the Names are ousted. My money's on Oschous."

"Gidula, I think. Oschous actually believes in the Cause. That's not good for a revolutionary."

Jacques rumbled once more. "Near as I can figure, I'm doing pretty much the same crap I was doing before. Just a different target list, is all."

"So, why one and not the other?" Domino Tight

asked from genuine curiosity. He had never decided whether Big Jacques had hidden depths or no depth at all.

"Oh, the quality o' the targets, of course. Takes more skill, more practice, more craft. 'The knife grows dull when the target is soft.' You move your man here yet?"

"Not yet. Pendragon's on-world protecting him."

"The hell, you say! How did he know we were going to move the Talker?"

Domino Tight shrugged. "'Three may keep a secret if two of them are dead.' Just makes it a bigger challenge. The target's night soil; just a matter of time."

Big Jacques nudged him with a forefinger. "There. Y'see? 'A bigger challenge.' But you may as well fold the play. If Pendragon's mother-henning your target, he's probably figured why he was in the cross-hairs in the first place. Whole point of moving our man into the Comm Center is that they don't know we done it."

"Oh, half a dozen cadre move up the ladder if the top dog's capped. Might not be obvious which we wanted moved. Tell me, Jacques. We chance-met here, or have you looked me up 'cause we're cobber?"

"Bone homey, we call it where I come from," said Big Jacques. The tavern-keeper brought him a large stein of uncertain content. The big man grumbled about something he called a demitasse and tossed it off in a single gulp. "Nah, just a call of the courtesy," he continued when the tavern-keeper had gone off to draw five more steins. "I'll be sending magpies out and your guys might cross paths with mine. Don't want no misunderstandings." He handed the smaller man a bubble case. "That's got the dance card for our FOFs. The identifier changes randomly, but that'll keep your guys in sync so they can know Friend or Foe. I'd appreciate the same info from you, 'cause while my main interest is that your boys don't pot my boys, I don't really want mine potting yours, either."

"Bad for morale," said Domino Tight.

Both Shadows took a moment to download the codes through their own intranets. "Who's your date, Big Guy, if you don't mind my asking?"

"Ekadrina Sèanmazy."

Domino Tight's magpies had been whispering the latest intel in his left earwig. He touched pause. "Ekadrina? She's on-world?"

"Not yet. She went to Ashbanal for the pasdarm. But she'll be stopping here to check with Pendragon on her way to Dao Chetty. She may have sent some of her magpies on ahead. You ain't seen any taijis drifting around have you?"

Domino Tight shook his head. "That . . . could send things up a gum tree. Ekadrina is a big bite to chew on. You have the teeth for it?"

Jacques grinned wide. "Who else you think could take her?"

"Oschous."

"Might could be. But we don't put our brains on the block. Gidula too, in his prime; which you might have noticed, he ain't. Maybe Dawshoo; and notice the 'maybe'."

"Manlius?"

"Not even a maybe. Only one who thinks he could is Manlius."

"There was Geshler Padaborn once," mused Domino Tight, "but she took him down in the end."

Jacques finished another stein. He smiled, as if to himself. "Sure, after he was already a prisoner, and had escaped her cordon."

Domino Tight nodded. "Speaking of the pasdarm, how did that play out? Which one retired, Epri or Manlius?"

"You have a way of asking things . . . Don't know. Message packets ain't caught up yet. I come here direct from Henrietta, but Oschous, Dawshoo, and them went to Ashbanal to collect Manlius. Which reminds me. They'll be looking you up soon. Big play coming, and you're the man for it. Or one of them. Seven Shadows in the play."

"Seven!"

"And our flocks too, I guess."

"What's the play? I suppose you already know, being in the Inner Circle and all."

"Yeah, I got it writ down somewhere. I'll let you know."

Domino Tight grimaced. "Well, I always did like surprises. Who else is in? Can you tell me that?"

"Oh, beside you and me, there's, lessee . . ." He counted on his fingers. "My copain, Little Jacques—I hit 'em high, he hits 'em low—Oschous himself, Ravn, Manlius . . . Oh, and Padaborn."

"Padaborn!"

"Yeah. Padaborn's back. Showed up on Henrietta

just after most of us left, courtesy of your old friend, Ravn Olafsdottr. She tracked him down over in the League, bagged him up, and brought him back."

The curly-haired Shadow finished his schooner. "How . . . interesting. Ekadrina know?"

Jacques grinned. "That's the problem with the Long Tall One. You never know what she knows."

"Padaborn . . ." said Domino Tight. "The greatest of the Shadows . . . He'll give the Cause a new life."

"If you believe in the Cause."

"Well, if Ravn could bag Padaborn and haul his sorry ass back over this side of the Rift, he isn't half the man he used to be."

"Way I hear it, he's four or five times the man he used to be. But they tell me he knows the way in."

"In where?"

Big Jacques gazed at the ceiling with pursed lips. Domino Tight made a sour face.

"Oh. By the way," Jacques added, "you know someone in the Secret City, doncha?"

Domino Tight nodded. "Tina Zhi. She works in the Gayshot Bo."

"Yeah, those smoochin' good looks of yours draws 'em in like a landing grid, especially the geeka girls in the Tech Ministry. She knows her way around there, don't she? The Secret City? Maybe has maps and floor plans and crap. Knows where each of the Names lives. Staff sizes."

Domino Tight smiled crookedly. "Maybe. But of course you can't actually tell me what the play is."

Big Jacques spread his arms. "I didn't tell you, did

I? See what you can get from her." He pushed himself to his feet and whistled, and five of the patrons in the bar stood, too. "Well, see ya 'round, Curly."

"Or not."

The Big Shadow left by the front, preceded and followed by his magpies. "Never leave by the way you came" was a maxim of the Abattoir. Domino Tight's Number Two magpie had been sitting at the bar. Now she came by the booth. "I don't even have to guess who that was," she said. "How's the analysis going?"

"I'm running a time series now." His instrument pinged and, without missing a beat, he said, "I've just finished running a time series." He glanced at the plot superimposed on a map of Cambertown. "Root! No wonder it took so long. The barycenter is nonstationary. Our bird is on the wing. He must have twigged, because it looks like *he's* probing for *us*. Tell the flock to fall back on refuge . . ." He struck a random number generator. ". . . three."

The magpie chirped. "Just like a pasdarm," she said. "With a planet-sized arbor."

A toss of the head gathered the other two magpies in the tavern. The banty man turned and for a moment locked eyes with Domino Tight before he professed interest in the engravings on the walls. "Out the back," Tight told the magpies. "Standard formation. Taverner, what does your surveillance say?"

It was not a nice neighborhood. The man behind the bar checked his screens. "Alley-the rear empty be-presently . . ."

They each pulled dazers from their belts and tugged their hoods up over their heads. The tavern-keeper pretended not to notice. Just another day in the Seventh District.

Standard formation meant Number Five and Number Fourteen would go out first—one breaking to the left, one to the right—and Number Two would go out last as a rear-guard. But at the last moment, Number Two tugged Domino Tight by the shoulder and pushed out past him.

And that meant that when the Shadow came out last, he had a perfect view of his Number Two magpie as she was shot down from ambush. Dispersal armor could dissipate the pulse, attenuate the load density; but not if the shot was in the face. Two fell backward, her face blackened, her eyes melted, her lips and tongues blistered and congealed. Domino Tight used her toppling body for a momentary shield and broke left, away from the main boulevard. He tumbled into a protective doorway.

"Got the bitch!" cried Number Five, who shared the doorway. "She was over behind the trash bins. No escape. Suicide mission." He glanced at his master. "Shoulda been you coming out third. Two had good instincts."

"Aye. 'Always do the unexpected.' See that she's tagged for pickup. She'll go in the Rose Garden. Assassin have a second?"

"Don't they always? Might have flown if he thought the primary succeeded. That's 'you' lying on the alley over there."

"Good theory. Test it."

Number Five stepped out of the doorway, but with his face averted.

The pulse took him on the armor and he convulsed and dropped. From the other side, Number Fourteen spotted the backup and sliced him up with a flechette gun.

Domino Tight tugged on Five's leg while Fourteen went to blacklight the two assassins. "You all right, mate?"

"Y-yes," said Five. "Just j-jangled. Dispersal armor b-better than n-nothing, but n-not all that much b-better."

The Shadow laughed. He had used that line himself.

"Pendragon's chrysanthemum," Fourteen told him over the link. "Both of them. Tag 'em for pickup?"

Domino Tight glanced at Number Two's body. "No. Strip their identifiers. If Pendragon's magpies think they'll never sleep in the Rose Garden, they may hesitate to do his bidding."

Fourteen looked at him from across the alley. "If we start pulling their identifiers, they'll stat pulling ours," he pointed out. "'The dead take no sides,'" he quoted. "Everyone agreed on that chapter from the onset. They're dead once, master. Why kill them a second time? What more can they do?"

Domino Tight sighed and wondered at the wisdom of a war fought with rules. "Very well, tag them." Then he opened the link. "Listen, my flock," he said. "The mum has found the lyre. Two has retired the service. Continue shifting. Who's watching the cross-hairs?"

"One and Twelve," came the answer.

Domino Tight sighed again. Another agreed chapter was "Don't spook the sheep." Removing the Yuts'ga Talker was supposed to be a tragic accident. If it looked like assassination, the sheep-cops started asking cui bono. "One. Twelve," he said. "Move the target. But move his protectors first."

"Ah, so *that* is how to suck an egg!" That was One answering. Close enough to winning a name to treat with her master as an equal.

"Do it." Domino Tight closed the link. "Right," he told the others. "Let's blow this place."

At that point, he learned that the dead did sometimes take sides. Both assassins had worn dead-man's packs, and when the timers ran out the blasts took Domino Tight and Number Five and left no trace of Number Fourteen but a thin film of oil on the paving.

"Not exactly what I meant," murmured Domino Tight before darkness took him.

Big Jacques set up a command center in an old warehouse along the River Cola in the Fourteenth District of Cambertown. He was the sentimental sort and saw no reason to site a potential combat zone in an area frequented by the sheep. "We're supposed to keep things on the q.t.," he reminded his flock.

When he had his equipment set up and linked to the string of microsatellites he had strewn in orbit on his arrival, he took reports from his flock. Seven would take the ship to the forward libration point, near the ruins of an old Commonwealth habitat. One had remained at Inbound to follow Ekadrina when once she had appeared.

Two, who was monitoring planetary news distributors, said, "That a good idea, boss, leaving One up there? What if *she* spots him? We should bushwhack her at Arrival Groundside. She won't be expecting you."

Big Jacques leaned back on the shipping crate he had appropriated for a seat and linked his hands behind his head. "First off, One has one of those baby faces that blends right in with the sheep. Looks innocent."

"No one's that innocent."

"Said he *looked* it; didn't say he was. Second off, a bushwhack at Arrivals ain't artistic. Thing that griped me most about the Life was hunting down all those sheep. A corrupt governor, an uppity businessman, an ambitious swoswai. All they do is whine and cower when you corner 'em. What sport, that? Third off, Yuts'ga's got five spaceports. Where do we set up the ambush?"

"She'll come down here, won't she?" the magpie asked. "At Number Three. I mean, she's coming to meet with Pendragon, and he's set up here in Cambertown."

"Yeah, and so's Curly. Getting crowded. But maybe she comes down at Spaceport Two and takes skimmers over here. Main Rule of Arrivals?"

Two sighed. "'Never the obvious.'"

"Yeah." Big Jacques looked around his command

center and wondered if he was being too obvious about using isolated locations. "Six," he said, "take a couple of the boys and set up a dummy command center somewhere else. Somewhere I might have chosen. No, don't tell me where 'less I got need-to-know. Keep an eye on the dummy from a sniper nest and see if anyone shows an interest. Make it a little more obvious than here. Use the playbook. Funnel all the comm traffic through there, but keep the link between here and the dummy site deep in the black. Two: Nothing goes in and out of *here* except through the funnel."

For a few moments bustle engulfed the warehouse as the subteam formed up, commandeered equipment, and departed. Two watched them go, then flipped up his data goggles. "Think Six is ready to solo?"

"Were you? If the ruse works, it works. If not . . ." The big man shrugged.

"If the ruse works," said Two, "Lady Ekadrina and her whole flock could come down on them."

"That's why they pay us the big bucks."

"Master, we are in rebellion. We are not getting paid."

"Oh, yeah. Then we're doing this for honor. Hey, drop the kid a message and remind him to have his boys sneak in and out of the center now and then. Foot traffic, you know."

"Nasty job," said Two, "when the prey is just as able to pot you. Give me the low hanging fruit any day."

"That's how you get soft, Two."

"Hold one . . ." Two held a hand to his ear, listened, then flipped down his goggles and started scanning the planetary network. "What was the name of that tavern where Lord Domino . . . The Mountain Dragon? The news dispensers here say there was an explosion there. Power cell overload or something."

Big Jacques grunted. "Or something. Body count?"

"Ah . . . The sheep are being assured that the tavern itself was undamaged and will be serving Bartholomew Black as usual in the morning. No mention of bodies."

"That's nice."

"Local bobs are investigating and the Riff of Yuts'ga is flying in from Great Hardwick in case there are Confederal implications."

"In case."

"Does the Riff know we're on-world?"

"Not if you ain't told him." Jacques tapped his comm box. "My skinny tells me the Yutsgar Riff is a loyalist. So Pendragon maybe gave him a heads-up."

"And . . ." Number Two listened again. ". . . Number One reports Lady Ekadrina's ship entering parking orbit."

Jacques considered that. "I hate coincidences."

Domino Tight felt a numbness all over his body, as if he had been sealed away from the outside world and nothing in it could touch him anymore. His head, lolling to the side, saw nothing but the back door of the tavern and the boneless body of Five. Something sharp had been accelerated by the explosion and protruded slightly from the back of the man's head, and

Domino Tight could see enough of it to be glad he could see no more. His ears rang, and sounds also seemed far away, beyond the barrier encasing him.

But his vision had brightened, and with it, his spirits. Some of his colleagues liked to talk about "a life unworthy of life," but when presented with the thing itself, Domino Tight found it always worthy enough.

The tavern door opened, and the banty man stepped into the alleyway. Oh, yes, he was in the Life! Look at the way he stepped, at the way his topaz eyes sought out threats, at the ready manner in which his dazer hunted out hidey-holes and snipers' nests. And only when satisfied, did he step clear and to the side of Domino Tight.

He walked at an eerily canted angle, but the Shadow recognized that as the way his head was resting on the ground. His common sense, that integrated all of his sights and sounds and kinesthesia into a common image, was not yet in sync. The alley smelled orange.

"Do you wish surcease?" the stranger asked him. He held his dazer to the ready, muzzle pointing straight up.

Domino Tight tried to speak. "Tina," he heard someone say, possibly himself, though it sounded like another. And why should he call on the young woman in the Gayshot Bo on far-off Dao Chetty?

The stranger's bristles crinkled with his smile. "No one who calls on a woman is yet ready to depart. Quickly, tell me. Are you with the rebels or the loyalists?" He had reached into his pouch and removed a packet of some sort.

The Shadow gasped, and whispered, "Which do you want me with?"

The other man laughed— and Domino Tight glimpsed teeth sharper than a man's ought be. He looked to the right, toward Fishbound Street. "I can't stay here. The smart move is to leave you, but . . . I don't like ambushes. Right after you left, the taverner finished his sentence by adding 'not' to the end. He laughed, like he'd done something clever. I took care of that for you, in case you need company on the ferryboat."

The stranger opened a tear in Tight's spun armor and pulled the rip apart. He placed his packet on the chest of Domino Tight; then he struck it hammer-wise with his fist.

The Shadow felt nothing. His body remained laminated by the concussion, and the blow might as well have struck someone else. But fire ran through his body. A tingling returned to his fingers and toes. "Th-thank you," he managed to gasp.

"Don't be too sure I've done you a favor. The booster won't set your broken bones. You'd best get yourself inside a meshinospidal right soon. For now, adieu." And the stranger stood, looked all directions, and vanished into the night.

Domino Tight found he could move his right arm. His right leg was not so fortunate, as he could see that it lay at more angles than knees and ankles could account for.

What the devil was a meshinospidal? His earwig had not yet resumed functioning; might need to be replaced entirely. It sounded vaguely like . . .

He snatched the spent emergency packet from his chest and held it to his still immobile face so that he could see the instructions upon it.

Printed in Gaelactic.

His savior had been a Hound of the Ardry.

Domino Tight laughed. He would take help whence it came and not ask too closely after it. He released the packet and the wind funneled by the alleyway caught it and it tumbled away toward Fishbound Street. "Tina," he said again.

And the air rippled and a woman stood before him, having just thrown a cloak back over her shoulder. Her mouth opened in an O and she knelt by his side, probing for his hurts.

Perhaps he was delusional from the concussion. First a Hound where no Hound ought by rights to be; then a woman appearing from nowhere.

"Tina!" he managed to say.

"I told you to call me if you ever found yourself in trouble. You should not have waited so long, my dearest." Then she unhooked her cloak and spread it over the both of them, and the darkness enveloped Domino Tight once more.

Oschous Dee Karnatika brought *Dark Horse* into High Yuts'ga Orbit, watching from the command chair in the control room with Ravn and Donovan to either side. Manlius, now hale, had returned to his own ship and was on his way to the Century Suns to meet with Dawshoo. Yuts'ga was a major node on the network of interstellar "tubes" and the number of ships in port was considerable. It was not a difficult docking for all that, as the Long Moon had plenty of facilities, and long-term parking was shifted by valet over to the First Equilibrium point.

However, no one touches a Shadow's ship but his trusted magpies. Oschous told Number One to "ping the parking" and see who was on-world.

Domino Tight and Pendragon Jones. Gidula. Big Jacques.

"Awfully crowded," Donovan commented.

"Yuts'ga is a major node," said Oschous. "Many pass through."

"I thought Big Jacques was tracking Ekadrina," Ravn said.

"He was. Either he gave up, or . . ."

"Or he didn't. Is *her* ship here?"

"Not overtly." Oschous dropped the screen to the table. "There's one other ship that didn't respond to the ping. Courier, maybe, passing through and traveling dark."

"I don't like this," Ravn said. "We're starting to go straight after each other."

Oschous swung his seat to look at her. "We've turned over glasses ere now. Some on our side; some on theirs. Ekadrina is probably just doing a face-check on Pendragon."

"I didn't mean her. I meant Big Jacques. Sure, sometimes, trying to move or to protect an asset brought us into conflict. But Manlius go after Epri, and now Big Jacques go after Ekadrina, and not in pasdarm."

"It's the way these things work," cracked the scarred man. "Gentlemen's agreements require gentlemen to keep them."

"Well, Yuts'ga big planet," Ravn said. "Perhaps not all gone to same district, let alone same township."

Oschous Dee grunted. "Don't tempt the Fates, Ravn. They'll send them there just to spite you. Number One!"

"Aye, master?" The magpie in the supervisor's chair swung to face him.

"Monitor the channels that Domino Tight and Big Jacques use. Gidula, too. Sift the other channels for sign of Pendragon or Ekadrina. Commandeer the Yutsgar Union's comsat network, if you must. And look for their personal satellites. Let me know what you catch. I don't like the way this is developing, and I don't want to go in blind. Ravn, Gesh, I'll see you again at lunch. If anything develops before then, I'll summon you."

In the gray and gold corridor outside the control room, Ravn slipped her hand through Donovan's arm. "Coom, my sweet," she said, leading him off toward the lounge. "Perhaps we will sit and chat and I will let you have your way with me."

Donovan allowed himself to be led. "Don't be too wishful of that until you know what 'my way' is. Do you expect a big rumble down below?"

"Roomble? Anoother Terran woord? You must mean fight, a passage of arms." Her teeth showed white against her lips. "Every thing will work oot fine. Once Ooschous pulls Doominoo off task, noo reason he and Pen fight. And Jacques maybe not find Ekadrina befoor she leave. Big woorld, noo?"

But Donovan shook his head. "No, it will all go to shit, and we will be in the middle of it."

"You are sooch cheerful ooptimist . . . Boot we keep you out of it. You are too valooable to waste on sooch squabblings."

"Why do I get the feeling that when you finally do waste me, it will be a really crappy situation?"

She patted his cheek with her free hand. "When oonly the best are needed."

"You know, it's not like I'm incapable . . ."

"Hoosh, my darling. Remember my advice."

"Oschous knows. There are no flies on him."

"Noo flies? You have the foony way of speaking. Come, in here."

The ship's lounge was broad and circular, decorated in silver and black. On the wall were embedded a shifting array of images: places where Oschous had been, magpies that had been in his service. Game consoles, spool racks, desks, and craft stations stood about the room. Save at the beginning and the end, interstellar journeys consisted primarily of doing nothing. Some of that was taken up in training and exercise, but there was such as thing as overtraining, so everyone in the crew had developed a hobby or interest. Magpie Four Karnatika, for example, was preparing an anthropological study of the Regensthorp Sector; Magpie Six engaged herself in clay sculpture.

Two magpies were present when Ravn and Donovan entered, one reading a screen, the other playing battle chess on a projection stage. Olafsdottr waved her arms about. "Go! Go, scat! Doonoovan would make passionate loov to me, and wishes noo audience."

The magpies laughed and one said, "I'd want no

audience either, was I him." But they gathered up their things and left the lounge, still laughing.

Donovan frowned. "Why did you tell them that . . . ?"

But Ravn scythed him with an ankle sweep and he fell onto the sofa with Ravn atop him. She wrapped arms and legs around him, and it was like being baled up in wire. He could not move. "What the hell . . . ?"

"Hush, my sweet," she whispered in his ear in the Gaelactic. "Listen, and listen. Oschous was bound to learn that you are hale. That could not be helped. But Gidula is the key. Whatever you do—and as long as we lie here on this couch, sweet, you may do whatever you wish—do not let Gidula know your sundry selves have come together. Billy Chins' last message told him that you were a broken man. That is what he expected when he had me fetch you, and that is what you must show him."

Donovan pulled his head back enough to see genuine fear in the eyes of Ravn Olafsdottr. "Why . . . ?" he whispered. But Ravn kissed him to stop the question; then, nuzzling his neck, she whispered again.

"Do not ask questions for which I cannot yet give you answers. The caution is sufficient unto the day. It is worth your life, and mine."

"Will not Oschous tell him . . . ?"

"Hush. Oschous is clever. Knowledge is power. He does not give it away. Mmm, you are good kisser."

"When I have to, I can play a role." Once again, he found his words smothered.

"Tell me," Ravn whispered between kisses. "Whatever. Become. Of Billy. Chins."

"He retired."

Ravn fell still for a moment. "How . . . sad," she said.

"He wasn't too happy about it, either; but I wasn't ready to retire myself."

"How fortunate for my present pleasures, then," Olafsdottr said and resumed her caresses. When a time went by with no further warnings, Donovan disengaged.

"Anything else?"

"Ooh, my sweet. We must not be too obvious that this roll was only a role; that this 'seduce' was but a ruse. Play the game to completion, darling. I told you before that we would become good friends someday. What better day than today?"

But if no drug could ever completely dull the whole of Donovan buigh, if no rite of meditation could ever completely entrance him, neither could the rush and flow of enzymes entirely engage his mind. The Silky Voice was seduced; but the Fudir stood aside, faithful to the memory of a woman who hated him, and Inner Child, as always, kept watch, and the Sleuth tried to deduce what it all meant.

Who does she want this conversation kept secret from? he asked the Fudir.

"Oschous. Who else has eyed and eared this vessel? The question is *what* did she want kept secret from him. Not the condition of our mind. He already knows."

Oh, that is obvious. What she conceals from our host is that Gidula mustn't know. And notice what she said.

Do not ask questions for which I cannot yet give you answers, the Pedant helpfully reminded them.

Cannot yet give the answers; not that she does not yet know them.

To a nonnative speaker, the distinction between "cannot'" and "can not" may . . .

Shut up, Pedant. How are Donovan and the others doing?

<If it weren't for the sheer terror of it all, they'd be enjoying this.>

Yes, thought the Fudir. There is more than a peck of trouble here, and it's not all down on Yuts'ga at all.

CENGJAM GAAFE: THE SEVENTH INTERROGATORY

It cannot be said that a woman of deep golden skin can flush, but Bridget ban has turned brass as Olafsdottr chants her seduction of Donovan buigh. Méarana has watched her mother tighten as the Shadow described each loose caress; and she smiles to watch, a little from alarm, but not entirely so. Graceful Bintsaif shows clear signs of distress and her tickler is half out from her holster. There are ways to stop this taunting torrent.

But Bridget ban cuts the narration short. She stands and trembles, fists clenched by her sides. "Faithless dog!" she snarls.

"Cu," says Graceful Bintsaif, hoping to assuage her anger. "Did you not hear? He was disengaged. His mind was elsewhere."

Bridget ban turns on her underling, waves an arm at the now-silent Shadow who watches, face composed in turn to the three women who interrogate her. "How would she know where his minds were?" the Hound snarls. "He has plenty enough to spare."

She holds that pose for a moment of silence which no one dares break. But at the juncture at which the accusatory arm has begun to lower, Ravn Olafsdottr speaks.

"To whom was he unfaithful?" she asks with a liar's innocence. "Was there someone perhaps with whom he had once exchanged a troth?"

Bridget ban makes no answer to this and her golden skin turns almost tin.

"If I foond soomthing discarded by the wayside," the Shadow continues in Alabastrine, "am I blameswoorthy if I clean it oop and care for it? Beside," she adds in Gaelactic, "I'm after promising him help in some small matter, and I have every intention o' doin' so. He is a despicable old scoundrel, but he is not without his charms."

Méarana wonders if she is the only one who has noticed the precise words of accusation her mother had flung out. Faithless *dog*? Of the three so entangled, which was the Hound? She bends over her harp to hide her smile, and begins to pluck out the melody of an old Die Bold courtship song. The Fudir had told her once that it was derived from a much older song of Terra, sung to a different purpose. She does not intone the words, but she knows that her mother recognizes them.

I fled him down the labyrinth of my mind
And hid from him with running laughter . . .

She notes from the posture of her mother's body that she has turned to glare at her, but she does not raise her head to meet that gaze, lest she herself burst out in laughter. She plays on, half-mocking, half-somber, for such matters are too serious for anything but jest. With the grace and intricacies of her finger work, she demands silence from the others, and receives it until she comes at last to the final unsung lines:

All you fancied lost I've stored for you at home.
So rise, my darling, clasp my hand, and come.

Only when she has stilled her strings does Méarana Swiftfingers look her mother in the eye. "Really, Mother, what did you want them to do? Ravn had to tell him something Oschous could not hear, but without making it obvious that she was doing so. Tell me you have never used similar ploys yourself."

This last, she adds with a touch of heat that surprises mother and daughter alike, for Bridget ban had once been notorious for such wiles. The silence between them is broken finally by Graceful Bintsaif, who says self-consciously, "There is another mystery here."

"Again," laughs the Shadow, "oonly one."

"What was Gw . . ." She stops at Bridget ban's gesture.

But Ravn completes her sentence. "What was Gwillgi Hound doing on Yuts'ga? Ooh, my sweet Doominoo may not knoow him, but thoose toopaz eyes I have seen before, to my great displeasure. It was sweet, what he did, and I can only pray the Fates keep the two of them from facing off in the pasdarm of life. Meanwhile, I cannot suppose that the Kennel has had no hint of our struggle, or that they have not sent observers to sniff around its edges."

"He was only observing, then," says Graceful Bint-saif. It is the dream of every young Hound that she will be sent one day on that most dangerous of quests. Few indeed have made that crossing; fewer still have returned.

"Ooh, what family engrossed in quarrel welcomes a neighbor's peep at window?"

"There's a deeper mystery," says Méarana—and she wonders momentarily if Olafsdottr had described her intimacies with such detail in order to distract Bridget ban from it. "That Hounds may spy within the Confederation is no great secret, but that your saga should brook bad art is."

"Yes," says Ravn Olafsdottr with a congratulating smile to the harper, "it is very troubling."

"What is?" asks Bridget ban, irritated beyond measure by her guest-prisoner, her daughter, and even her protégé. She has been diverted by her own thoughts, but now reviews what has been said and nods. "Oh. Of course."

Olafsdottr's smile is grim. "Aye. Domino Tight has a lover in the Gayshot Bo on Dao Chetty, and this lover just happens to be in a back alley in Camber-town when he is wounded? Ah, my sweets, that begs too much of chance. The Fates are ne'er inclined to aid romance."

VIII. YUTS'GA: JACQUES, IN A BOX

Domino Tight was neither so clever as Oschous, nor so powerful as Big Jacques. He was neither so agile as Little Jacques, nor so wise as Gidula. What he was, was charming. He could charm, it was said, the skin off a snake. He had, all unwittingly, charmed the Technical Name.

"Unwitting," because had he known Tina Zhi's true nature, he would have run very fast in another direction, in any other direction. The loves of the Names were like their other passions: too vast and too intense for any lesser vessel to contain. It would burn him out, use him up.

Though it is not clear whether, however fast and far he ran, he could have escaped, because it may have been less his charm than her choice. Charm, after all, depends a great deal on a willingness on the other part to be charmed. Perhaps she saw him one day and was struck by the curl of his hair, where it lay across his brow. Perhaps she simply wondered what life was like outside the Secret City. Or perhaps mere cold calculation moved her. With a Name, you could never tell, and all three might be one. But however it befell, his charm was no less real, and no less effective.

When Domino Tight came to his senses once more, he found himself in a downy bed set upon a flag-stoned patio in a bower of oak and laurel. Birds sang intricate and unfamiliar songs and a dull orange sun was approaching his zenith in an amethyst sky. The breeze was cool and comforting and brought with it a scent of lily and hyacinth. The sheets that draped his naked body were warm, despite their diaphanous weave. Domino Tight considered his body, counted the scars that ornamented it, and found more than his wont.

He raised himself on an elbow and looked out through a gap in the trees down a rolling valley of pleasant green and yellow grasses to a meandering stream bordered by towering plane trees. The land-scape had been artfully arranged to appear natural: shapes and contours led the eye, colors complemented, sounds soothed and roused.

The bed conformed itself to his movements, becoming a divan. The songs of the birds changed, became more resolute. He saw one sitting on a perch in a cam-ouflaged cage. It was called a "king löyingmu" in the Confederal tongue. A "lovebird."

Domino Tight might not equal Gidula for insight, but that a lovebird's song greeted his first stirring he thought a message of sorts. As too the artfully dis-guised cage in which the bird sat.

He had not yet figured it out, but he had begun to realize that there was something to figure out. Thus are always the first stirrings of wisdom. Tina Zhi was obviously not as she had represented herself, a minor functionary in the regulation of technology. But he had not yet chased that fox to its burrow.

Sitting, he examined his shattered leg. He detected no breaks, evoked no pain. He wriggled his toes and was gratified to find those members responding with enthusiasm.

Tina Zhi entered the patio through doors that had replicated the bower and so had appeared a part of it. Domino Tight glimpsed the interior of a house in black and silver and red: comfortable chairs, a carpet, a ramp curling upward. Then the doors closed and there was nothing but the trees and the yellow lilies and blue hyacinths that bordered the patio. He looked up, but saw no sign of a second floor to which the interior ramp might have led.

She wore white, translucent robes with billowing sleeves and silver borders. A silver cincture girded her waist. A necklace, also of silver but with turquoise highlights, encircled her throat, and seemed in constant motion. Her short-cropped hair had been silvered as well. Her skin was dusky, her nose long, her cheekbones high. Her body was softened by the fat of youth, yet her eyes seemed immeasurably old.

"Ah, my Domino," she said as she swept toward him and gathered him to lay his head in her lap. "You are awake at last."

Domino Tight had never seen the point of telling someone what he already knew. "How long was I in a coma?" he asked, thinking it might be a very long time indeed if his leg were so completely healed.

"Oh, a day, two days. Who can say when we flit from world to world?" Her hands fluttered, her voice trilled. But the flightiness that he had once found so endearing now seemed too contrived. The robes, when they billowed, were solidly opaque; but where they draped, they may as well have been spun glass. As she moved, parts of her body made brief cameos before ducking coyly behind the curtains. Her hair dye, he saw from his vantage point, overlooked no patch; and the complementary nail colors extended to her decorative nipple caps.

"How did you happen to be on Yuts'ga?" he asked. "How did you find me so quickly?"

"Oh, love." She brushed his lips with her own, stroked his forehead, brushing back his curls. "I am never far from you. Love entangles us."

"That sun," he said, nodding toward the great orange disk now nearly atop the sky. "It's not the Yutsgar sun, and no world lies but two days sliding from her."

"An age before an age ago," she told him in a singsong voice, "the god Aspect decreed that two hearts that had beat as one would beat always together, however far apart they wandered. And this same is true of patches of space.

Any two states, however distinct,
May by this admonition
Coexist in any complex
Linear superposition.
And what is true of the tiniest specks
Must hold for their larger assemblies.

"For this reason, it is called a 'quondam state,'

from an ancient word that meant 'in the past,' 'in the future,' and 'sometimes' all at once, because what was one in the past will be one in the future. Do you understand?"

Domino Tight bobbed his head. "No."

"It is Technical, with many prayers in the hailipzimou, and so understanding is not given to all. Thus the mystery must be tightly guarded by those of us in the Gayshot Bo. But the consequence is this: that by entering the quondam state at one place, you may exit from it at another. I entangled with you when first we met and so I can be at your side *quondam*."

"I've never heard of such a thing!" And he thought, *Should Padaborn and the others possess this techne, the Revolution is won!*

She kissed him gently once more. "And neither would you have, save that your life wanted saving. There are vestiges, the Seven Wonders, and the world must be guarded from them. Yet necessity and the Fates rule us all. I could not let you die."

"And I thank you. My life is yours, now and forever." He pulled her head down to meet his, and kissed her deeply. But more deeply inside him there was that hard nut where no Shadow ever allowed Love's entry, and affections were wedded always to craft. Seven Wonders? Kept from the world? Another of the Wonders was undoubtedly what had healed him so swiftly and seamlessly. What were the other five?

"Vestiges," he said. "That means 'remains, leftovers, widows.' Remains of what? The Commonwealth? The prehumans?" His hand found an opening in her robes and ran lightly up her back

Tina Zhi laughed like wind chimes. "Oh, the storied Commonwealth! Everything wonderful is given to it. But it fell from pride and arrogance, and its pride came from its techne. We use techne judiciously, with what wisdom we can muster—because every change in technique means a change in culture; and when a culture has been perfected, as ours has, any change would lessen that perfection. That is why the Vestigial Virgins guard them from impious use."

Domino Tight laughed and drew her to him once more. "You are no virgin!"

"Oh," she touched a finger to his lips to silence him, "it is just a name."

Was there something in the way she said "name"? Domino Tight shivered, and not entirely from her strokes. "Tell me about these techniques," he said. "I want to know all about them."

She disengaged and stretched out beside him on the divan. She searched him out and held him. The blankets were lighter even than silk; they may as well have been air. "I can make you strong," she said. "I can make you fast."

"I'm already strong and fast." He laughed.

"Not like this. And I can let you . . . see things."

He squeezed her gently. "I'm already seeing things."

"No. I will give you special lenses that you wear directly on your eyes. With them, you can see my colleagues when we wear our Cloaks."

"What cloaks are those?"

"These." And Tina Zhi whirled her robes about her, and disappeared.

For a moment, Domino Tight lay amazed and

unmoving on the divan. Then he grew aware of her warmth next to him, the sough of her breath on his neck. He reached and found that which he desired, and heard again the wind chime of her laughter.

"Yes," she said. "I am still here. This too is one of the Seven Vestiges."

"But . . . How is it possible?"

Tina Zhi hesitated, then said,

"Light flows like a river
Through the channels of the fabric
Around the obstructing one.
The eye sees straight
While the light bends."

Then, dismissively, "It is Technical. It can be imitated, but not understood. The ancient god Fengtzu wove it on his loom in the age before the age."

Domino Tight, who believed in the gods only inasmuch as he scorned them, translated that to mean that long ago there had been a man who actually did understand. "And your special lenses will enable me to see those who wear such Cloaks?"

He was no longer certain that he wanted the ability to see the Cloak-wearers, for he now understood who Those must be.

"Yes," his lover told him, throwing her clothing aside and appearing once more very much in the flesh. "But none of them may you hurt . . . save this one." Her voice hardened again at the last and her eyes grew very old. She flipped her hand, palm up, and it was as if her palm were a holostage—for a tiny figure appeared in the space above it.

It was a woman of deep chocolate brown and hair

bound up in a complex weave that left neck and shoulders bare. She had the solid, muscular grace of a swimmer and in the image was emerging naked from the ocean. The image captured not an instant, but a moment: The figurine stepped toward Domino Tight as she unbound her hair, and it fell cascading to her waist.

Domino Tight was more charming than wise, but he was wise enough not to voice his thoughts to his lover. *By the Fates,* he thought, *that is the most desirable woman I have ever seen! It would be a sin punishable by the fire to mar that perfect skin.* "Why?" he asked, and then asked again with a steadier voice, "Why do you wish her dead?"

"Not dead." Tina Zhi laughed. "But if she were hurt . . . If she bore a scar on her face . . . That would be fit punishment. Jimjim Shot abetted a foul in one of your pasdarms. You will hear of it from Oschous when I return you to Yuts'ga. That act violated . . . certain rules that had been laid upon her. Her punishment has been willed."

"Willed. By whom?"

"Are you certain, Domino Tight, that you wish to know the answer to that question?"

There was something in her voice, a loss of flightiness. It no longer soared. And her eyes had grown hard. There was love in them still, but there was something else beside. Looking back, much later, he thought that was the moment when certainty had him.

She looked into his eyes for a long and lingering moment. "Ah," she said sadly. "You have guessed. Well, fear not, my Deadly One. No harm will come to you. My loins ache for you; my heart longs for you. Together, we will foil *this one's* plans." And she closed her hand into a fist and extinguished the glowing figurine.

When Domino Tight was returned to Yuts'ga, he was half machine. Limbs of titanium enfolded him, multiplied his motions, responded to his thoughts and desires. Wearing this exoskeleton, he could race with the wind; he could strike like a hammer. His eyes could pierce the Cloaks that shrouded Those of Name. He wore such a Cloak himself. "I am become like one of the gods of old," he told himself as he sprinted unseen through the streets of Cambertown.

"Lyre," he said over his link, but received no response. The link was dead. High overhead, he knew, his personal satellites had been sanded out of orbit, probably the very night of his ambush. He sampled one of Big Jacques's channels—and found himself shunted to Oschous's network.

What he heard was gibberish, but that was because he had not Oschous's codes. He waited for what he hoped must come. Further gibberish directed to Big Jacques's network, then instructions directed to the lyre! Those messages he could read, and without breaking stride, he flipped down the goggles on his shenmat and studied the map thus presented. An old warehouse on the edge of town. Pale green dots showed the movements of friendlies. Red dots showed foes. He studied the dance for a time, then asked his belt node to find the best route and set off on it.

As nearly as he could determine, Big Jacques was

under siege by Pendragon's men, who had been taken in the rear by Oschous, who had in turn been surprised by Ekadrina in a classic double envelopment. He flipped over to the frequency used by the city police and with trifling decryption learned that the Riff of Yuts'ga had ordered them to stay clear of the brawl. The Riff was not overtly taking sides.

The heads-up told him that but five of his own magpies lived, Four being senior. Domino Tight thought of pinging him, but decided that if everyone thought him dead in the tavern ambush, he may as well make use of that. So he studied the map, searching out where the pressure was greatest on Oschous and Jacques. He would undermine those attacks; relieve some of the pressure.

He was on the edge of the battle space when he remembered. Tina Zhi had been hidden from his sight, but not from his touch. (Oh, by the gods! Not from his touch.) And that meant that a ramjet round that augured his body by wildest chance would kill him just as dead as one that had been properly aimed.

But in for a minim, he told himself, in for the credit. The Cloak gave him an edge; it did not grant invulnerability.

The first body he encountered was that of a magpie wearing a golden chrysanthemum. One of Pendragon's boys. Domino Tight analyzed the forensics—the placement of the charring and the angle of the fall—and turned to a nearby building set upon a small elevation, long overgrown with saw grass. Domino climbed this until he stood just below the window. One of Big

Jacques Delamond's boys dangling there. Number Six, he saw on the brassard.

A sniper's nest to cover the operation center, it provided an excellent field of covering fire, and he gave Magpie Six Delamond kudos for choosing the site. From below came the *buzz-snap* of teasers, the whine of dazers, and the louder reports of slug throwers. For sheer stopping power, there was nothing like a high velocity slug of metal plowing through the target and transferring its momentum. Now and then, he heard the *bang-and-whoosh* of ramjet rounds. He saw nothing, of course. Shadows did not act in order to be seen. It may as well have been a pleasant summer's day, the whines no more than the buzzing of insects.

To the right, on the north side, was a large block of a building: the warehouse proper. A lower extension ran southward, where sealed doorways marked one-time loading docks. Embraced between these two arms, the foreground lay open. It had once been a car park and staging yard, through the plast-seal of which tufts of triumphant grasses had broken. Not even a shadow could cross that expanse unseen and the defenders by the loading docks and inside the main building had it well quartered.

A knot of defenders clustered behind derelict containers and jenny-trucks barring the attackers from reaching the docks. Among them Domino recognized Ravn Olafsdottr. On the farther left, at the south end of the lot, stood a smaller building that had evidently once been a guard shack for security inspections of incoming jenny-trucks. If there had ever been a pad for ballistic shipments, it lay outside the security perimeter.

The besieging shadows had an advantage over Oschous's boys. The black horses were trying to fall back on the warehouse where Jacques was holed up, and so from time to time they had to show themselves and run; at which point either Ekadrina or Pendragon would try to pot them. Domino Tight studied the pattern, deduced from it whence the shots came, and set himself to observe.

Patience was rewarded. A tuft of grass moved in a way that the wind wound not. The setting sun rolled out a shadow for which there was no evident caster. An incautious shift by a magpie chanced a glimpse of shenmat. Domino Tight marked his targets, grinned fiercely, and after some self-consultation, pulled a mace from his belt.

Then he ran down the little hill—Oh! How he flew! The exoskeleton amplified his motions; the gyros maintained his balance. He swung the mace as he closed behind the first magpie, who crouched on his left knee. Brains spattered, the man fell prone without a word. Simultaneously, and with his other hand, Domino fired an EMP burst across the empty lot, to strike a Sèanmazy magpie lying behind the cover of a composite block. The pulse was weak at the distance, but it would have seemed to the taijis that it had come from Pendragon's ranks.

In swinging the club and firing his dazer, Domino Tight had shown himself briefly. He closed the Cloak once more, but he knew better than to linger for anyone's second look. Three more magpies to his left wriggled forward through the tall grass in a triad support formation, infiltrating closer to the warehouse compound. Domino exchanged mace for variable-knife and telescoped the blade to arm's length. Then he ran across the line of magpies, swinging upstroke-downstroke-up, leaving three throats laughing behind him.

But the grass rippling in the wake of his progress drew fire from black horses pinned down by the old loading docks. It was called "friendly fire," but Domino Tight saw nothing companionable in it. He changed course to avoid the grass.

His potshots across the lot into the taijis had begun to annoy the latter, and more than a few were wondering if the mums had switched sides. It was not unheard of. Someone shouted an insult and one of the mums, not yet realizing what was happening on his right flank, hollered back. A slug from the black horses entered his open mouth and exited the back of his head.

"Nicely shot," said Domino Tight over Oschous's link.

("Who said that?" demanded Oschous's voice. "Who's on my links?")

Domino resumed link silence, for he had seen the object of his desires. He had deduced from the survival of only five of his fifteen magpies that the ambush behind the Mountain Dragon had been but one in a set of coordinated strikes. And there stood Pendragon Jones, who had orchestrated it. He was behind the guardhouse, shielded from the fighting, but directing his flock over his link.

A Shadow uses *his emotions,* Domino remembered his one-time master, Delator Landry, saying. *He does not let them use him.*

Domino Tight withdrew his blade to nub position. He took great calming breaths; grew cold inside. *The key to creating a future, my magpies,* the Landry had said, *is to have a clear vision of it. What you imagine, you can achieve.* And so Domino imagined Pendragon dying; as in fact having already died. His fate accomplished, his body lies on the ground, bleeding out. Yes, and he must know before that end whose hand it had been that had launched him on *the unreturning journey.* That knowledge must be the last thing to fade from those eyes on the blood-soaked ground.

Next, he envisioned a change-path from his present state to the imagined future state, though this took less time to complete than to describe: penultimately, he must do *thus*; antipenultimately, *this.* And before that, *so.* Mentally, he worked his way backward from Pendragon's cold, dead body to the present.

Domino Tight had always been fast and ferocious. With his exoskeleton assisting, he moved swiftly, avoiding the grass, dancing from construction block to tumbled construction block, moving ever closer to Pendragon's position, remaining outside the man's line of sight by sheer habit. When he landed on the ground two arm's lengths from his target, he stepped on a strew of crispies.

At the crunch, Domino did not hesitate, but leapt high and to the side. But Pendragon did not fire at the sound. Instead, he squinted about—and fixed on

Domino. "There you are," he said with a touch of petulance, "and about time. Yes, yes, I can see the quiver in the air. I told you those things weren't perfect. Your darling Epri is pinned down on that rooftop . . ." He pointed to the edge of the warehouse extension. "The trident preplaced submunitions and booby traps up there. If Epri can reach the main roof, he can drop cluster bombs through the ventilation shafts into the warehouse where the rest are cowering."

Domino Tight did not think that anyone was cowering. The return fire was too crafty, too focused. He followed the pointing arm. Yes, there was Epri on the rooftop, sheltering behind an air regenerator with three of his own magpies. A remote-controlled fire center had him neatly interdicted. He could neither advance nor withdraw.

"I entreat you, Lady," said Pendragon, more politely if a bit peremptorily, "to act posthaste."

Domino Tight stepped forward, closing the distance between himself and Pendragon. When he was within arm's reach, he pulled the Cloak away and pressed the nub of his knife against the man's belly. "So I shall," he said, and extended the blade to maximum.

Dispersal armor was well and good against energy weapons, and its thixotropic properties made it useful against moderate velocity projectiles. But for bladed weapons, the Shadows liked to say, you may as well wear cotton.

The blade squeezed between the threads of the armor and shot through Pendragon. He spasmed, arched backward. The blade exited high from his back, and Domino saw the incredulity in his eyes. "But . . . you're dead," he heard the dead man say. Then he nubbed the blade and Pendragon Jones crumpled to the ground.

"Those reports," Domino told the corpse, "were greatly exaggerated."

He had seized the man's link from his hand as he fell and now spoke into it, modulating his speaker to imitate Pendragon's voice. "Mums! Fall back!" he said. "We are betrayed!"

At this, the right flank of the assault began to dissolve, as the magpies there in swift obedience to their master's voice began to withdraw. But Domino Tight saw one of the fighters with Ravn fall and he aimed a bolt at Epri on the roof. Epri, caught from an unguarded quarter, spun and fell.

Domino Tight saw a shimmering in the air on the rooftop, like a heat ghost.

Ah, that is what Pendragon had meant! He blinked his eyes as Tina Zhi had taught him and the whole vista faded to gray scale in which one solitary figure stood out. It was the woman that Tina had shown him, Jimjim Shot, and she was bending to tend to the wound that Epri had sustained. With her left hand, she maintained an inaccurate harassing fire on Olafsdottr's squad.

The woman was bilateral, then, but not a trained fighter. The Mayshot Bo, Tina had told him, dealt with control of the arts, as the Gayshot Bo dealt with the control of technology. He took aim at her.

He did not fool himself. He knew he was about to fire on a Name. But then, what was this rebellion about if not overthrowing the Names? Why quail at this? Was it only long conditioning that held Those persons sacrosanct?

No, it was a sin to mar such perfect beauty. The lenses by which he saw through her Cloak revealed all. There was not a blemish upon her.

Automatically, he calculated distance and adjusted the power on his dazer so that it would burn, but not kill.

"Do it," he heard Tina Zhi's voice say. Disconcertingly, that voice came through his own lips. "Before she can take the quondam route."

Domino Tight sucked in his breath. His arm wavered, then steadied.

And then Jimjim Shot stood up and away from Epri and stared directly at him, and her eyes were the red of flame. She saw him and saw his lust and saw his hesitation, and her lip curled in contempt, and she raised a weapon that Domino Tight did not recognize.

And Domino Tight shot her in the face.

The scream unnerved the battlefield, for it seemed to come from nowhere. It was a scream of surprise and anger and pain; and both sides in the firefight hesitated, creating for a moment a simulacrum of truce.

Inside the warehouse, where Oschous Dee Karnatika directed the defense, the fox-faced Shadow took a report from Ravn, who was outside and under desperate straits. "Oschous," she said, "the mums are withdrawing. There is confusion on their right. I thought I saw someone fall from behind the guardhouse. Could have been Pendragon. And three or four of his boys that I had marked, they haven't moved in a while."

"That might be tactical," Oschous warned her.

"Might be, but I think one of ours is out there behind their lines. Someone took a couple shots at Epri up on the roof, and it wasn't us. Do you think one of the boys in the sniper's nest survived?"

"I don't think," Oschous told her. "I count the dead. But . . . The iron's hot, however the fire was blown." He switched links to Big Jacques's channel. "Jacques? It's time."

Domino Tight watched the Beautiful Name scream and clutch at her face, and he wept that her beauty had been destroyed, for it was more a desecration than an honorable blow. Over the mum link, he heard Magpie Two Pendragon rallying the remainder of his flock. They would learn the deception soon enough. Number One Pendragon was undoubtedly making his way to the guardhouse to verify in person the order to withdraw from the fight. That made this a place not to be.

Below the rooftop where Epri had crouched, some taijis had noticed the disruption and had glimpsed Domino Tight when he had opened his Cloak to stab Pendragon. Two were directing speculative fire at his position, so he shifted to the other side of the guardhouse and went to ground. If he played it right, he might get the taijis to fire on Chrysanthemum One when he arrived.

Domino Tight was still using the special lenses, and so saw a second cloaked figure appear on the rooftop, one who in appearance might have been a male version of Jimjim Shot. Perhaps a fraternal twin; or an identical twin altered in the womb. He rushed to aid the Beautiful Name, and Epri himself scrambled back from the rage in his eyes. *Yes,* thought Domino Tight. *Take her away from this. It is not mete that she should be here.*

The newcomer seemed altogether more accustomed to a battle and bore the instruments of valor on his belt. He knelt by Jimjim, touched her gently, and then glared across the battle space with the pitiless gaze of a raptor.

And his eyes found Domino Tight. His mouth set into a grim line and he spoke into his balled fist. Then with calm deliberation, he lifted a hand weapon of unfamiliar design. Death was no more than Domino Tight deserved for marring the perfect beauty of Jimjim Shot, but long years of training in the Abattoir had given his body a will of its own and he raised his own dazer and fired first.

Perhaps it was surprise that he saw in the face of the man of golden bronze, as if he had not expected so defiant an act. If so, it was followed closely by the rage it had momentarily displaced. Domino's bolt had no apparent effect on him, and he continued to aim.

Domino Tight cloaked himself and ran in a random direction, knowing that he was surely visible to the man of the roof. He changed directions like a rabbit, using the random number generator in his shenmat. Then something hit him hard and he flew aside as if swatted by a great open hand.

It might have been a fatal swat, had his gyros not stabilized his flight and brought him down on crouching feet directly beside Ravn Olafsdottr and three of Oschous's magpies. He staggered, blocking two of their shots and taking a third on his dispersal armor before he could identify himself.

"Well, well," said the Ravn, who alone had not fired. "You are quite spry, Domino Tight, for a dead man."

Big Jacques and most of his magpies had waited in his main headquarters until he had been certain that Sèanmazy had committed herself to attacking the decoy. As soon as he had learned that Pendragon had taken down Domino Tight and most of his boys in one fell swoop, he had sent two more magpies to the decoy site with orders to simulate greater activity, had shut down the link to the main site, and had folded up shop.

Oschous Dee Karnatika had discovered the fighting and had rallied his own flock to its support, attacking the mums in the rear. Big Jacques had not planned on that, but it added a greater touch of authenticity to the defense of the decoy and not incidentally had saved Big Jacques's considerable butt. Sèanmazy had waited for likely rescuers before closing in with her taijis. Had Oschous Dee not triggered the trap, it would have been Jacques caught in the pincer.

Now, Jacques would add a final touch of irony to the entire engagement, ambushing Ekadrina in turn.

Unless there were still another Shadow on-world to attack him in turn. He laughed.

"Ever play jenga?" he asked his team. A few nodded; the rest looked puzzled. "It's a game where you stack a bunch of wooden blocks, and the players take turns pulling out one block at a time—until the tower collapses. Whoever collapses the tower loses the game."

"All shut down, chief," said Number One, as he buckled his weapons harness. "Best we be a-getting over there." His accent revealed roots on Broad South Continent, on Brannon's World.

Jacques sighed and pushed to his feet. "Twenty, you shepherd the jennies to the spaceport. Don't balk, kid. You ain't got the seasoning yet. Contact Seven and tell him to bring the ship down from Elfour and be ready for a full catch. Make sure our boat's prepped and ready."

He sent outriders ahead on scooters and the rest of his flock followed in a ground-bus they had commandeered earlier. A mile from the battle space, his tridents disembarked and made their way on foot through a wooded park across the roadway from the battle space. There, they waited Oschous's call. Jacques dispatched Three and Nine to reconnoiter the loyalist positions, and they vanished without a sound. Then he unrolled a holomap on the ground and a glowing miniature of the surrounding terrain rose from its surface. His flock clustered about. "Second Section," he told them, pointing. "The black horses chewed up the mums pretty good in the original ambush before the taijis drove them into the warehouse. But don't discount them. Suss 'em out, locate them, then strike hard and fast on my click. First section. Ekadrina is mine, but her flock is tough and ain't been through the grinder like Pendragon's boys. Oschous Dee tells me she's reinforced by Epri Gunjinshow and a couple of lilies. We'll get support from the black horses and the rest of our boys what took refuge inside the warehouse. So don't shoot long if you can help it. There's a white comet over there, too. A free lance named Olafsdottr who took Gidula's service. And, boys, Padaborn's with them."

The name ran like fire across the lips of his magpies. Padaborn. Padaborn's back.

Big Jacques, and his senior magpies, said nothing. Twenty-four years ago, Geshler Padaborn had been a traitor, an experiment gone bad. And Jacques himself had been in the team that assaulted the Education Ministry. They had killed Issa Dzhwanson, the actress who had been the voice of the Rising during that mad, tumultuous week. Her last words, broadcast to all Dao Chetty, had been: *They shall not silence us.* But of course they had. On the rooftop, he had found a mixed squad of magpies and commoners who could not even be dignified as walking wounded, left behind as a rear-guard. The magpies had died fighting, of course; but Padaborn himself had somehow escaped the net.

"Yeah, Padaborn is directing the defense," he told his flock. He doubted it was true. Any direction was Oschous's doing. Way he heard it, Padaborn was not up to snuff. But if it fired up the boys, the lie would serve.

Nine slipped back into the caucus. "Mums in confusion. Some withdrawing. Mum Two trying to rally.

Pendragon out of link. Saw three, maybe four mums throats cut. Fresh kills. Nice precision close-in work. Black horse sortie?"

"No. They're bottled up pretty tight. Prick your spots on the map here."

While Nine was detailing the mum positions and movements, Three slipped back with the intel on the taijis. "I saw a couple take pots at the mums. Someone over there was firing into Ekadrina's people, and wounded Epri up on the roof, so some of them think the mums flipped. Something happened on the roof, but I couldn't make out what they were saying. Didn't want to get closer and risk blowing the play, so I folded up my parabolic and came back."

Big Jacques considered that, and the positions pricked on the map. "Okay, change of plan. One, you take *half* of Second Section—even numbers—against the mums. Someone out there done half your work already. Don't let 'im show you up. Odd numbers, you're with me and First Section against the taijis. Upload the map, boys and girls. Same rules as before. Locate, mark—two apiece, I think—click when ready and in position. When you hear my click, strike hard and fast. That should give us near simultaneous kills and take out at half the loyalists before they even know we're behind them. Understood?" He gathered their nods. "Great plan, right? Expect it to go wrong. Remember, an estimate of what the enemy will probably do is important, but don't be surprised when he does something else. Combat is always complicated by the presence of the other side."

That earned him some chuckles. Nineteen swallowed hard and looked to One for assurance. The kid had promise, and Jacques hoped he would last the night. He touched his earwig. "Right. Just got the word from Oschous. Shift."

And hardly did the words leave his lips than the clearing was empty. A fern trembled where Nineteen had inadvertently brushed against it. Then it was still. Jacques smiled. They were good boys. Then, he too stepped into the woods and vanished.

Ravn Olafsdottr had never seen a man as rattled as Domino Tight. Even for one so recently resurrected, he seemed unnerved. He crouched behind the old shippers and rasped, "They've come. They're here." But who had come and who was here he did not clarify.

"That was good work you did behind their lines," she told him. "I assume it was you that scattered the mums and got the taijis potting them."

One of the defenders behind the shipper was a lyre. "Good to see you quick, boss," he said, but the Shadow hardly reacted.

This was not the Domino Tight that Ravn remembered from the disaster relief work on Nanq'ress. That had been a man quick-witted and cool.

So why not assume he remained quick-witted? "Who is here?" she asked him. "Has another Shadow joined the play? The Riff? Surely not Gidula! He is too oold to play at these games."

His answer, if any answer had been forthcoming, was forestalled by Ekadrina Sèanmazy, who tossed an incendiary onto the rooftop of the south extension. The fire nests failed to interdict it and the resulting explosion wiped out four of the remote guns that Ravn had planted up there. The screens went dark and she could no longer see through their eyes or fire their weapons. The other nests, being farther back, had escaped, and she switched rapport to them, expecting Epri to launch an assault behind the explosion. "He better be right quick aboot it," she murmured, "for the roof is to catch fire." Then she toggled Oschous. "Black Horse, two taijis have entered the south annex ground floor at the far end. That zone is no longer interdicted."

"So noted," said the Fox.

"Has our mutual friend decided yet whether the fight is his to wage?"

"He is a remarkably stubborn man."

Ravn made a face. What game was Donovan playing? It seemed sheer lunacy to her. If they lost this fight, no one would pause to ask him if he were neutral. Perhaps Gidula had been right all along . . .

At that point, the trident struck the attackers from the rear. It seemed to Ravn that a third or more of the attacking force fell silent, and the mums ceased to exist as a coherent force. Epri's boys on the roof had begun aiming fire to their rear; and Ekadrina, on the verge of following her magpies into the annex, whirled about.

"Oh, well struck, Jacques!" cried Oschous over the link. "Let's close the trap."

Ravn acknowledged and told her task force to move forward, enfilading to the left to take advantage of the mums' collapse. There were trenches—employed perhaps by mechanics to work on the undercarriage impellers of old ground trucks—and the magpies slipped into them, one by one. Ravn switched her fire nests to remote so she could work them while she shifted location. She shook Domino Tight. "Let's finish this."

"He—he's on the roof!"

A glance showed Epri being evacuated by his boys and the roof of the annex beginning to smolder with thick black billows. "There's no one on the roof." Ravn switched her fire nests to automatic so they would take down anyone who moved toward them. Unlikely, now that the roof was igniting, but other fights won had been lost at the last because something unlikely had been tried.

"No! *He* is on the roof."

Ekadrina Sèanmazy was at the far end of the annex, firing toward her rear. Ravn swung a long arm strapped to her back and aimed through the scope. A long shot, but not impossible. Her finger trembled on the trigger, stroking it, then withdrawing. Big Jacques had claimed Ekadrina for his own, and honor required that she refrain; yet, honor was not all that kept her finger from the trigger. She rather liked the Long Tall One and she grieved over the state to which the Lion's Mouth had fallen. It was one thing to play the game by maneuver, shifting the sheep, seizing positions and offices. Quite another to betray one another. After the issue was settled, would Prime ever be able to reassemble the Lion's Mouth? Would there be a Purge, as in the far old days? Would there be years of ambush and murder by die-hards of the losing side?

If the Revolution succeeded, there might not even be a Lion's Mouth afterward. And what would it be like to be an orphan?

Ekadrina Sèanmazy spun three-quarters about and fell to the ground. But in the fall, she rolled, and moved into a shadow—and was gone. Moments later, Big Jacques appeared; but he was not so foolish as to appear completely. Ravn saw him only because she expected to see him and knew where to look.

But of course Ekadrina expected the same, and Big Jacques recoiled from a bolt that flashed across his dispersal armor; and he too vanished.

Tridents began to appear in the spaces previously occupied by mums, and had linked up with the mixed bag of magpies Ravn had sent out. The taijis were backed up against the burning annex, safe from the rear only in that their rear was become an inferno.

"Another one!" cried Domino Tight.

Irritated beyond measure, Ravn Olafsdottr started to reprimand him, but bit her words short.

A man stood in the angle between the two annexes. Hard muscled and hard eyed, wearing body armor of a strange and ornate kind that seemed to glow in a sullen ruddy color, enclosed by sparkling lights, he turned slowly and surveyed the battle space with a studied contempt. His eyes seemed to pick out each combatant individually.

Fire in the battle space had died off while taijis and tridents, black horses and yellow lilies, assessed this new arrival and wondered who it was and what he portended. No one fired at him, for it was not clear which side he intended, and something about his appearance, so suddenly and so indifferently in the very midst of the battle space, indicated a level of power not lightly to be aggrieved.

Then he laughed, and his laugh was like the booming of a cannon, and he lifted to his shoulder a tube. And he turned and fired into the tridents who had taken the mums' positions.

An eye-searing flash blossomed and spread linearly to left and right, followed moments later by the sharp *clap* of an explosion. Simultaneously, a casing flew from the tube.

A missile of some sort. "Foul!" she heard Oschous say. "The chapters forbid the use of military-grade weapons."

The man in the marshaling yard must have heard, because he laughed, and his voice boomed over the links. "How can there be rules when men murder men?" And he pulled another missile from his belt—it was about a forearm long—and fed it into the tube and fired again: this time toward the guardhouse.

But the tridents there had wasted no time. The fates of their brothers near the auxiliary building had been all the warning they required, and they had already melted into the brush beyond. The rearguard and the black horses in the main warehouse directed fire on the newcomer from their own weapons and from the prepositioned remotes and submunitions. But the golden cage of fireflies that enclosed the man simply flickered more brightly and neither bolt nor pellet penetrated to wound him.

Ekadrina Sèanmazy appeared once more, bloody and with one arm dangling. She raised a long knife in her other fist and gave the ululation of the taijis. At this, the taijis set in pursuit of the tridents.

And the man in the yard turned to the warehouse and pulled a third missile from his belt.

Ravn took careful aim with a pellet rifle, but with no hope that her bullet would penetrate where others had failed. And a hand stilled her arm.

It was a stranger's hand: a woman dressed in silver armor similar to that of the man with the missile tube. Her close-cropped silver hair was bound in a metallic band that was almost a crown. "Do not draw Ari Zin's attention, yet," she said. And she turned to Domino Tight and handed him a curious two-barreled weapon. "Hold this horizontally so that the sights bracket him. That will 'short' his armor. You, black-woman, when his armor snaps off, shoot him. But aim well, for armored or no, he is a fighting man. Quickly now, before he reloads."

"Who . . ." said Domino Tight.

"The Woqfun Bo is angry because you shot his wife. Her brother summoned him. Now fire, each of you, for it is your lives to hesitate."

Domino Tight steadied the U-shaped weapon in both hands so that one barrel was left and the other right of Ari Zin. The firing stud rested under his thumb. He exhaled and, at the nadir of his breath, gently pressed the stud.

Ravn had followed his rhythm and his breath with her own and, an instant after Domino Tight had fired, her own weapon barked, one-two-three.

The protective glow winked out, but the first shot

glanced off his ruddy armor. The second bullet penetrated. The third struck him in the hand. He howled and clapped the hand to his chest, smearing the golden bands with blood. Whirling, he saw Tina Zhi with the defenders, raised a hand and wagged a finger at her, once, twice; but if he meant to say anything, it was cut short by his abrupt disappearance.

Bullets cut the space he had occupied, too late to slay him.

"Domino Tight," said Ravn Olafsdottr, "when we have the leisure, you will explain. And you . . ." She turned to their silver-clad savior to find that she too had vanished.

"She said," said Domino Tight, "that they had all been recalled." He stared at the smoke-embroiled roof of the annex and what he saw there—or did not see there—must have comforted him, for he relaxed for the first time since sailing through the air to land at her side. "Now we have only Ekadrina to worry about."

"Only!" said Ravn Olafsdottr, who, but moments before, would have named her the deadliest individual in the battle space. "Where have you been, sweet Domino? You have made new friends."

"There is no time now," he said. "But, here . . . In case . . ." And Domino Tight aimed his interface at her and downloaded what she supposed must be an accounting of his suit record. She would review it later; if there was a later.

The taijis still had the tridents on the defensive. They would pick them off at retail. Ravn closed her eyes and thought; but she did not think long. Finally, she sighed. "What banner," she asked Oschous over the link, "did Padaborn fight under?"

"Forest-green," he answered, "under sky-blue. Why?"

But Ravn Olafsdottr was reprogramming her shen-mat so that her waist and legs were green and her blouse and sleeves were sky-blue.

"What are you doing?" Domino Tight asked.

"Forgive me, Gidula," she said. Then she pulled the white comet from her arm, set aside the long arms, and hung her belt with close weapons, checking the loads or the edges as the case might be.

"We must rally them," she said, "before Ekadrina can drive home the counterattack that Ari Zin creature opened up."

Domino Tight peered around the edge of the shipper. "Where is Big Jacques? The tridents have fallen back onto the woods across the roadway. The taijis are closing in; but a few are still watching the warehouse against a sortie."

Ravn nodded. She thought about Gidula, about Oschous, about Donovan. She remembered long nights with Domino Tight. She turned her grin on him. "Follow me."

She backed away into the loading docks, then turned and ran through the building, ran through the main warehouse, crying "Padaborn! Padaborn is back!" She did not look to see if Domino Tight followed. Jacques's magpies, those that had been inside the warehouse, saw her colors, cheered, and leapt up to join her. "Padaborn!" Half of Oschous's magpies did the same, though surely they *knew* that Donovan was supposed to be Padaborn. Perhaps they thought now that Donovan had been a diversion, and that Padaborn had traveled with them sub rosa.

She had a moment to glimpse Donovan's astonishment and Oschous's widened eyes, then she was past them, into the burning annex.

"Through the fire?" she heard Domino Tight ask, though when she turned her head she did not see him.

"From which corner are we least expected; from which stage might we more dramatically enter the fray?" Ahead, framing had caught fire and the paneling was peeling and dripping into the main gangway. "Explosive rounds!" she called to the magpies following her. The truck door at the end of the hall must be weakened from the flames. "Plant your munitions around the frame, by the numbers. Call out!"

The boys behind her hollered, "One, Two, Three . . ." and she noted that half of them, even the black horses, had altered on the fly the colors of their shenmats, so that they too sported the colors of Geshler Padaborn. Gidula had been right about the inspirational power of his name, though wrong about so much else.

"Someday you must tell me, Domino Tight," she said conversationally, "how it is that you have become invisible."

"Don't be too sure you want to know," a voice beside her said.

The heat in the annex was intense, the flames a

tunnel through which they sped. A portion of the ceiling came down in a shower of sparks. The runners scattered and danced around the debris, shaking off the fiery fragments. She heard one of the boys holler, loud and shrill, and Ravn thought the girl had been burned on the face. Breathing, even through the filters, was becoming difficult; and the heat was approaching the top of the shenmat's rating. "Standard breakout, seventh modulation!" she called to the others above the sound of the crackling and snapping joists.

"Padaborn!" they shouted in return.

And there was the metal door ahead of them. It was the sort that rolled up into an overhead bin. On the floor, consumed in flames, lay the two taijis who had entered earlier, felled by the fire nests that Oschous had emplaced, dead well before being offered as a holocaust. Ravn measured the paces to the door.

"On my call, fires explosives. After breakout, fire as opportune to relieve the tridents. Ready, three, two, one, fire!"

Fire, indeed! A dozen guns let loose, each aimed at a different point around the door, and the rounds bored into the putty-soft walls and exploded as nearly simultaneous as made no difference. The door shuddered loose from the structure even as Ravn's combat team hit it, feet first, and it toppled like a loading ramp onto the ground beyond. They poured out across the door, breaking in all directions, still shouting, "Padaborn!"—and three taijis too slow to realize that they were dead fell with their backs still turned.

Ekadrina Sèanmazy turned a scarred and bloody face toward the newcomers who had burst so unexpectedly out of the inferno of the annex. She whipped a flying star in a single fluid motion even as she dove for cover and summoned the rest of her flock over her link. The star struck someone in the attack team, pierced the cords of his armor, but did not bring a cry to his lips as he fell. "Padaborn!" they shouted. Padaborn? She saw a green and blue apparition bear down upon her and she fired her dazer.

She did not wait to see its effect, but whirled in a three-point tumble to come down behind an old truck barrier, where she rolled to the side and brought a pellet gun to bear. The dazer should have jangled Padaborn, slowing him, allowing the bullets opportunity to pierce the armor.

But never be surprised when the enemy does something else. Padaborn had sidestepped just before the dazer pulse and was nowhere to be seen. Ekadrina quickly ducked back behind the barrier, disappointing several bullets eager to meet her.

Save for the crackling and collapsing annex, silence lay over the battle space. Of the combat team that had burst from the annex there was no sign; of her own taijis not a trace. This was not going well. Or rather, it was seesawing too wildly for the orderly tastes of Ekadrina Sèanmazy. First, the unexpected presence of the black horses, when it should have been the tridents caught in her pincers. Then the attack from the rear by tridents who should have been bottled up in the warehouse. The fight with Big Jacques from which they had both withdrawn bloody by mutual and unspoken consent. Then the intervention that Epri had so grandly promised succeeded brilliantly, only to unexpectedly collapse. Now Padaborn had returned from the living dead.

She lay still for a moment before, in a controlled, economical gesture, she strewed crispies to the other side of the old truck barrier, so no one could approach from that quarter without a betrayal. Then she flipped her wrist and extended a see-me-more fiber scope that she slaved to her goggles and extended above the lip of the barrier.

Nothing. Discreet pops and snaps from across the roadway told her that the fight with the tridents continued. "Odd numbers," she whispered over the link, "disengage from trident. Padaborn had a troop lying in reserve. Some will try to relieve da tridents."

"Padaborn!" said her Number One, and the way he said it made her wish she had not mentioned the name.

"He's a sick old man," she told Number One. "I have dat on best authority. Dis is a desperation play." That the play had her pinned down behind a plasteel barrier did not make it any less desperate.

"Taiji," her Number One said, "the flock is down fifty percent. Perhaps we should disengage."

"I have never departed a kill space in defeat."

"No, ma'am. But no one leaves here unharmed. Pendragon is slain and most of the chrysanthemums. Domino Tight is slain along with the lyre. The black horses were mauled. Big Jacques is badly wounded and the tridents as battered as we. You are badly wounded. And . . . *Others* were wounded. Perhaps that is sufficient for the day."

Ekadrina's left eye had spotted motion through her fiber periscope. She logged the coordinates into a smart gun and launched a pinwheel bomb. The explosion came as a flat slapping sound but the truck barrier kept the blast from reaching her.

If she withdrew now, the one sure winner would be Oschous who, so far as she knew, had sat untouched in the warehouse directing the battle like a spider in the center of her web—and Padaborn, whose unexpected entry into the battle space would be seen by all as the tipping point.

No, she must first harm Padaborn. Only then could she withdraw with face.

She paused a moment to curse Epri and what he had brought into the fight. The ruddy man had to have been the Woqfun Bo, a man who should have been supreme on any field, but who had by his use of shoulder-launched missiles introduced a further escalation in the Shadow War, but who, far worse, had shown himself fallible.

"Are these the men that we protect?" she asked, half-aloud.

She heard the distinctive crinkle of crispies stepped upon, grinned and rolled to her knees, and aimed . . .

And there was no one there.

A lesser Shadow might have paused and gaped; but Ekadrina Sèanmazy had not reached seniority through being lesser in any respect. The only reason for making a sound in front of her was to approach behind her. She whirled.

And there was Padaborn only two strides away, already raising a pellet gun for a fatal armor-piercing shot.

Ekadrina, who had already chambered her gun to fire on the crispies, fired on this new threat.

The bullet caught Padaborn on the chest and the transferred momentum knocked him backward, even as the recoil pushed Ekadrina back.

Oh, fortunate recoil! A flying star scissored through the space her body had occupied, and Ekadrina executed a dancing pirouette and laid down fire toward the location where no one stood. The shot caught something, however, for the air rippled and brightred blood seemed to blossom unsupported. Then that something leapt away, higher and faster than a man might leap.

A clever play, whatever it had been. Epri had possessed such a Cloak, but it was apparent now that Others had been equally generous with the opposing side. She did not like the implications of that, but filed it for later consideration. Now was not the time for introspection.

She walked over to where Padaborn lay on his back, spread-eagled to the sky, and stared into the face.

The black face of a Groomsbritch, and a woman's face at that. She smiled up at Ekadrina. "This hurts moore than I thoot it wood."

"You are not Padaborn!" Ekadrina said. An accusation, an outrage, an affront.

"No," said a new voice. "I am."

And there at the gaping entry to the burning building stood the hook-chinned old man she remembered, wearing the green-and-blue shenmat and a belt of weapons and bandoliers.

IN THE LION'S MOUTH

And there stood gaping at the entry to the vault, unaffected, the peak-chinned Oh, pale the enormous trowsmin the system and blue shimmer and a belt of weapons and bandoleer.

CENGJAM GAAFE: THE EIGHTH INTERROGATORY

So," says Graceful Bintsaif, "he joined them at the last."

Méarana explores the battle with dancing fingers. Her harp howls and twangs with sudden-plucked strings; she runs a nail down their lengths to evoke the whine of energy weapons. Domino Tight leaps about in octaves; Names appear in discords. "Or perhaps," she says over the chaotic jangle of the music, "it was they who finally joined him."

"Fash! What nonsense," her mother says. "It was not *that* he joined, but *why* he joined."

Ravn Olafsdottr smiles at her. "You think?"

Bridget ban smiles too, but it is a smile that few have rejoiced to see. "I think you are more clever than you let on."

"Ne'er mind yer chawin'," says Méarana, stilling her chords. Then, to Olafsdottr: "How did Fa—How did the Fudir fare against Ekadrina?" She thinks that if she does not call him "father" his loss will not hurt as badly.

The Shadow shrugs. "Understand. I was unconscious, and when I awoke they were gone, all of them, and the wind blew leaves and papers across an empty lot. What I learned, I learned later, from my suit's recorders after I awoke—and that only what passed before their sensors."

"I am surprised you awoke at all," Graceful Bintsaif interjects from her corner behind the Shadow.

The Ravn turns to her and smiles. "Noo lace than I," she adds. "Boot the surprise is always pleasant."

Méarana strikes an imperious chord. "But ye can tell us how the struggle ended, however supine ye might hae been during the fighting of it!"

"I think," the Shadow tells her with a nod to Bridget ban, "that your mother suspects."

"You've come here on a fool's errand," the Hound responds cryptically. "Tell me, for I am passing curious, why you donned the garb of Geshler Padaborn and pretended to be himself."

A shrug. "Someone had to do it."

But Méarana judges the indifference feigned. "To rally the rebels."

Ravn leans forward, arms on her knees. "They needed a Padaborn; I gave them one."

"You gave them a false one."

The Shadow flashes her teeth, leans back on the sofa, and spreads her arms along the backrest. "Did I?"

"No," says Bridget ban. "She gave them the true quill. He was impervious to every persuasion but the last. Revenge, glory, or the liberation of Terra—these three things could not sway him. But that you had been felled acting in his place brought him forth at last."

Ravn dips her head. "Such was the plan."

"Your plan!" says Graceful Bintsaif. "You might have been killed. Had Donovan held back, you would have been."

Teeth flash. "It seemed like a good idea at the time."

"Tell me, Ravn . . ." Bridget ban straightens, "who gave you the scars? Ekadrina? Did she vanquish the old man as she vanquished you; then hold you afterward for kaowèn? Or did Oschous lash you, for losing him the Padaborn card in his play for power?"

"No one *gave* me the scars, Red Hound. I *earned* them. They are most seemly wounds, and well acquired beside; for principle might merit lash, and wear such welts with pride."

IX. YUTS'GA: THE MAIN ARGUMENT

What words may capture combat grim
Whose course evades narration's ken?

Surprise holds hesitant bold Ekadrina;
The scarred man's passion recks no such pause
Nor 'tis shackled by single thought. First shot is
  his!
And Ekadrina falls! But falling, rolls; and so
  evades
The fatal blow, and vanishes midst swaying grass.
The parking lot becomes a hiding place. She finds
Still forms there who once had followed her,
Gazeless eyes on golden sky affixed, weapons all
  a-scatter.
Those hands that lately clutched them clutch at
  naught,
As if they seize at things unseen. Or else were
  seizèd by them.
Shadows never more, they are become but shades,
To plow a vague existence shorn of fleshly joys.
They fade as holograms from aging substrate
  plucked.

"How sweeter than the king of all the dead,"
Achilles once proclaimed, "it is to slop my father's
    swine alive."
But who can fight when fueled by thoughts like
    these?
And failing fight, could hope the gods to please?

Ah, what blows were struck, what feats performed! Only a portion of the combat passed before the receptacles of Olafsdottr's shenmat, to be recorded, pondered, honored in later leisure. Despite the shock of Padaborn's unexpected advent, Ekadrina survived his first onslaught, and from stealthy and ever-shifting positions took potshots at her foe.

But Padaborn's psyche had been split for just such affairs as this. He could consider options with half a mind while the remainder focused on the task at hand. No such fool as to trust his first shot fatal, he had winkled straightaway to a new position, one concealed, from which he might take his second.

Had he been in more constant practice, he would have prevailed. And had she been uninjured, she would have prevailed. As it was, the fell combat joined an equity of impairments, so that while victory might elude them both, defeat could fall to either. Around them, as companion stars do orbit a bright primary, the remnants of the taiji, the trident, and the black horse battled in contests lesser to any but those whose lives depended on them. The flames of the warehouse had already spread to the underbrush, sought out nearby dwellings, overleapt the Endicott River at the Narrows, and even then stalked the skirts of Cambertown herself. Several magpies struggling in the nearby woods must have found their deadliest enemy not in one another, but in the encroaching flames.

But much of this befell beyond the Ravn's ken. Prone as she was, her shenmat's view was limited and from an odd perspective. Padaborn showed himself briefly to draw fire and performed the Play of the Bundled Sticks. Ekadrina, from some location unseen, wafted a glider grenade, a spinning saucer that sailed across the grass tops before exploding. Only such fragments as these were recorded of this most celebrated struggle.

But the Long Tall One was badly wounded. Earlier, she had battled Big Jacques to a draw—no mean feat in itself—and the brief, but intense combat with the masquerading Ravn and the encloaked Domino Tight, though it had ended improbably in her victory, had not been exactly a restful entr'acte. The passages had taken their toll, and when at one point she limped directly by Ravn's unconscious form, the seeping blood on her left side glistened against the flat black of her garment.

But Padaborn was little better off. Some of Ekadrina's shots had told. The glider grenade had perforated his right leg and only the shenmat's self-knitting powers had firmed up and staunched the wounds. And he had not fought a man à outrance since he had retired Billy Chins from the service nearly two years since.

In the end, the Play of the Spider was his winning play, or should have been. Fortuitously near Olafsdottr's body ran a depression in the ground, and into this depression Padaborn insinuated himself by inches, bringing himself to lie as one dead in its concealing embrace. He scattered crispies not about his own position but farther off, to his left. Then he waited, as still and patient as Death. The wind, excited by the growing fire, whispered through the grasses and weeds and through the more distant trees and carried with it the occasional snap of weapons.

Betimes, the best stalk is to remain still and wait for the prey to come. It is a play oft used in extremity by those whose woundings hobble them. Stillness vanishes into the backdrop of the world. It is motion that catches the eye.

And soon enough came Ekadrina creeping. Soundless, rustling not the grasses, she seemed to *flow* through the landscape, embracing it, making it her own. Not for her the *snap* of the crispies. She spied them sparkling in the even-grown sun and, smiling just a little, sidled to her left to avoid them.

Padaborn erupted from the ground, seizing her by the ankles and toppling her like a caber. Her pistol went a-fling and she fell upon her back with a great *whoof* of breath, momentarily stunned.

Padaborn—or perhaps one should say the Brute—seized hold of her ankles and dragged her, intending perhaps to swing her by the heels against the broken wall of the old guardhouse. But at that juncture a spaceship's lander screeched across the skies above, and distracted even the multifaceted Padaborn, if only for an instant. But in that instant Ekadrina Sèanmazy hurled a chance-snatched stone at Donovan's head while she scrabbled for her dropped gun.

The Brute rolled, the stone missed, and the scarred man came to his feet with his own gun once more in hand, and ...

... And there they stood, panting, gun arms extended, at point-blank range, both of them dead but for a moment of mutual hesitation.

Into the hiatus, Ekadrina inserted a grin. "You look like shit."

"You, too. You've never been prettier."

The lander canted and circled above them. Neither combatant spared it so much as a second glance; nor did they speculate on the allegiance of its owner. It fired impartially on all sides, but only to encourage evacuation of the battle space, and the remaining magpies melted away. Neither Donovan's weapon nor his enemy's wavered in the slightest. Each waited for the moment when a flicker of inattention would allow murder without effecting suicide.

"Why not shoot?" the loyalist asked, perhaps from genuine curiosity. "When will you ever in your soon-to-be-foreshortened life have a bedder chance?"

"I'd ask you the same, but I don't want to put ideas in your pretty little head. This is what Terrans call a 'Mexican Standoff.'"

"Mexican. Ack. And how do dese 'standoffs' end?"

"Badly, usually."

Each remained poised, each pondering the purposes of the approaching lander. Reinforcements, perhaps—but for which side? Peacekeepers sent by the Riff? The boots, goaded finally beyond endurance by the destruction wrought by the Deadly Ones? Perhaps the neutral Shadows had joined the fray at last, "against all flags"?

And still Ekadrina did not fire. A wager, perhaps, that the lander brought assistance. But perhaps also prudence. A Padaborn mutually slain in glorious combat with the loyalist champion would be almost as great a coup for the rebels as one that lived and fought. Greater, perhaps, since a dead Padaborn could never go on to tarnish his mon with mistakes. She would much prefer to kill him without being killed herself.

There was a slight wobble in the Tall One's stance. Her blood gleamed in the long sun of evening when she swayed. The Taiji was weakening.

And not to split hairs, but the scarred man was not so steady on his feet, either. There is only so much adrenaline to go around. But neither did he pull the trigger, despite Ravn Olafsdottr lying motionless nearby.

The lander settled onto the old parking apron and the ship's guns took aim at both combatants.

Ekadrina Sèanmazy might be loath to create a martyr, but if she thought herself about to die anyway, she might as well take that martyr along to man the ferryboat.

But the Fudir forestalled her. "Had he wanted to kill you," he cried, holding his left hand palm out, "he would have done that from the air already."

Calculation arose in the eyes of Ekadrina. She skipped over the motivations of the newcomer and went straight to those of her foe. "And why would *you* zee me liff?" Her 'Zarmayan accent emerged more strongly when stress had stripped it bare.

"I would see you dead," he answered, "to avenge the Ravn. But there are things you and I must speak of first, matters that lie only between us. Afterward is time enough to die."

Ekadrina blinked. "Shall it be a pasdarm, den? One of dose old traditions you and your ilk would o'ert'row?"

"No, I will stalk you and kill you from ambush. Or hire it done."

"Dat is a hard t'ing. But what a pasdarm it would be! Da banquets, da entertainment. T'ink on da Shadows dat would gadder for da honor to watch. T'ink of dose who would offer demselves for prelim bouts! To be a prelim to da meeting of 'Kadrina and Gesh would win more glory dan top billing in any lesser contest. An ambush? A hired assassin?" She spat on the ground. "Where is da glory in dat?"

Donovan stared at her. She was dead serious. He could almost see the skull emerge from underneath her skin. He could almost smell the smoke of her burning corpse. She was already dead, and only the details of time and place remained yet unsettled. "There is something more than a little mad in your 'traditions.' By the Fates! I had thought the Hounds tightly wound, but beside you they are lackaday, de'il-may-care Peacockers. The Hounds may flirt with Death, but you are in love with Him, all of you. You kiss Him on His rotting lips."

"Evert'ing is relative," his enemy agreed. "Our lives are short, and fleet in a universe dat does not care. Dey are an insignificant blip in da march of time. So what matter if dey be shortened a tiny bit more? Dat is why we will win da Long Game. Da man who does not care too greatly for his life has da advantage over da man who might hesitate for love of it."

"The problem with the love of death," the scarred man told her, "is that it is never unrequited. Tell me, Ekadrina . . ." And he tapped the side of his head with his free hand. "Did you do this to me?"

The loyalist understood. "I oversaw da work. It was willed by Dose whose will is done."

"And were there others like me?"

"What do you t'ink? Practice makes perfect."

"Another day, then?" Donovan returned his dazer to his holster.

Ekadrina glanced at the lander, whose nose-gun twitched suggestively. Then she laughed. "Anodder day, den," and holstered her own weapon. "And where," she cried in affected indifference, pointedly looking about the field, "did I leaf my staff of office?"

Donovan sagged against the low stone wall, the air draining out of him.

Doors opened on the sides of the lander and a flock of magpies emerged and took up security positions. That both combatants were battered, injured, and had downed arms did not diminish their caution in the least.

"Comets," said Ekadrina. "Da old fool, Gidula, shows himself at last. I wonder if he will show da forbearance you have shown." There was something in her voice that sounded like, *If I go down beneath Gidula's guns, I will not die before I can draw and burn you through.*

"*I give you my word,*" the Silky Voice said through

Donovan's lips. "*If Gidula breaks our tacit truce, I will fight at your side.*"

Ekadrina looked at him sharply, as if she had heard the shift in personality. "*Your* word . . ." she hazarded with a shrug and began pulling first-aid kits from her bandolier and applying them to her hurts. "Tell me dis, Geshler Padaborn," she added without looking up from her task. "Why are so many of your newfound allies dose who fought against you da first time?"

SĪDÁO ZHWÌ: THE FINAL INTERROGATORY

When I awook," the Ravn says, "Gidula's lander was beside me, and I was soon aboard his ship, tubed and wired in the autoclinic, for Gidula wished me hale."

Bridget ban considers her for a long moment. "Yeees . . ." she says, drawing out the syllable. "I'm sure he did."

The Ravn's face grows impassive. "I believe Donovan knows long-first this truth, and keep pretense for that sake. For that I forgive him his last betrayal."

Méarana plucks a question mark from the strings of her harp. "What the de'il are ye twa randering on aboot?"

"We are alike," the Shadow tells her, "your mother and I, in so many ways."

"In too many ways, I think," Bridget ban adds, low. She turns to Méarana. "Ravn was concealing from Gidula the fact that Donovan had recovered his faculties. Donovan betrayed her by stepping forward as Padaborn to challenge Ekadrina. *That*, she could not conceal."

"Ah," says Graceful Bintsaif. "That explains her scars."

Olafsdottr runs a hand along her right shoulder and down her arm, and cranes her head to study Graceful Bintsaif. She smiles wanly. "Scars far too easily won to merit honor."

Méarana frowns. "And Gidula had to be deceived because . . ." She pauses, and cocks her head. How alike is daughter to mother, not only in that gesture, but in the powers of imagination that the cock betokens. "Ah. He *wanted* a damaged Padaborn."

"Yes. He fetch Geshler *because* his mind destroyed. Billy Chins tell him so. Rebels rally round Gesh, but lose heart when ruined old man falter and fail."

"A subtle play," says Graceful Bintsaif.

"Disappointment subtle knife," says the Ravn. "But subtlety his life's blood."

"Was he subverting the Revolution, then?" says Bridget ban.

"Gidula not want Revolution, only Rebellion. The stables must be cleaned, he told me; but not burned down."

"And in all that," Bridget ban continues, "you were his willing instrument."

The Ravn shrugs. "What concern you which side I fight? *Not your fight!* Rebels tear apart Lion's Mouth, despoil all what is loved. Abrogate ancient traditions; pull down revered ancestors; extinguish trust and bond among us. *And for what?* So *these* Names rule instead of *those*? Bother!"

The outburst provokes a moment's silence. "You

must be," says Bridget ban, "the one last patriot in the Lion's Mouth."

The Shadow ponders that accolade in silence, wrings her hands together, stares at the floor. "No," she says quietly. "Others, too. Poder Stoop. But . . . aye, few enough. Very sad thing, when brothers fight, sisters fight; old comradeships forgot."

"And all along it has been a power struggle among the Names," says Méarana.

"Obvious now, no? No noble rebels with freedom in teary eye. No stalwart defenders of ancient ways standing firm in doorway. Dawshoo and Ekadrina both puppets, dance to strings."

"And Gidula?"

"A string. Oschous, I think, suspects much, but also thinks he maneuver powers to himself, so even clever men may be fools."

"But you turned against Gidula," the Hound points out. "Otherwise, ye'd nae have advised the Donovan tae conceal his health."

"Donovan dead man if Gidula know."

Méarana's hands close hard on the frame of her lap harp, but she fears to ask. She will not ask, though the words press hard against her teeth. Because Ravn had said only a moment ago that Gidula had finally learned.

"An' wha's that tae ye," Bridget ban asks, "if Donovan be a dead man? Why should ye care?"

Olafsdottr cocks her head so deeply that it seems to lie on her shoulder. "Is it soo soorprising, then," she asks the Hound, "that soomeone might?"

Bridget ban peers at her intently, then looks away. She rises from her chair and walks to the bay window. Already, the Dōngodair Hills lie in shadows. A few pinpoint lights mark old Clanthompson watchtowers, now in this more enlightened age mere beacons for travelers. She thinks about Donovan. Dead, now? Or sucked wholly into that unholy civil war amongst the Names. In either case, lost to the League; lost to Méarana. Lost even to herself, who never really had him. The long uncertainty now resolved. She need no more expect his unexpectedness: his knock at the door, his tread upon the carpets, his arms . . . She need no longer look for the unlooked-for return.

It ought to relieve her.

She remembers how Donovan had gone with Méarana into the Wild to search for her, despite his belief that to do so was death. She remembers that he was the first thing she had seen when she had awoken from that death-in-sleep into which the guardians of the Commonwealth Ark had placed her. She remembers too that he had been coming to Dangchao at last when Olafsdottr snatched him up on Jehovah. Should she condemn the Shadow for that, or thank her?

She knows at last what the Shadow has come to ask and it grieves her sore that she cannot grant it.

"We'll have dinner presently," she says gruffly. "Have ye any preferences?"

"I'm not hungry," her daughter tells her. But the soft notes that drift from her harp hunger nonetheless.

"Something light," says Graceful Bintsaif in a hesitant voice. "A tomato sandwich perhaps."

"Ooh, what is the dish that the Beastie boys favor?" the Confederal Shadow asks. "Since at loong last I am oon Dangchao, I may as well savor it."

"It's called 'fry-pan,'" Méarana tells her. "It's pretty much anything to hand—potatoes, sausage, onions, beef ends, peppers—fried up in an iron skillet and mixed with egg and flour into a casserole of sorts."

"It soonds delicious."

Bridget ban smiles without humor and turns from her contemplation of the empty and darkling prairie. "Did you hear, Mr. Wladislaw?"

"Aye, mum," a voice replies. "And yourself?"

"A Crenshaw Salad, I think. Addleberry dressing." Then, arms folded across her chest, she faces the Shadow. "You have not come all this way to tell us nothing, Ravn Olafsdottr. How came you to awake in Gidula's ship?"

The Shadow bends forward over arms resting on knees. She looks to the floor as if searching for something lost in the carpet. "Gidula," she says in a low voice. Then, more loudly, "He monitor battle from afar; and when he see Geshler fight the Long Tall One, he knew himself betrayed. A heroic Geshler heroically returned was not at all to his taste. And so he intervened." She looks up and catches Bridget ban by the eyes. "Gidula told me that Geshler had been defeated, but I know he lies for no better reason than the practice. He scattered the fighters from the air—both sides—and only Geshler, Ekadrina, and my unconscious form remained when he landed. He told Ekadrina to withdraw and salve her wounds and, as she was no fool, she did as he bade. Then Gidula took

Geshler and me aboard his shuttle. This I know from what he told me and what he failed to tell me."

Bridget ban nods. She glances at her daughter, who has essayed a small geantraí on her harp: a happy, triumphant tune that is more premature than she realizes. "And what did Gidula tell you?"

"That he had rescued us from death at Ekadrina's hand. But I knew where matters stood with him and, more importantly, he knew that I knew. We had collaborated to bring a lackwit Geshler back. Even had he died fighting Ekadrina, he would have inspired the rebel cause. Gidula could allow neither victory nor defeat, and so he deprived him of both. For the same reason, he could not slay Geshler and leave him for Oschous to find. Oschous *would* have used him to inspire the others. And so he put me to kaowèn." She looks up. "Yes. That why he need me hale. But kaowèn for question only, never punishment." She laughs without humor. "One more tradition lost."

Méarana sucks in her breath and Bridget ban glances at her sharply. "Could you have expected anything less?" she asks the Shadow.

"From time we fight Frog Prince together," Olafsdottr answers, "I see no other end but that."

"And yet you brought him back regardless," says Méarana. Then she stops and her mouth rounds out. "No, *he* brought *you* back."

"Yes," Ravn says in clear Gaelactic. "Just how clever is Donovan buigh? He knew that those fetching him had only Billy Chins's initial report that his mind was still shattered and he was an ineffectual old drunkard. To whose benefit was it to bring such a man into the fray? To no friend of the Revolution, I think. Perhaps that was his first betrayal. That he *knew* and said nothing. Perhaps he always meant to join the Revolution, for his vengeance; but at his own time and on his own terms."

"No," says Bridget ban almost to herself, "that was not his first betrayal."

"By your own account," Graceful Bintsaif says, "you fought well in the defense of the warehouse. You even fought in Padaborn's colors. Sharp work for Gidula's man."

"What? I should break cover? I fought well because to fight less than well was suicide. Who in battle space ask opponent polite, 'Be you dooble agent?' And beside . . ." She stops and shakes her head in annoyance.

"And beside," Méarana finishes for her with a little laugh, "you had come to like them. Oschous, and Domino, and the rest."

"You still not oonderstand, young harper. I admired them all. Ekadrina and Oschous, both. Domino Tight had been my brother in the Abattoir. Epri had been my teacher. Dawshoo and Gidula were legends whose exploits I had long studied. I betrayed my own master for love of Donovan buigh; but it was only in that battle, when the Names intervened *on both sides*, that I came to see that they must be overthrown."

"'For love of Donovan buigh,'" Bridget ban quotes her.

But the Shadow shrugs. "He is many enough that more than one may love him."

"He joined the fight only when you fell fighting as him," the Hound points out. "I think *he* fought for love of *you*."

"Think what you wish, Red Hound. Little enough do you know of such things."

Méarana laughs and the others all turn to her. "I told you," she says with a pluck at her harp stings. "It was *they* who finally joined *him*. He put on the colors of Geshler Padaborn only after Ravn fought truly for the Revolution. Tell me, Dark One, though I think I already know, why you came here this night to tell us this tale; for I see it has no end to it."

The Ravn shows white teeth. "Is it not oobvious? Gidula has Donovan buigh and has taken him to his citadel. He left me behind when he passed through Delpaff. I was no more use to him, but for sake of my former use he did not 'retire' me. Sentimental old fool! What mere planetary prison can hold the likes of me? A throat cut here; a palm crossed there . . . Steel and silver won me free. The Delpaffonis do not even know I have escaped." She hugs herself. "Ooh, I am soo clay-ver!"

Bridget ban returns to her chair and sits. "And you desire what of me, O so clever one?"

"You know. You have known this while. To free Donovan from Gidula's citadel, of course. I am very good, but I cannot do *that* alone."

Bridget ban barks an involuntary laugh. "But the two of us might? What are the chances of two snow-balls in hell?"

"Very good, I think. On the Groom's Britches, our legends say Hel is froozen."

"Would your friends nae help?" Méarana asks the Shadow. "What of the other rebels?"

"Domino Tight would help, for old times' sake. Perhaps Big Jacques, simply for the challenge. And he might persuade Little Jacques. They are old collaborators. But of Dawshoo and Oschous and the others, I am unsure. Dawshoo would not believe in Gidula's treachery; and Oschous, who I believe has deduced much already, may see Padaborn as a potential rival. But for me . . . This is for me to do. Donovan and I are gozhiinyaw. How do you say it in Gaelactic? 'Brothers-because-they-have-spilt-blood-for-each-other.' "

"Blood brothers," Méarana tells her.

"Ah, so. Blood brothers." She looks to Bridget ban through lowered eyes. "A close relationship, and one he shares of old with others. It makes, I think, you and I blood-sisters-in-law."

The Red Hound smiles crookedly. "I hae ne'er heard of such a law. Where is Gidula's citadel?"

"On Terra."

Méarana stops playing. Bridget ban tosses her head back. "And so he receives the gift he has always wanted. He makes his hajj to Terra, after all! Tell me. Why would he wish to be freed, or if freed ever to leave that place?"

"Ooh, I can think of a reason, maybe even two."

Bridget ban crosses her arms, flings one leg over the other. " 'Tis nae possible. Terra lies in the Triangles, in the heart of the Confederation, no more than a day or two from Dao Chetty, New Vraddy, Old 82 . . . No, he may as well be held in the Perseus Arm."

"Mother!"

"Nae, wean. We lost him long ago. If he were anywhere here in the Periphery . . . If he were even in the Wild, as I was . . . If he were even in the Confederal borderlands . . . If I even thought yon Ravn has told us the whole truth . . . I'd owe him that much to fish him out. But not to the Triangles, darling. Not to the Triangles. Only three Hounds have ever gone there— and but two ever returned, and only one hale."

"But you should . . ."

"If he is half the man he once was, he is more likely to come to us than that we should go to him. He has escaped more tight places than most men have e'er squeezed into. Friend Ravn glossed over her escape from a Delpaffoni prison as if it were no great thing; but Delpaff is one of the oldest colony worlds, barely younger than Dao Chetty herself. It was no ramshackle frontier stockade our Ravn claims to have slipped from. And what she could accomplish, Donovan could accomplish nine times over."

"Do not be soo sure, Hound. Gidula's citadel staffs three Shadows and over a hundred couriers and magpies."

Bridget ban cocks her head at her prisoner. "You have a strange way of persuading me to attack it."

"But Mother . . . !"

Bridget ban slaps the arm of her chair. "Don't be such a fool, Méarana! While ye've been a-playing that harp, yon Shadow has been playing you. What if the whole purpose of this farrago has been to lure a Hound of the Ardry to stick her haid in the Lion's

Mouth? What chance then that it remain attached to her shoulders?"

Ravn speaks quietly. "I give you my woord."

"Oh, there's hard currency for you."

Olafsdottr sighs and her eyes retreat and look inward. "I have failed, then. Will you at least allow me to leave this place? My honor demands that I make the effort, even if it is doomed."

"Is blood, then, thicker than oaths?" Bridget ban asks.

"Thick enough. Gidula dissolved my oath to him when he abused kaowèn to punish me. He made a most grievous error."

Bridget ban nods. "I can see he did."

"What was the error?" Méarana asks.

Graceful Bintsaif tells her. "Never do your foe a small injury."

Olafsdottr grins. "That which does not kill me," she says, "has made a grave tactical error."

Bridget ban nods as if to herself, then glances at her protégé. "Yes," she says finally to Olafsdottr. "There are some few points we still need to discuss; but after that . . . Yes, you may leave with my blessing."

The Shadow laughs out loud. "Yayss. One more faction added to that stewpot of a Revolution cannot help but advantage the League. Well, it cannot help but advantage the enemies of the Names, wherever they may dwell. But please, Mistress Hound, do not confuse enmity for the Names with a disloyalty to the Confederation."

"You know which matters want discussion, of course."

The Shadow flips her hand. "Oh, 'vestiges,' one supposes. But I know no more about them than what Domino Tight downloaded to my shenmat."

"But that is so much more than we have ever heard of them that I cannae but suppose there may be one or two other details that we would find interesting."

"I will tell you what is mete for you to know. Does the League too practice kaowèn?"

Bridget ban stiffens. "Only in restricted cases; not with the gay abandon of the Confederation."

"Ooh. You are oonly a wee bit pregnant, then?"

The door opens then to admit Mr. Wladislaw and another man wearing the red-and-yellow livery of Clan Thompson, although in his case the colors are muted to tawny and break his silhouette with camouflage patterns. It is difficult to see him straight. He and Bridget ban lock eyes for a moment and he shakes his head very briefly and waits orders.

The Ravn chuckles. "Is my flier missing? Perhaps I walked."

"Ignore her jibes, Mr. Tenbottles. She is overimpressed with her own cleverness."

"Are ye quite sure, Frannie-ban, that she is *o'er*-impressed?"

"Ne'er ye mind that, Hang. Resume your duties."

"Before we eat," suggests Méarana, "can we nae take a rest break?" As they rise, she says to Ravn Olafsdottr, "I have been wanting to ask you about the poetic form you have been using to chant the story. 'Tis very different from what we use in the League. It teeters on the verge of prose but ne'er quite topples in."

Bridget ban and Graceful Bintsaif follow them to the rest room just outside the sitting room and, the other two women entering engaged deep in discussion of poetic forms, they take stations just outside the door.

"You don't fear that she will take her hostage, do you?" Graceful Bintsaif asks with a nod at the closed door.

"No, Méarana has more sense than to try that." Then she laughs at the junior Hound's look. "To what end would she do so? We've promised to release her."

"Aye, when we've wrung her dry. Do you think she trusts that promise?"

"Shadows are not like Hounds. They have a peculiar code of brotherhood, a convoluted notion of honor."

"Peculiar, I would say! They send them out in pairs, with the second tasked to kill the first should he fail in his assignment. What sort of brotherhood is that?"

"A close one, I would think. Their lives are ever in each other's hands. And their sense of honor leads them to acts that we would regard as rank foolishness."

"Such as a single-handed assault on Gidula's fortress?"

"Very much like that. What are they talking about in there?"

Graceful Bintsaif listens at the door. "The Dark One says that the style is called the Old Northern Saga."

"Northern? North of what?"

"The Ravn does not know. Oh, now Méarana is

singing something. I cannot make it out. Your daughter really has a fine voice. Wait, I recognize it. It is a passage from her *Dancer Cycle*. 'The Call to Hounds.' That was the meeting my old master called on *Hot Gates*. You came, and Gwillgi, and Grimpen. I was na Fir Li's second Pup, but he had sent Greystroke off on a mission. Oh, those bass notes capture Grimpen very well."

"Bass notes . . ." Bridget ban steps into the hallway and calls, "Mr. Wladislaw, is Méarana's harp still in the sitting room?"

"No, mum."

"Please alert Mr. Tenbottles. Graceful Bintsaif, would you open the door, please?"

The junior Hound tries the hoígh plate, but the door does not respond. "It's locked, Cu."

"Did I ask ye whether it be locked or nae; or did I tell ye to open it?"

"Cu!" Graceful Bintsaif pulls a device from her belt pouch and places it against the door plate. The light on it turns from red to green and the door slides open in its accustomed manner.

The lavatory is empty, of course. On the vanity a voice synthesizer cracks on about abstruse modalities in poetry and song. Bridget ban picks it up and studies it, finds a button, and silences the faux voices. How, she wonders, did Olafsdottr smuggle the device in with her? Surely, they had searched her every cavity! But then she remembers that the intruder had taken a little longer than needful to make her way from the yards to the sitting room. She had paused to stage this here. Oh, that was coolly done, and argued that she had always foreseen the need to employ it.

"They escaped through the ventilation," Graceful Bintsaif says, and she points to higher on the wall, where a cover screen dangles from a single fastener.

"How clichéd of our Ravn," murmurs the Red Hound. "I would have thought better of her." Then she curses. "No, the ventilator is where she hid her devices and weapons before she entered the sitting room. She brought a Cloak with her. Two Cloaks. And when we walked in, they walked out, as cool as you please."

"Then . . . your daughter went with her willingly?"

"I don't doubt she broached the whole notion. Or that she thought it wholly her own. But that scheming skald of a Shadow led her to it by her pert little nose. Presenting herself as a poet and storyteller; claiming a love for Donovan buigh. The lying little . . ."

"What! Was none of it true what she told us?"

"Oh, all of it was true. That is the best kind of lie."

"What now?" The junior Hound spreads her hands helplessly.

Bridget ban nods to the voice synthesizer. "Olafsdottr came to fetch me, not my fool of a daughter. And since I would not go and help her free Donovan, she took Méarana."

"But what sort of aid could a harper provide . . . ? Aah. But, Cu, all of the reasons you gave for not going to Donovan's rescue apply to . . ."

"Graceful Bintsaif, probabilities do not matter in this case. No, we will do as Méarana asked." She nods deference to the voice synthesizer. "We will call to Hounds."

NOTES FOR THE CURIOUS

It's a big Spiral Arm and the technology of thousands of years from now is about as imaginable as airliners would be to Assyrians. It helps that there were intervening dark ages, lost technologies, and deliberate suppression of innovation. That lets us get away with over-the-horizon science and technology of here and now. Take some stuff that we maybe almost know how to do, and then suppose that we can do it really well. The list below can be thought of as the acorns from which the oaks of some Spiral Arm technology have grown.

1. **"Subway tunnels" through space.** Just a gleam in the physicists' eyes, for now: http://www.npl .washington.edu/AV/altvw86.html
2. **Meat vats.** Dr. Vladimir Mironov of the Medical University of South Carolina, as well as researchers in the Netherlands, are presently working on the growth of "in-vitro" or cultured meat: http:// news.yahoo.com/s/nm/20110130/sc_nm/us_food _meat_laboratory_feature
3. **Gravity grids.** Depend on antigravity. Recent

citings found here: http://www.npl.washington
.edu/AV/altvw83.html

4. **Domino Tight's exoskeleton.** We're already
making their precursors: http://www.technovelgy
.com/ct/Science-Fiction-News.asp?NewsNum
=2174

5. **Invisibility cloaks.** We can't make them yet, but
see here: http://www.cnn.com/2010/TECH
/innovation/11/16/space.time.cloak/index.html
?hpt=T2

6. **Self-assembly and self-repair of shenmats, equipment, and systems.** Self-healing polymer mixtures
from Oak Ridge National Lab and the University
of Tennessee: http://www.ornl.gov/info/ornlreview
/v42_3_09/article15.shtml
Nanoparticles assembling into complex arrays at
Lawrence Berkeley National Laboratory: http://
newscenter.lbl.gov/press-releases/2009/10/22/new
-route-to-nano-self-assembly/
A University of Illinois polymer with self-sensing
properties that can react to mechanical stress:
http://news.illinois.edu/news/09/0506polymers
.html
Raytheon HEALICS Technology incorporates
self-healing into a complex system-on-chip (SoC)
design, providing the capability for the chip to
sense undesired circuit behaviors and correct them
automatically: http://raytheon.mediaroom.com
/index.php?s=43&item=1410&pagetemplate
=release

7. **Teasers and dazers.** At Old Dominion University,
nanosecond long, high-voltage pulses that punch

holes in cell membranes could be used for a
Taser-like weapon that stuns targets because the
pulse temporarily disables human muscles: http://
www.newscientist.com/article/dn16706-shocking
-cancer-treatment-may-also-yield-weapon.html
8. **I-ball.** Thrown cameras with image stabilization
have been developed in the United Kingdom:
http://news.cnet.com/8301-13639_3-10101293
-42.html

Shadow culture is based loosely on the decadent
Franco-Burgundian knighthood of the fifteenth century, the main source for which is Johan Huizinga,
The Autumn of the Middle Ages. Many of the anec-
dotes, events, and poems are based on actual anec-
dotes, events, and poems of that era, including the
sudden passions of cruelty and sentiment. Extravagant oaths, such as Manlius's pledge to eat standing
up until he had bested Epri, are typical of the era.
And in fact, a Polish knight admitted into the Chi-
valry of the Passion by Philippe de Mézières took just
that oath. The pasdarm on Ashbanal is derived from
the *pas d'armes la fontaine des pleurs, l'arbre Char-
lemagne* ("The Fountain of Tears, the Arbor of Char-
lemagne"), fought in 1449/50. The ceremonial chains
the combatants wear reflect those worn for the combat of Jacques de Lalaing and Jean de Boniface, 1445.